DISTANT WHISPERS

CATHY M. DONNELLY

Copyright 2012© Cathy M. Donnelly

All rights reserved.

ISBN-13: 978-1507799093
ISBN-10: 1507799098

DEDICATION

For my beautiful sisters, Wilma and Linda.

PROLOGUE

As he approached the house along the darkened street, he knew many eyes watched him. He was not afraid. He had waited a long time for this day. Even when death snapped at his heels and weariness made him reflect on the darkness he once held in his heart, he knew this day would come.

The door opened as he reached it and a man filled the space where it had been. They looked at each other—men who had once been enemies but who now shared a common cause. Despite this, their mistrust of each other lingered.

The man bid him enter and pointed to the wooden chairs by the fire. Four others in the room watched them.

'You know why I am here?'

The man's face held no expression 'You were told it would not be possible.'

'Everything is possible. You of all people should know that.'

'Not this.'

'You do not trust me? Do you know how I have spent these last years? I have worked tirelessly and achieved much.'

'We heard.'

'Then why can I not see her? You know I would never betray her.'

'Why is it so important to you?'

'You ask me that? You, who had moments I can never have and who live free of the regrets that are like a giant rock chained to my body. You think you have the right to decide if I am worthy to see her?' He felt the tension build in the silent witnesses to their conversation. 'After all I have done, you still doubt my purpose?'

'You seek reward for your works?'

'No.' He stood up, sending his chair crashing to the floor. He stared down at the man he had once tried so hard to destroy. Then a calmness, a sadness, overcame him. 'No,' he whispered. 'I want only to see her.'

The curtain at the far end of the room opened. She walked slowly towards him. She smiled and held out her hands to him.

He wept.

1

"For what is it to die but to stand naked in the wind and to melt into the sun? And what is it to cease breathing, but to free the breath from its restless tides, that it may rise and expand and seek God unencumbered?"
The Prophet, Kahlil Gibran

England, April 1665

His heart beat in time to the pounding of the horse beneath him and as he raced through the fields he gradually felt the knot in his stomach unwind.

By the time Edward reached the first of the trees the anger had left him and he was able to appreciate the beauty around him. Not even the smallest of clouds blemished the bright blue sky and the warm breeze was filled with the smell of grass and wild flowers. Once under the shade he brought Pharaoh to a trot. A memory stirred of when he came here as a child. He would run from one of the shafts of sunlight that pierced the canopy of leaves to another, each time closing his eyes and imagining he was in a land far away.

Edward dismounted and released the reins, allowing Pharaoh the freedom to nibble on whatever patch of grass was to his liking. He sighed. Did he really have to wait another two weeks to go to London? It had only been a month since his last visit but he sometimes felt time passed much slower in the country than in the city. Here, life was governed by routine and the seasons but in London no two days were ever the same. He loved his family and his home but he could not control his growing feelings of restlessness and confinement. He craved excitement and unpredictability.

The rule of Oliver Cromwell and his Puritans no longer lay like a blanket of darkness across the land. Even in the poorest parts of the city laughter could be heard. Fun was no longer regarded as sinful. The court of King Charles II was lavish and colorful. There, Edward met learned and interesting people who talked of things that did not include the weather and the prospect of a good harvest. He experienced a different side to life and hungered for more. He knew he would one day have to settle down and run the family estate, but not yet—this was time for adventure. Why did his father not understand this?

Perhaps a swim in the pool would relax him. The trees were sparser there and allowed the sun to warm the water and the bushes to bloom in the light. In really hot summers the family would sometimes come here. Perhaps it would ease his impatience if he lingered on those happy memories.

Edward heard singing as he approached the clearing. The words were not familiar but the voice was sweet and clear. He strode towards its source, puzzled as to who it may be. The pool was on his family's property so no-one from the village came here, especially not to bathe—for many that thought was abhorrent.

Then he saw her, and the image took his breath away. She was walking out of the water, her skin glistening with moisture and her dark hair clinging to her shoulders. He had never seen a completely naked woman before. Her body was slim and perfectly formed, her skin flawless except for some dark marks over her right hip. Her small breasts were erect and he was sure he could have spanned her waist with his hands. She stood in the sunlight, slowly stretched her arms above her head and looked to the sky. The light seemed to radiate to her and from her and he thought she might disappear in its brilliance. He could not turn his eyes away. Slowly she lowered her arms and looked straight at him.

His cheeks burned and he quickly turned his back. 'My apologies, Mistress. I did not mean to disturb you.'

'I will be but a moment dressing,' she said.

He was glad of the time to regain his composure. He realized how foolish and inappropriate he had acted and hoped she was unaware of how long he had been staring. He turned when he heard her approach. She was simply dressed in a cream blouse with a ruffled collar. She smoothed down her long brown skirt as she walked.

'I am Rachel.' She smiled at him as she pulled her wet hair over her shoulder, squeezing out the water.

'My name is Edward. I am pleased to make your acquaintance.' Her eyes were the deepest blue, framed with long dark lashes. 'I offer my apologies for...for...'

'There is no need. Your heart is good.'

'I did not recognize the language of your song,' he said, anxious to change the subject.

'My mother taught it to me a long time ago.' She looked away from him and sighed. 'The sun grows hot. I think I will rest a while in the shade.' She walked towards a fallen log under a giant oak tree.

'May I sit with you?'

'That would please me.'

The warm air was still and the only sound was that of the birds singing above them. Even though he sat at a respectable distance from her, Edward thought it strange that his body felt as if it was touching hers. 'Do you live nearby, Rachel?' he asked.

'I live with my aunt and her husband at Cloverdale.' She pointed to the west.

'Tom and Grace Clarke?'

'Yes.'

'They are good people,' Edward said. Tom had been his father's tenant for as long as he could remember. 'Have you lived there long?'

'Only a short time.'

'Where do you come from?' he asked. Her voice held a hint of an accent he did not recognize.

'I have lived in many places.' She squeezed more moisture from her hair.

'The day is very pleasant,' he said. She turned to him and he felt his heart race at the beauty of her smile.

'On a day such as this it is not difficult to believe that all is well in this world. Do you also live near, Edward?'

'My father owns the land around here. I live that way, to the south, at Riverbank Manor.'

'Ah, you are the son of Samuel Mills. Tom has spoken of your family.'

'Then we are not strangers, Rachel.'

She stared at him, not blinking. 'We were never strangers, Edward.'

He was about to ask her what she meant but was distracted as two large blue butterflies came fluttering towards them. He thought how they were almost the same color as Rachel's eyes.

She raised her left hand slowly and they both came to rest on her fingers.

'They seem unafraid of you,' he said.

'They know I will not harm them. They will come to you if you ask them.'

'Ask them?' I do not understand.'

'Close your eyes and hold out your hand. Send them thoughts of love. You do not have to use words.'

He laughed at this strangeness. 'How do I send them love?'

'Think of their beauty and fragility. Ask them to share a moment with you.'

Her gentle voice made him think all things were possible and so he slowly put his hand outwards and closed his eyes. He pictured them in his mind—their delicate wings and the way they floated effortlessly in the air. Sitting there with Rachel, he felt a sense of peace, as if nothing mattered but that moment in time. Then he felt the lightest of touches on his hand. He opened his eyes and saw both butterflies resting on his finger, their wings lifted towards the sky. He held his hand steady and after a few moments they slowly, without any sign of fear, fluttered away.

He could not help but smile. 'When I was a small child I would chase butterflies but I never attempted to catch them. It did not seem right.'

'This world is filled with so many joyous creatures,' she said.

She was right. And he thought her the most joyous.

'I must go now.' She ran her fingers through her hair which had almost dried. Shiny strands framed her face.

'Do you come to the pool often, Rachel?'

'This is my first time. I was searching for a particular plant and came across this place. Perhaps I should not be here, on your property.'

'You are welcome whenever you wish. Will you come tomorrow?'

She closed her eyes for a moment. 'Yes, around this time.'

'May I escort you home?'

'Thank you, but no. I will look for the plant on the way back.'

Rachel walked over to Pharaoh who was patiently waiting nearby and gently stroked his flank. Edward saw her lips move close to the horse's ear but did not hear her words. The horse nuzzled her face and she laughed.

'I will see you tomorrow,' Edward said. He watched her walk away and his heart leapt when, just before she disappeared among the trees, she turned and waved.

He stayed there for a long time, reliving every second he had spent with her. She was unlike anyone he had ever met. And she was so beautiful. A rush of heat rose through his body as he remembered her standing naked in the sunlight. He laughed. His impatience to return to London had somehow disappeared.

2

'Edward, where have you been?' Elizabeth Mills asked her son. 'Your father has been looking for you.'

'I rode further than I intended and then stopped at the pool on the way back.' He gently kissed his mother on her cheek.

'Your father is not pleased. Mr. Newman is here. Go quickly and change. They are in the library.'

'I will make all haste.' He smiled fondly at her, gave her another kiss and hurried up the staircase.

Elizabeth watched him take the steps two at a time. His dark hair was thick and straight and touched his shoulders. His sparkling dark brown eyes were his father's but everyone said he had her smile. He had a liking for fine clothes and his tall, firm body was well suited to them. She saw how Edward attracted the admiring glances of the young ladies of the area and the looks of anticipation on the faces of their mothers who thought what a fine match the son of Samuel Mills would be for their daughters. At gatherings he would compliment the young ladies and make them laugh, but he did not single out any for special attention. He was kind to everyone and was well liked. He knew every one of the servants by name and always treated them with respect. The younger ones would blush when he spoke to them and he always managed to get a smile from the older ones.

Elizabeth walked slowly into the drawing room and sat down by the window, her violet silk dress rustling against the delicately carved legs of the chair. The pleasure of Edward's kiss lingered. Elizabeth had two sisters and a brother and her parents had always been openly affectionate to each other and to their children. Her mind wandered back to those days and the remembrance of that physical display of caring warmed her heart.

Although their marriage had been arranged and she had not loved Samuel on their wedding day, Elizabeth's deep feelings for her husband slowly crept up on her. She thought him a handsome man when they first met. He was tall and strong, and carried himself with an air of someone totally in control of his world. Although he had not smiled much on his first visit to their home, his dark eyes held hers whenever she looked his way. She could not describe him as a man of great affection but as one who showed consideration. After meeting Samuel's father, Elizabeth understood why any show of affection in public embarrassed him. Samuel's mother had died giving birth to him, her first child, and he had been brought up without a woman's influence by a harsh father who considered women's only purpose in life was to do their duty to their husbands and take care of their families. His father had never re-married and she imagined Samuel's childhood to be one of loneliness.

When Edward was born, Elizabeth showered him with love and affection. Samuel loved their son, she knew that, but he found it hard to overcome the embarrassment it caused him to show it. Only Margaret penetrated his stern exterior when she was born six years later. Their daughter only had to smile at Samuel and his heart softened. She knew Edward did not understand why he was not shown the same affection and although he gradually seemed to accept the reality of it and content himself with the love and adoration freely bestowed on him by the rest of the household, Elizabeth sometimes wondered if his heart held any resentment.

Recently she and Samuel had become concerned about the somewhat frivolous life Edward was involved in with his closest friend, William Overton, whose father had been appointed to the King's court in London. The young men were often invited there for parties and other social occasions. Although Samuel spoke to Edward about his need to work harder at learning to manage the estate, Elizabeth suspected her husband still held guilt about his relationship with his son and compensated by allowing Edward certain freedoms he would not otherwise have permitted. Edward was used to getting what he wanted but Elizabeth also knew he had a kind heart and a gentleness of spirit.

The sound of laughter brought Elizabeth from her thoughts as Margaret and her friend Sarah came in through the entrance from the garden, closely followed by Pepi. Wherever Margaret went, her little black and white spaniel followed.

'What are you two giggling about?' Elizabeth asked.

'We were just discussing what dress Margaret should wear to dinner tonight,' Sarah said. 'I brought a blue one and we did not want to wear the same color.'

'Perhaps you two young ladies should have a rest before dinner. You have been rushing around since early this morning and we would not want you to fall asleep at the table.'

Margaret laughed. 'We would never do that, Mother.'

Elizabeth loved her daughter's enthusiasm for life. Her green eyes were always sparkling with excitement and her smile added to her natural beauty. It seemed she could hardly wait for each new day to begin to fill it with love and laughter.

'Sarah, your parents will not want you to look exhausted when they arrive. They will think we do not take care of you when you visit.'

The two girls looked at each other. 'We will rest, Mother, I promise.'

'Has Edward returned?' Sarah asked.

The Griffins had moved to the area about four years ago and the families became close. Margaret and Sarah were both 12 years old at the time and formed an immediate affection for each other. Margaret always followed Edward around like a puppy and Sarah eagerly joined her. Elizabeth became aware that Sarah was beginning to feel a different kind of fondness for Edward when she overheard the girls talking two months earlier about how wonderful it would be if Sarah married Edward and they could truly be sisters. Sarah was an extremely pretty young woman with long fair hair that flowed in natural curls. Her blue eyes seemed to follow every movement and her petite figure was always dressed in the most exquisite of clothing. With the growth of her breasts it was impossible to hide the fact she was anything but a young woman. Edward showed no romantic interest in Sarah whatsoever, instead treating her in the same manner as he did Margaret. When Elizabeth discussed the matter with him, Edward was surprised but said he would take note of her advice to be more careful in his actions and words when in Sarah's company.

'He is with my husband and his guest in the library.'

'Oh.' Sarah's smile disappeared.

'Do not worry, Sarah,' Margaret said, 'we will meet at dinner tonight. Come, I have still to decide what to wear.'

At few minutes later Edward returned. He had changed from his riding clothes and was wearing dark green breeches, an embroidered waistcoat of the same shade over a ruffled long sleeved white shirt and a white cravat flowing down his chest. On top of this he had a dark green coat. William had introduced Edward to his tailor in London and this was one of the outfits he had brought back from his last trip.

'You are so handsome, Edward.'

He smiled as he bowed to his mother and then blew her a kiss before heading off to the library.

Edward took a deep breath and entered the room.

'At last. Come and meet Mr. Newman. Richard, this is my son, Edward.'

As his father moved away, Edward was able to see the man he had been talking about for some weeks. He had told him Mr. Newman was a man of property like himself. He had recently bought land in the area and had moved from London.

'I am pleased to meet you, Sir.' Mr. Newman was small and slim, almost fragile, and wore expensive but dull clothing. His hair was tied severely at the back, accentuating his long nose and thin lips. His smile did not reach his eyes.

'I told you Mr. Newman bought the Henson property, Edward, but he has also accepted the position as our new magistrate.'

'Congratulations, Sir.'

'Thank you. I feel it is my duty.' He took a sip from his glass. 'The end of the Puritan influence has again allowed evil to spread. There are those who take advantage of the situation to rob and murder and I want to see our country rid of these people. I feel I can serve this community well.' He took another sip and settled himself into one of the high-backed winged chairs.

'Pour a glass and sit down, Edward,' Samuel said. Edward did so and sat down in the chair opposite Mr. Newman. He could not understand his instant dislike of this man or the uneasy feeling he had in the pit of his stomach when he looked at him. Edward had never reacted like this to anyone. He mentally gave himself a shake and tried to concentrate on what Mr. Newman was saying.

'My particular interest is witches. Such vile creatures. Not enough of them were sent to the gallows. I particularly admired the work of Mr. Matthew Hopkins who rid us of so many of them.'

'Ah, the Witchfinder-General,' Samuel said. 'Such a pretentious name I think. We do not have that kind of problem these days. I have not heard of a witch being accused around these parts for quite some time. I believe Mr. Hopkins was particularly cruel with his methods and did not need much proof to send someone to the rope.'

Mr. Newman shook his head. 'He was greatly misunderstood, Samuel. Hopkins was deeply committed to sending those in league with the devil straight to hell and their master. It was a difficult task, for witches do not make themselves known to us. They are cunning creatures, evil and manipulative. They pretend to help others. They make up potions to cure illnesses. They are clever and deceitful. Through their acts of apparent kindness they seek to steal the souls of good Christian folk.'

'If they show kindness to others, what exactly is it that makes them witches?' Edward asked. He had never met a witch but was sure she could not have a heart as cold as the man opposite him. Fifteen minutes later Edward was still regretting having asked the question as he watched what he could only describe as hatred in Mr. Newman's eyes as he continued his discourse on the evil of witchcraft.

Edward found it difficult to concentrate on the conversation at dinner that evening. Mr. Newman seemed to love an audience. Charles and Agnes Griffin appeared intrigued with his tales of the criminals he had dealt with during his time as a magistrate in London. Eventually Edward stopped listening to what he was saying. It had also not taken Edward long to realize this man had no liking for women. He was respectful to the ladies and answered the questions of Margaret and Sarah, but his eyes only lit up when he talked about himself or conversed with Edward's father or Charles Griffin.

When the conversation steered towards witches, Elizabeth tried to intervene. 'Gentlemen, I think perhaps this is not a topic for discussion in front of Margaret and Sarah.'

'Nonsense, Elizabeth,' Samuel said. 'It is better they know something of the evil that exists in this world in order that they may recognize it if it is ever presented to them.'

Edward saw a slight smile touch Mr. Newman's lips at this dismissal of his mother's objection.

'I assure you I will not go into details too gruesome for the delicate ears of these young ladies,' he said. 'Your husband is right, Mistress. One of the reasons the evil craft flourishes is that it is not a matter for discussion. It is a hidden thing and because these creatures disguise their true intent with the pretense of helping their fellow man, the damage is often done before they are found out. It is said they can destroy crops with a spell, and even cause the death of someone who displeases them. It is best people are aware of this evil so they may be on their guard.'

Edward saw his mother frown but she held her tongue.

'Are there witches around here, Mr. Newman?' Margaret asked.

'Indeed there may well be. Although many were sent to the gallows, the ones who remained became more skilled in hiding their true purpose. There are still those among us who quietly and carefully practice their craft—still subtly trying to win souls for their evil master.'

'How would one recognize a witch, Mr. Newman?' Sarah asked.

'It is not easy. They could be your neighbor or a friend.'

'Must we be on guard against people we have known all our lives?' Margaret asked.

'Samuel, I must insist.' Elizabeth said.

'Yes, yes, my dear. I think you may be right. The young ladies are becoming overly excited, Richard, let us change the discussion.'

'Certainly. Please, accept my apologies. I am not used to the company of such fragile and delicate creatures.'

'Mother, we are not ...'

'Margaret, the subject is closed,' Samuel said.

Silence followed for a while as everyone concentrated on their food.

'Did you enjoy your ride today, Edward?' Sarah asked, 'You were gone a long time.'

Edward's mind immediately drifted to the pool and his meeting with Rachel.

'Edward, Sarah is speaking to you,' Elizabeth said.

'Yes, it was a very pleasant ride. I did not intend to go so far.'

'We thought we might all have spent some time together while Sarah was here,' Margaret said. 'You know she is returning home tomorrow.'

Edward exchanged a glance with his mother. 'I regret it has not been possible this time, Sarah, but I promise that next time you visit I will spend more time with my little sisters.'

'It is pleasing that you think of Sarah in such a way, Edward,' Agnes Griffin said. The look on Sarah's face clearly showed her annoyance at being considered so.

'We are hardly little, Edward.' Margaret said. 'Sarah and I are old enough to have husbands.'

'Husbands!' Samuel almost choked on his wine. 'Husbands!'

'We are 16, Father.'

'That is too young, far too young to be discussing husbands.'

'But you married Mother when she was only 16.'

'That was different. Your mother was a mature young woman for her age.'

'You do not think I am a mature young woman?' Margaret fluttered her eyelids.

Samuel laughed loudly. 'Well, I suppose if the right young man came along I would consider it. Mind you he would have to be from a good family and have suitable prospects.'

'I would, of course, be of the same mind,' Charles Griffin said. 'The young man of Sarah's choosing would have to be of good stock indeed.'

The girls laughed. 'Father, we are talking about a husband, not a horse,' Sarah said. The others joined in, except for Mr. Newman, who managed only the briefest of smiles.

The rest of the conversation went well enough with no further talk of witches or husbands, and Edward was glad to have the evening end. When Mr. Newman left for home and everyone else had retired, he went out into the garden. How he loved this house. His family had lived here for over three hundred years and each generation had added to the beauty of the place. The front rooms faced the manicured lawns and gardens which benefited from the love and care of his dear mother. The gardeners on the estate willingly followed her every instruction and took great pride in their work.

As Edward stood watching the cloudless night sky, he thought how brightly the stars sparkled. He could hear the sound of an owl in the tree nearby and the occasional neighing of the horses in the stables. Now he had time to think of Rachel.

There were beautiful young women among his family's friends and neighbors and he had made the acquaintance of many of the ladies at court, but none pulled at his emotions like Rachel had when she looked into his eyes. He smiled. Only minutes before meeting her he thought of getting away to the excitement of London and now he only thought of when he would see her again. He quickly dismissed his thought as to why she had shown no embarrassment whatsoever at being caught unclothed. He shrugged. He did not want to think of that now.

3

Edward arrived at the pool just before noon and stood quietly under the tree, waiting. It was warm and the sky cloudless. He caught sight of a butterfly and smiled as he remembered the previous day. He laughed. His father would certainly not have approved of him standing under a tree in the middle of the day thinking of butterflies.

Then he saw her. She was standing at the edge of the clearing, watching him. She smiled, stepped into the sunlight and walked slowly towards him. His breath caught in his throat. Her hair hung down her back, allowing him to see her face clearly. She was wearing a light grey dress over a white blouse. She had a simple beauty that needed no adornment. She held his gaze all the way, with no shy little glances, as most young women would do.

'Rachel.' He loved the sound of her name.

'It is good to see you again, Edward. It is another beautiful day is it not?'

'It is. Shall we walk a while?'

The leaves in the trees above them rustled in the warm breeze. Edward thought how there was music in that sound.

'Tell me about your life, Edward,' Rachel asked.

'I live with my father and mother, and my sister Margaret. Your aunt would have told you that. I help Father run the estate which covers a large area. We have cattle and sheep, and we grow crops. There is a well-stocked river and we have a mill for the grain. We have many servants, most of whom live on the estate. There is always much work to do.'

'You are a happy family?'

'Yes. My father is strict but it is only that he has expectations of those around him. He sets high standards and those who respect him try to live up to them. I do not always meet his expectations but I do try.'

'And your mother?'

'She is truly a wonderful woman, so gentle and caring. She surrounds us all with love. I cannot imagine our home without her. Although we are all obedient to my father, she can gently guide him to her way of thinking. She is a very clever woman. Margaret has just turned 16 and is a great beauty. She used to think only of horses and reading; now it is gowns and husbands. My father has no other family but we see my mother's family at least once a year. They are like my mother, joyful and a pleasure to be around. Tell me about you.'

'Grace is my father's sister. She is all the family I have.'

'Where did you live before you came here?'

'France.'

'My mother used to sing Margaret and I lullabies in French when we were children. Sometimes she still sings them when she is working in the garden. Is the countryside there as beautiful as England?'

'Some of it is very beautiful.' She fell silent. Her thoughts seemed far away.

'You were not happy in France?'

She did not reply.

'I hear the King has a magnificent court and is very powerful.'

'They call him the Sun King. He likes that. It is important to him to be powerful.'

'You speak as if you know him.'

'I met him once,' she whispered.

Paris, two months earlier

'You are weary, Rachel. You must rest.' Jean Paul put his hand on her shoulder.

'Later.' She turned back to little Colette who lay so still on the soiled bed. The room was cold and damp and sadness radiated from its walls. Poverty and death had overwhelmed any joy there had ever been in this house.

'Can you help her, Mademoiselle?' Colette's mother asked. 'She is the only child I have left. The others all died. She is all I have.' The woman began to weep.

'Be still, Madame. Let Rachel do her work.' Jean Paul guided the woman to the other side of the small room. He sat down with her on a worn, dirty bench and took her hand in his.

Rachel watched him for a few moments. She loved Jean Paul dearly but not the way she knew he had come to love her. She told him they shared a destiny but knew it was small compensation.

Rachel had been leaving the house of a woman who had just died from hunger and neglect. She had comforted her in her passing but was saddened she could do no more. Again she was reminded that the choice was not hers to make. She saw Jean Paul kneeling in a doorway helping a man whose bones protruded through his pale and scabbed skin. Together they helped the poor fellow to a nearby church where the priest gave shelter to those who needed it, although there was only dry bread softened in wine to feed him. That was many months ago and together they now tended the sick in the streets of Paris. She knew he wondered at her power for healing and so she trusted him with her secret. She was thankful he believed her.

They worked long and hard. Sometimes they had nothing to eat. They would go back to the little room they shared and she would make him close his eyes. They would pretend they were eating a sumptuous feast. She described every detail of the dishes until they could actually smell and taste the food. When they had mentally eaten their fill, they toasted each other with cups of cheap wine, pretending it was the finest in the land. They would laugh and talk and then wearily fall asleep. Rachel slept on the only bed while he lay on a thin mattress on the floor.

Jean Paul came from a wealthy family with many business interests but he had always known he would be a doctor. He had received the best education money could buy but when he was ready to go into the world, his father disowned him because he set up his practice in the poorest part of the city. Jean Paul never regretted his decision, even when the despair and hopelessness which permeated the streets threatened to overwhelm him. Rachel thanked God for allowing her to share part of Jean Paul's life.

Rachel returned her thoughts to the child on the bed. Much later, when the flow of energy eased, Rachel opened her eyes. Colette moaned softly. The mother rushed to her daughter's side, tears streaming from her eyes. 'Mademoiselle, thank you, thank you.' She kissed the child and then threw her arms around Rachel.

'You are an angel, Mademoiselle, sent by God. I feared she would die but you healed her. You have given her back to me.'

Rachel shook her head. 'No, Madame, God healed your daughter. Give your thanks to Him.'

Later that day Rachel and Jean Paul enjoyed a meal at the inn near where they lived. They had tended to the owner's wife the week before.

'Thank you for your kindness, Henri,' Rachel said.

'It is nothing. My wife is well. A meal is little trade.'

They thanked him again and walked out into the bright afternoon, pulling their cloaks tightly around their bodies against the cold wind. When they heard the pounding of hooves in the street behind them, Jean Paul put his arm protectively around Rachel and guided her towards the wall. They stood there waiting for the coach to pass but it came to a halt before reaching them. When they looked around they saw a magnificent carriage accompanied by four soldiers in the uniform of the King's guards. The soldiers dismounted and one of them opened the door of the carriage. An elegantly dressed man alighted.

'Are you the girl they call Rachel?' he asked.

'Yes. I am Rachel.'

'You are to come with me.'

Jean Paul pulled her closer. 'Who are you and what do you want with her?'

'She is to come with me,' the man said.

'She is going nowhere until you tell me why you want her.'

'The King wishes to speak to her.'

'Why?'

One of the guards placed his hand on his sword.

'It is not for you to question the King,' the man said, dabbing his nose with a small white handkerchief.

'Tell me why he wants to see her?'

The man glanced at the guards who quickly drew their swords.

Rachel put her hand on Jean Paul's arm. 'I will go with them.'

'No.'

'Please, do not worry.'

'Then I will come with you.'

'The King has requested only the girl,' the man said.

She touched Jean Paul's cheek. 'I will return when I can.'

Rachel stood in the center of a small but magnificently decorated room, the furnishings rich and abundant, and the deep blue carpet thick and soft. There was a large portrait on one of the walls. The man's long dark wig hung in curls to below his chest. He was wearing a red velvet hat edged with white feathers. His doublet was heavily decorated with white and gold braid as was the blue overcoat. A white scarf hung around his neck, meeting in a perfect blow at his throat. His legs were covered in white stockings and his black ankle boots adorned with silver buckles.

Suddenly the door opened and the man who had taken her from the street entered.

'My name is Monsieur Duval. I have come to take you to the King.'

'What is it that he wants of me?'

'One of the King's friends told him you cured a favorite servant of his. The servant was near to death apparently but has now regained full health. The King wants to find out if the story is true. I hope for your sake that it is.'

Rachel followed Monsieur Duval along corridor after corridor until they reached a door guarded by two soldiers. Without a word they stepped to the side and one of them opened it.

Monsieur Duval turned to her. 'Do not speak to the King unless he asks you a direct question. Do not approach him. Do not look at him. Do not touch him. If you ever repeat anything he says to you, you will die. Do you understand?'

'Yes.' Rachel took a deep breath and followed Monsieur Duval through the door into the presence of King Louis XIV of France. The King stood looking out of large windows to a magnificent garden that stretched into the distance. The furniture shone and light glistened off the large crystal chandeliers. Everything seemed to be decorated with gold. Rachel felt the King's energy and lowered her gaze as he turned towards her, but not before she recognized him as the man in the portrait.

'You are Rachel?' the King asked.

'Yes.'

'You have the gift of healing I am told.'

'I do what I can,' she said quietly.

'I am told you help the poor and ease the suffering of my subjects. Is it true you can cure sickness?'

Rachel did not respond. 'Answer me, girl.'

'God grants me the gift of healing but the spirit must be willing to receive His grace.'

'I do not understand you. You can heal or you cannot. Come closer.'

Rachel walked slowly towards the King and stopped a short distance from him. Still she did not raise her eyes.

'I have a...an inconvenience. It is the pressure of work. I spend almost every hour of my day tending to my people's needs. I have much to do. At the end of the day I want to relax. A King must relax in order to regain his strength for the work ahead. My people depend on me.' The King walked around her as he spoke. 'All the hard work, these worries, cause problems to my health. Because of these pressures, this constant caring for my people, I have no strength left. You can heal this condition?'

Rachel did not answer.

'Look at me, girl.' The King stopped in front of her and she raised her eyes. His did not seem kind.

'I am your King,' he said. 'I command you to heal me. If you do not, then I will assume you are a liar and a fraud. As such your punishment will be harsh I can assure you.'

'What are your symptoms, Majesty?'

'I told you. I weary from the trials of running the affairs of state, the affairs on my people. The lower part of my back aches constantly. Sometimes I work for many hours and then sit in my apartments, seeing no-one for days. I worry. I get melancholy about not achieving all that I want for France. When I want to relax I cannot. I need the comfort of a woman's embrace but I am too weary to satisfy my needs. I want you to cure my malady.'

'I cannot cure you, but with God's help I will do my best to help you.'

'Your best?' The King suddenly grabbed Rachel by her hair. 'I am your King. I command you to cure me.'

She felt the depth of his rage. 'I will try, Majesty.'

'You will do more than try, Mademoiselle.' He threw her to the ground and strode to the door. The King whispered something to Monsieur Duval who looked quickly at Rachel before leaving the room.

The King ignored Rachel and went to his writing desk where he studied some of the many papers lying there. Rachel quietly moved to a kneeling position and closed her eyes. She slowed her breathing and relaxed her body. She pictured herself floating on the still water of a beautiful lake. She imagined the white light of the full moon penetrating her until she felt only peace. She was unaware of time passing. She was brought back to reality by the sound of knocking.

'Enter,' the King shouted.

She heard the sounds of scuffling but did not look behind her.

'Rachel.' Jean Paul's gentle voice stirred her from her thoughts. Her heart ached at the sight of him. Two guards were holding him by his arms and his legs hung useless from his body. Blood ran from his head and over the bruises on his face.

'Jean Paul. Oh, what have they done to you?' She tried to reach him but guards stopped her. 'What have they done to you?'

'I have a proposition for you, Mademoiselle. You cure my malady and I will allow no further pain to be inflicted upon your friend.'

'I will try.'

'Try. Yes, you will try.' The King turned to the guards. 'Take him away and hurt him no further. For the moment.'

The King removed his thick blue velvet overcoat and lay on the plush red divan. Monsieur Duval stood slightly behind her.

Rachel knelt down beside the King, closed her eyes and brought her hands together in prayer. She then placed them above his head and slowly moved them down his body, being careful not to touch him. She felt the disruption of his energy before she reached his waist.

She connected to his emotions and memories. She felt his disgust at himself when he ate more than his fill of the rich and varied food put before him, which caused him to be tired and listless. She felt both his overwhelming desire to be a great king and his fear of failure. Rachel knew all these emotions contributed to the disturbance in the flow of his energy. She worked on him for a long time. Eventually she sensed him become calmer. She had done what she could and knew the rest would be up to him. She stood up and stepped back.

The King slowly stood up and Monsieur Duval assisted him to drape his coat back over his shoulders. 'I feel better,' the King said.

Monsieur Duval smiled. When the King felt good, he did too.

'Majesty, I was able to alleviate the symptoms but I cannot help the cause. Only you can do that.'

The King stood up and smiled at her. 'And pray tell your King what you think the cause of his problem is.'

'It is not my place to tell the King.'

'You have the King's permission,' he said.

'My examination shows you need more balance in your life.'

'Balance! You think I need more balance?'

'I think it would help you if you try to balance your work and your pleasures a little more.'

By the way the King put his hand to his chin and the silence that followed, Monsieur Duval thought he was reflecting on what the girl had said. He was wrong. Rachel knew what the silence held.

'I am interested, Mademoiselle. You think the King enjoys too much pleasure?'

'No, Majesty, I think more balance will give you more energy.'

'That is what you think?'

'Yes.'

'I do not know where your talents come from, Mademoiselle, but you have eased my discomfort. But tell me this. Why would I need to balance, as you say, my work and my pleasures if I have you to tend to me?'

'I will not always be here, Majesty.'

The King smiled at Monsieur Duval as he walked over to Rachel.

'You will not always be here, Mademoiselle?'

'I cannot stay. I have work to do.'

'There is greater work than administering to your King?'

'Many of your people are sick and dying. My work is to help them.'

'They are more important than your King?'

'No, Majesty, but there are so many of them. They are your people.'

'Mm. I think Mademoiselle may need a little balance in her own life. Put her with her friend. Give her time to think of her priorities. Perhaps she should see up close his pain and bear in mind that if she does not comply with her King's wishes how much greater that pain can be. Take her away. I will test the effects of her healing tonight.'

Rachel stood in the darkness. The coldness made her shiver and the smell of blood and human waste overwhelmed her senses.

'Jean Paul.' She called his name into the darkness. Her eyes adjusted slightly, assisted by the light of the torch outside the door. She saw him then. His back was up against the wall and his broken legs lay out in front of him.

'Jean Paul.' She rushed to his side and knelt down beside him on the soiled, damp hay. 'Jean Paul. It is Rachel.'

His eyes opened and he smiled. The blood dripping from the side of his mouth had already soaked his shirt. She gently dabbed his mouth with the hem of her skirt, then placed one hand on his head, the other on her heart, and closed her eyes. Almost immediately she felt him relax as the weariness of the pain left him. She put an arm around his shoulder and he rested his head against her.

'I am sorry,' she whispered.

'You have nothing to be sorry about, Rachel.' Jean Paul coughed and more blood ran from his mouth.

'I have brought you much trouble.'

'No, Rachel, no. You are the joy in my life. No amount of pain can take that away. You shared part of your life with me. I am honored.'

'Oh, Jean Paul.' She kissed him on the forehead.

Gradually it became brighter and the foul smell was replaced with the sweet scent of flowers. Before them stood a young man in a white robe. His golden hair hung to his shoulders.

'Michael!' Rachel stood up and held out her trembling hand. He took it gently.

'What is happening? Who are you?' Jean Paul tried to get up.

'He can see you,' Rachel said.

'Yes. I have allowed it.'

'You have come for me, Michael?'

'Not you, Rachel.'

'Oh.'

The young man knelt down and put his hand on Jean Paul's shoulder. 'Jean Paul, my name is Michael. I am an Angel of God. I have come to take you home.'

'Home?' Jean Paul stared into the stranger's eyes. Then he smiled. 'Yes. Home.'

Rachel laid her hand on Michael's shoulder. He turned and smiled. Her love for him had never been greater. 'Thank you,' she said, a tear sliding down her face.

She knelt down at Jean Paul's side and gently cupped his face with her hands. 'You have blessed my life, Jean Paul. You and I have a bond that will not be broken. Even when I cannot see your beautiful face with my eyes, I will see you with my heart. I will always love you.'

'I loved you from the moment I saw you,' he said.

'We will meet again, my dear friend.'

Jean Paul reached up and wiped the tears on her cheeks. 'Yes,' he whispered.

She lowered her lips to his and kissed him on the mouth.

'It is time,' Michael said.

Rachel watched as Jean Paul stood up and walked to Michael's side.

She felt the darkness and the cold now that she was alone. She gently kissed each of Jean Paul's hands before laying them across his chest. His body still held warmth although his spirit had departed. She cupped her hands in prayer and asked for guidance.

Sometime in the night she had a vision and when she awoke in the darkness she knew the Guardians were near. When the jailer came for her in the morning, he did not look at Jean Paul. Rachel followed him up the stairs to where Monsieur Duval waited.

'Come,' he ordered. As Monsieur Duval approached the King's rooms he turned to find her no longer behind him. Immediately he called the guards to search for her and with a heavy heart he entered the room.

'Where is the girl?' the King asked.

'She escaped, but the guards will find her. She will be found and brought here immediately. My apologies, Sire, I should have been more diligent.' Monsieur Duval waited for the King's outburst. It did not come. The King went to the window and gazed out.

'It matters not,' he said. He turned to Monsieur Duvall and smiled. 'Get my architects and master builders. I have much work to do.'

Edward felt now was not the time to ask Rachel what happened in France but perhaps when she knew him better she would confide in him.

'You are happy living with your aunt?' he asked.

'Oh yes. She and Tom have shown me great kindness.'

'Is your home now with them? You will stay?'

'I do not know.'

They talked of flowers and spring happenings that day. There was no awkwardness in their times of silence, only a drawing together of hearts. Edward knew this day would stand apart from all others in his life. His whole being seemed to be alive with feeling. Whatever else happened to him, this day he would remember.

When they came again upon the pool, Rachel sighed and turned to him. 'I must go now.'

'I...will you meet me here again?' he asked. 'Tomorrow?'

'Not tomorrow. Perhaps in two days?'

'I will be here.'

She walked away, and as she had done before, she turned and waved before disappearing behind the trees. He was overcome with the urge to run after her, to take her in his arms. He stood there a long time but gradually a seed of doubt arose in his mind at her strangeness and his lack of control over his need for her.

4

Rachel stopped wiping the table and watched Grace hang sprigs of rosemary by the window. She had met her aunt for the first time only a few weeks ago but Rachel felt she had known her always. After the Guardians had rescued her from Paris, they wanted to take her to a safe place where they could protect her. To them it was their duty and they would not let go of the responsibility easily. Rachel stayed with them for five days and they came to know one another. She shared her memories and spoke of her visions and eventually she persuaded them to bring her here. They left her reluctantly but Rachel knew they would be always be there if she needed them.

Grace had not seen her brother, George, since he left home over 25 years ago and she welcomed her niece with open arms. She and Tom first gave her food and left her to sleep for nearly two days before asking her about her life.

Rachel was born in Spain and her mother, Helena, died when she was three. Rachel's grandparents had not approved of their daughter's marriage to George and blamed him for her early death. Although wealthy and with much influence, they refused George's request to take Rachel into their home where she could be educated and learn the finer ways of life. George spent the next three years doing the best he could to raise Rachel but when he was killed by a runaway carriage when she was six, the nuns of a local convent gave her a home. Rachel told Grace and Tom of her journey to where she was now and held nothing back, although she knew her story must have sounded so incredible as to be the workings of a deranged mind.

Grace and Tom shared with her their sadness at having lost their precious son, William, to fever when he was 10 and how they faced each day with profound loneliness. Rachel was able to banish that dreadful emptiness so instantly that they accepted the truth of who she was.

Grace looked over at her and smiled. 'You seem in a happy place this morning.'

'I met a young man in the woods and I liked him very much.'

Grace laughed. 'And does this young man have a name?'

'It is Edward Mills.'

'Glory be! And you say you like him?'

'Very much. We met yesterday and the day before. We talked of many things.'

'And did he show fondness for you?'

'Yes.'

'Will you see him again?'

'I hope so.'

'You do not know our ways here, Rachel. Some would see it inappropriate for you to meet with him so. You will be careful.'

Rachel stopped what she was doing and went over to Grace. She put her arms around her and kissed her on the cheek. 'I will take care, I promise.'

It was almost noon as Edward rode towards John Booth's house. He had matters from the previous day to discuss with John who managed much of the work on the estate. He liked John. He was a tall, thin man with a full head of grey hair that always seemed to be in disarray. He was always cleanly dressed and his wide dark eyes took in everything. He was honest and hard-working. Although he always showed respect for his employer, John offered his advice or opinion completely as he saw it, whether it was what Samuel wanted to hear or not. As a result John had their complete trust.

He thought the day too long without seeing Rachel and was glad of the opportunity to keep busy. His need to go to London had waned and he thought he would put the trip off for a while.

A pillar of smoke spiraled from the chimney of John's small cottage. Mary Booth's garden was well kept with vegetables and herbs. He had met Mary often when he called at the cottage to speak to John although he had never been inside their home. He knew they had four children, but it occurred to him as he dismounted how little he knew of the lives of these people. He tied Pharaoh's reins to the stake and just as he approached the door, it opened and John stepped out.

'Good day to you, John. One of the men said you had gone home to see your wife. I hope all is well.'

'Master Edward.' John stood holding the door open.

'Rachel!' Edward could not hide his surprise as she stepped from the house. 'I did not expect to see you here.'

'Mary is ill, Master Edward. Rachel has been helping her.'

'Oh.' Edward could not help feeling put out as he realized her reason for not meeting him today was to tend to Mary. He was instantly ashamed of this thought. 'I am sorry to hear that, John. Perhaps I could pay my respects to your wife while I am here.'

'She will be pleased to see you.'

'I will make sure Mary is ready to receive a visitor.' Rachel disappeared back into the house.

'You did not mention your wife's illness to us.'

'She had been getting tired and had pain in her joints. Sometimes the pain was so bad she lay awake all night, trying not to cry. I had great concern for her.'

Rachel emerged from the house a short time later, with two young boys clutching her hands. 'Mary is ready to see you now, Edward.'

The main room, albeit sparsely furnished, was neat and tidy. Rachel opened the door to another room and Edward followed her through it. Mary was sitting up in bed, her hair neatly brushed and the covers arranged around her. There were smaller beds in the room and Edward realized the whole family must sleep in this one room.

'It is good of you to visit me, Master Edward. Please sit.'

'I am pleased to see you again, Mistress Booth, but sorry to hear you have been unwell.' Edward sat on the chair next to the bed.

'I will take the children outside to play.' Rachel said.

'Is there anything I can get you, anything I can do to help?' Edward asked.

'It is kind of you but I have everything I need. John takes good care of me and Rachel has been an angel. I feel my strength returning and the pains are easing. I hope to be walking around soon.'

'Good news indeed. Having four children must keep you very busy.'

'They are a lot of work but it is a labor of love. We are very fortunate.'

'They seem fond of Rachel.'

'Oh aye. She has such a way with children, with everyone. You feel good when she is around.'

Edward wanted to ask more but held back and concentrated on Mary. They talked of her garden—apparently Rachel was tending to that also—and the children. When an appropriate time had passed, Edward made his farewells and followed John outside. Rachel was playing with the children. The girl was about ten, a boy about five and the two younger ones he had seen previously. Both Edward and John watched them in silence for a while. Rachel had a scarf hiding her eyes and the children ran around her, squealing with laughter, as she reached out blindly to catch them.

John smiled. 'She is a fine lass.'

Edward could not remember ever having seen John smile before and thought how much younger it made him look.

'I do not know how we would have managed without her. I think I would have lost my Mary if not for her.'

'It was that serious?'

'I could see it in her eyes. The pain was just too much for her. She tried hard for my sake and the children, but she was fading.'

'And Rachel helped her?'

'She brought flowers and herbs and boiled them up and made Mary drink the broth. She spent days here just holding her hand and speaking gently to her. Now Mary is feeling better and wanting to leave her bed but Rachel is making her rest. The lass cares for the children and helps with the cooking. We have some fine neighbors too and they help as much as they can.'

'I am glad to hear that, but you should have told us how serious it was and we would not have expected you to work.'

'I need to work, Master Edward. With help from God and our friends we have managed.'

'I can see you have, but you must promise to tell us if you ever have such troubles again.'

'Thank you, Master Edward,' John said before looking back at the children.

Rachel had caught one of them in her arms and the others screamed with excitement. She took off the scarf covering her eyes and planted a kiss on the child's forehead before putting him down on the ground.

'Again, Rachel, again,' they all shouted. Rachel looked over at Edward and John standing by the door.

'In a moment. I will speak with your father first. Here, Jenny, you put on the scarf while I am gone and see if you can catch one of the others.' Rachel tied the scarf around the girl's eyes and turned her round in a circle. 'I will return shortly, I promise.' The excited cries started again as Rachel walked over to the men.

'Mary would have enjoyed your visit, Edward.'

'She did, Rachel,' John said. 'Her cheeks are quite rosy.'

'Good.'

'She still wants to leave her bed.'

'I know, John, but just another day and she will be able to get up for a while and sit in the garden.'

Edward could not take his eyes from Rachel. Her cheeks were tinged with pink and her blue eyes sparkled with light. He desperately wanted to be alone with her.

'I will take my leave of you now, John,' Edward said.

'I will be heading back to the top field soon. You wanted to talk to me,' John reminded him.

'That can wait. We will speak tomorrow. Rachel, may I escort you home?'

'Thank you, but I promised the children I would return to play.'

'Oh.' He had thought her as eager as he to be together. 'Well then, I will see you on the morrow, John.'

Edward walked to his horse and mounted. He heard the children shout excitedly to Rachel but he did not look back. He rode Pharaoh hard back to the stable. He could not shift the feeling of annoyance. She could not meet him today by the pool because she was tending to Mary Booth and then had refused his escort home because she had promised the children she would play with them. Perhaps she did not find his company as interesting as he found hers. He refused the stable boy's help to unsaddle Pharaoh. This he did himself, deciding to give the horse a good rub down.

His annoyance had spent itself by the evening when he joined his family in the garden after dinner.

'Sarah will be here on Friday, Edward. Promise me you will leave time to come riding with us.'

'Edward, your sister is speaking to you.' His father's voice brought him back from his daydreaming.

They were seated in the shade in the garden. Elizabeth Mills was working on her tapestry and Margaret was doing some lacework.

'My apologies, Margaret, what did you say?'

'Your thoughts always seem elsewhere these days. I was saying Sarah is coming to visit again on Friday and I wanted us all to go riding.'

'We will, little sister, if the weather holds.'

'Do you think Sarah is pretty, Edward?'

He shared a glance with his mother. 'Of course she is pretty. You are both very pretty and talented young ladies.'

'She thinks highly of you, and has a great affection for you,' Margaret said.

Edward shifted in his chair. He did not like the way the conversation was going. 'She is your great friend, Margaret. I share your affection for her.'

'You know that is not what I am saying.'

Edward did not answer.

'She comes from a good family, Edward,' his father said, looking up from his book. 'Or do you have someone else in mind? Someone in London perhaps? Is that why you are anxious to return there?'

He could feel the heat in his cheeks. 'No. Now can we please end this discussion?'

'You are blushing.' Margaret put down her work and stared at him. 'You do have someone in mind. Who is it? She cannot be as pretty and as good a person as Sarah. Tell me who it is.'

'I do not wish to discuss this.' He got up from his chair. 'I will bid you goodnight. I am going for a walk.'

'Edward!' He ignored Margaret's call and strode off towards the stables. The horses had been fed and bedded down and the stable hands had gone off for their supper. He opened the gate to Pharaoh's stable. The horse nuzzled him and Edward stroked his neck affectionately.

'What I am going to do, Pharaoh? They are trying to find me a wife.' A picture came to his mind of Rachel walking from the pool on that first day. He felt a warmth spread through his body but then discomfort. Again he wondered how she had she spent her time in France and why she was unaffected by the improprieties of swimming naked and agreeing to meet a man she barely knew without a chaperone? Did he really want to know?

5

Edward was at the pool before noon. Although he was anxious to see Rachel, he enjoyed the feeling of anticipation. Then he saw her.

'Edward.' She said his name softly.

'Rachel. You are well?'

'Yes. It is a fine day is it not?' They followed the same path they had taken previously.

'It is. And how is Mistress Booth faring?'

'Much better. She sat out in the garden for a while. She so hates to be inactive but her strength is coming back.'

'And that has been due to your ministrations?'

'Not mine. God allowed me to help.'

'Are you very religious, Rachel?' He assumed she was Catholic if she came from France.

She smiled. 'There are people who say I am not religious at all, but I know what I believe.'

They walked in silence for a while. Edward fought the urge to take her hand.

'You were offended when I did not accept your offer to accompany me home,' she said.

He thought he had kept his annoyance concealed. 'Not offended. I just wanted to spend time with you and I thought you might want the same.'

'I do want to spend time with you but I made the children a promise.'

'They would have forgiven you, I am sure.'

'When I make a promise I try to keep it. Otherwise I would just be saying words that have no meaning.'

'Are some things not more important than others?' he asked.

'For me a promise can never be empty words.'

'I will try to remember that, Rachel. Now tell me how you spend your day. When I think of you I want to picture in my mind what you are doing.'

'You think of me?' she asked.

'I think of you often when I am not with you. You find this strange?'

'No. I think of you also.' She smiled. 'My days are full. I help Tom in the mornings with the milking of the cows and collecting the eggs. I help my aunt to bake bread and do household chores.'

'And you help Mistress Booth,' he added.

'Yes. I help Mary and others like her who are sick and cannot manage. I know of nature and herbs and flowers. I combine them to make medicines.'

'Where did you learn this? France?'

'I think I have always known.'

'You will soon put Dr. Brown out of business?'

'I do not think Dr. Brown would agree with my ways. He appears not to know much of what nature has to offer.'

'It would appear you do not have good thoughts of him.'

'I try not to judge.'

'You have obviously received a good education?'

'I have the best of teachers. I am fortunate. I learn quickly in some things. On others lessons I am still working.'

'Did you leave many friends behind when you left France?' He remembered her sadness when she had previously talked of the place.

She momentarily stopped walking and closed her eyes. 'Yes.'

He recognized pain in that one word. He wanted to ask more but did not wish to disturb the harmony of their day.

'And what of you, Edward?' She smiled and her lightness returned. 'What is it that you do with your day?'

'I help Father as much as I can. He is teaching me all aspects of business. I attend to the bookkeeping and I oversee what is happening on our estate while he is in London. I accompany him there on occasions, but not as much as I would wish.'

'You like London?' she asked.

'Very much. It is so alive with people and much takes place there. I have a friend in King Charles's court and there is always something happening and interesting people to meet. On my last visit I met a man called Samuel Pepys. We talked for hours about music and ships. And he writes profusely. He knows everything about the city. I accompanied him and his wife to Greenwich which I greatly enjoyed. I am to dine with them when I next return. Father thinks I go there too often by myself but when I go with him it is all business and there is no time for pleasure. Mother thinks he wishes to hand over more of the running of the estate to me but first he wants me to take a wife and settle down.'

'He has someone in mind for you?'

'Perhaps. Our friends, Charles and Agnes Griffin, have a daughter, Sarah. She and Margaret are great friends and the families spend much time together. I think my father is beginning to see Sarah as a good match for me. I have spent many years thinking of her as a dear friend of my sister so it is hard for me to think of her in a romantic light.'

'Would she make you a good wife?'

'She is very pretty and pleasant company. She can play musical instruments and sings quite sweetly. She rides well. I am sure she has been taught how to run a household. Margaret certainly thinks she would make me a good wife. My father is an only child so it is up to me to carry on the family name. One day I will marry and have a son but there is time yet.'

'A child would be expected, I can see that,' Rachel said.

Edward saw sadness in her eyes. 'Let us talk of the present,' he said, 'not the future. John's children seem very fond of you.'

'And I of them. We went to the river this morning and picked wild flowers and played games. The laughter of children always fills my heart with hope. We saw frogs. At first the children were afraid of them but then they sat so quietly just watching them. Children are not taught enough of the wonders of nature or what is around them. Imagine being afraid of a frog.'

'They are not exactly the most handsome of creatures.'

She laughed. 'Oh Edward, not you too. I find them most beautiful.'

'I think you find everything and everyone beautiful.'

'There is beauty in every living thing if we look hard enough so it is not difficult.'

'Not for you, but not everyone sees the world the way you do. Sometimes you encounter someone who possesses no beauty of heart or soul.'

'Do you know someone like that?'

'He is a new friend of my father. I met him recently. I felt a coldness surround him. I wanted to get away from him. He was polite enough but I felt he was not a good man. He talked of evil but I think the evil came from within. I would be pleased not to see him again but I think that will not be possible.'

'It is not easy. I too have not always loved when I should.'

She put her hand on his arm. He saw the color disappear from her cheeks. Her touch became a grip as she stared ahead, her eyes glazed. She let go of his arm and sank to her knees, repeating words he did not understand. He knelt beside her.

'Rachel, are you unwell?' She did not appear to hear him. 'Please, tell me what is happening.'

Slowly she removed her hands from her face and ceased her chant. He took her arm and helped her to stand.

'I am sorry. An old memory stirred.'

'Come, you are trembling. Let us sit under the tree for a while. This memory was not a happy one it seems.'

'No, but it was a long time ago.' She pushed her hair back from her face and looked at him. 'Tell me about your father's friend.'

'There is not much to tell. He bought some property in the district and is the local magistrate.'

'You really did not like him?'

'No. He talked of witches and evil-doers as if it was his mission in life to destroy them. Rachel, your memory, was it of someone who hurt you?'

'Yes.'

'Was it someone you loved?'

'No. I did not love him.'

'Then you hate him?'

'I hope not. Our Lord taught us to love our enemies.'

'It must be hard to do that, to love someone who has caused us great pain. I do not think I would find it easy.'

'It is not, but we must try. If our hearts are filled with hate then we cannot feel love. But first there must be forgiveness. If we are able to forgive those who have caused us pain then it will be easier to love them. I have forgiven. I think perhaps I still have work to do on the loving part.' She smiled and he saw color return to her cheeks.

'Is this man able to hurt you again?'

'If I fear him perhaps he will.'

'Who is this man who would hurt you? I will not allow it. I will protect you. Please Rachel, let me protect you. Tell me who he is?'

'I have not seen him in a long time. Perhaps we may never meet again. I thank you for your concern, Edward, but we each have to walk our own path and you cannot walk with me on mine.'

Edward felt a sinking of his heart. He wanted to walk her path. He told himself he was foolish as he had not known her long but he knew it mattered not. He would bide his time but he would be with her.

'Oh, look at that beautiful hawk,' Rachel said.

He looked up into the sky where she was pointing. 'Where?'

'Just below that little white cloud. Do you see it?'

'Yes, yes, I see it.'

'She will lay her eggs soon.'

'How do you know that?'

'I just know.'

He laughed. 'You are a strange one. You know so many things. Are you sure you are not a nymph of the forest in disguise?'

'It is easy to know the things of nature. You just have to listen and to watch. The creatures of the earth want to share with us. We are all equal in the eyes of God.'

'You really believe that?'

'Yes. We are all connected to each other, every living creature, and our purpose in life is to make that connection. We have to learn to love each other unconditionally.'

'Do you think the day will come when the world will be like that?' he asked.

'I know it will come.'

'I do not have your faith, but I hope what you say is true.'

'We can all help to change the world, Edward.'

'Do you really think one person can make a difference?'

'I know many who have.'

'I believe you also are one of those people, Rachel. I think you make a difference.' She smiled and he felt he had known this woman all his life.

The rest of the time was spent discussing the things of the forest. When they returned to the pool, the clouds were moving over the sky.

'Ride with me and I will take you home. The rain may come soon.'

She looked upwards for a few moments. 'Not until evening. Thank you, but I would like to walk.'

Edward laughed. 'You can predict the weather also? 'Is there no limit to your knowledge?'

She smiled but did not answer.

'Will I meet with you tomorrow?' He tried to keep the pleading from his voice.

'I have much work to do. I do not know if I can come.'

'I will try to come as often as I can around this time. I will not expect you but if you are here I will be very happy to see you.'

'Thank you.' She held his gaze and seemed reluctant to leave.

He lifted up one of her hands with great tenderness and kissed it. Rachel did not pull away and although he did not want to let it go, he released it. She smiled once more, a smile that radiated to a place deep within him, and then turned away.

6

Edward emerged from the library where he had been discussing business with his father to find Sarah and Margaret waiting outside the door.

'You promised to go riding with us.'

Edward tried to hide his impatience. It was almost noon and he wanted to go to the pool in the hope Rachel would be there. They had not met for four days. He had gone with his father to buy some new horses some distance away and only managed to go to the pool on one day. She was not there. The time apart made him realize how much he missed her and at night his dreams were only of her.

'I have things to do, Margaret.'

'You promised, and we are ready. Please.'

Edward remembered his conversation with Rachel. He did not want to make empty words of his promise.

'I will change and meet you in the stables.' He smiled at their pleasure. He would go to the pool tomorrow.

'Do hurry.' Margaret shouted to him as they rushed out the door.

They rode slowly, side by side. The girls talked endlessly and Edward tried to keep up with their conversation. He could not stop thinking he might be missing a chance to be with Rachel.

'We are riding too slowly. Follow me!' Margaret suddenly spurred her horse and raced off. Sarah laughed and did the same. Edward could only follow. Margaret was a good rider and soon they were heading across the fields. Margaret sensibly slowed her horse as she approached the trees. By the time Sarah and Edward reached her she had dismounted and was stroking her horse.

'That was fun?'

'I can see it is so. Your cheeks are quite rosy. After we have rested the horses I think we should head back.'

'Not yet. We have not been gone long. Let us walk the horses for a while. We should go to the pool. We had such fun there when we were younger, Sarah. It is so beautiful and peaceful. I cannot think why we have not taken you there before this.' They led their horses by the reins. 'I hope summer lasts forever. It is so restricting not to be able to leave the house when I wish.' Margaret, like Edward, loved to be outside, even when the weather was not so inviting.

'I think for a respectable young lady you are allowed far too much freedom, little sister.'

'It does not seem right that it is proper for you to do what you want and not me. I think I would rather have been born a man.'

'I think not. You like to be pampered and taken care of.'

'How can you say that? You certainly do not pamper me. You are always making fun of me.'

Smiling, Sarah listened silently to the playful conversation between them.

Edward stopped when he realized they were almost at the pool. 'I think we should turn back now.'

'We cannot come this far and not at least see it. It is so pretty in the summer. Come Edward, it is still early in the day.'

He realized it was well past noon and unlikely Rachel would be there, although the thought that perhaps she might be excited him.

'Here we are!' Margaret let go of the reins and rushed over to the water. 'It is so clear. See how it sparkles in the sunlight. If you watch very closely, Sarah, you can see small fish. When Mother brought us here when we were children we used to try and catch them but they always seemed to get away.'

All three turn around at the sound of rustling in the bushes behind them. Rachel came out of a clearing, her arms filled with wild flowers. She did not seem surprised to see them. Edward thought again how beautiful she was.

'Edward, it is good to see you.' She smiled at him and then looked at the girls.

'Rachel.' Edward said her name so softly that both girls turned to stare at him. 'This is my sister, Margaret, and our friend, Sarah.' Both girls stared at the newcomer. 'Margaret, Sarah, this is Rachel.'

'I am happy to meet you,' Rachel said. Still the girls did not speak. Rachel put down her flowers by the trunk of a large tree and walked over to them. 'It is a beautiful day to be outside.'

'Yes.' Margaret at last found her tongue. 'You are an acquaintance of my brother? I have not heard him speak of you.'

'Rachel and I met one day when I was out riding.'

'Oh. So this is where you ride to each day. And what is it you do here?' Margaret's tone was hard.

'Margaret! I will not have you speak like that. Rachel and I are friends. My apologies, Rachel. My sister has been taught better manners.'

'It matters not.' Rachel's smile did not fade.

'I apologize. I did not mean to offend. I was just curious as to how you know my brother.'

'As he said, we are friends. I must go now. I trust you will enjoy the rest of your day.' Rachel smiled at them, gathered up her flowers again and walked away.

'She looks like a servant girl. Who is she employed by?' Margaret's harsh tone returned. You can tell by her dress she is not from ...'

'Stop! I will not have you discuss Rachel in this manner. She is a good person and has my respect. We are leaving now. Get on your horses.'

The girls looked at each other and decided to do as they were told. Edward was silent on the way home and rode slightly in front of them. When they reached the stable, he handed the reins to the stable boy and strode off into the house without a word.

7

In his room he sat down on the chair by the window. His thoughts were in turmoil. He must speak to his father. He changed from his riding clothes and made his way downstairs. His father was crossing the hallway.

'Ah, Edward, I have matters to discuss with you. Join me in the library.'

'I wish to talk with you also, Father.'

Samuel took his seat behind the desk and Edward stood by the window looking out into the garden.

'I think we need to employ more people for the harvest this year. The crops have done well with the mild winter. Will you see to it for me? Speak to John. I am sure he will know some honest men who would do the job well.'

'I will do it today.'

'Good. I have invited Mr. Newman to dinner this evening. I get the feeling you do not like him, Edward?'

'I will be honest, I find him unusual. He does not appear to have the nature of a man required to sit in judgment of others. I sense no compassion in him.'

'You may be right, but we need a man who is prepared to do the job well. I would ask you to give him a chance.'

'I will try, Father.' Edward thought it unlikely he could change his mind about the man.

'And you said you had a matter you wanted to discuss with me?'

'Yes, there is.'

Samuel had been writing while he was talking but his son's serious tone made him put down the pen and give him his full attention.

'I know it is your wish that I take over more responsibility for the estate. You said you would first like me to… to marry.'

'Ah!' Samuel's delight was obvious. 'Sarah? Or did I guess correctly that you have met someone in London?'

'No. I only wish to discuss the possibility. I have made the acquaintance of the niece of Tom Clarke.'

'Tom Clarke. He is good and honorable man, but Edward he…'

'Please hear me out. I know you would like me to make a good marriage but I do not wish to wed someone I am not fond of.'

'Are you not fond of Sarah?'

'Yes, but not the same way I am fond of Rachel.'

'Rachel. So that is her name. What do you know of her?'

'Tom's wife Grace is the sister of Rachel's father who is dead. Grace is her only living relative. She has come lately from France. She is a respectable and kind woman. She helps others. Did you know John Booth's wife had been ill?'

'No, he did not mention it.'

'The illness was serious. Rachel helped care for Mistress Booth and the children. John said he would have lost her if it had not been for Rachel. She is an angel, Father. Well educated. She can talk on many things. She is...'

'Beautiful?'

'Yes.' Edward smiled.

'I can see you are quite taken with this girl. And is she fond of you?'

'I think she is.'

'And when did you make her acquaintance?'

'Only two weeks ago. It is long enough for me to know I wish her to be my wife.'

'Edward! You cannot decide on marriage after only two weeks. What does Tom say of this?'

'I do not know if he is aware of our friendship. I have not spoken to him.'

'He knows nothing of this?' Samuel stood up and walked around the desk. 'Edward, how did you meet this girl?'

'We have been meeting in the woods.'

'In the woods? She had no chaperone? You met alone with her in the woods?'

'Yes, Father, but it is not as you might think.'

'A respectable woman would not agree to meet you alone in the woods.'

'Please listen to me. Our friendship has been innocent. We walk, and talk about many things.'

'She knows who you are; who your family is?'

'Yes.'

'Did it not occur to you she might have enchanted you, compromised you, knowing you come from a wealthy family?'

'No. Rachel would not do that. I have told you, she is fine and honorable.'

'You have a kind heart, Edward. Your mother taught you that and I am grateful to her, but you are too trusting. I have seen it in your dealings with others. You are too quick to believe that what people say is the truth.'

'But Father, I know Rachel. I know she has a true heart.'

'Listen to me. It is not respectable to meet a young woman alone in the woods. How can you expect me to accept someone as your wife who has no self-respect, no thought for propriety? How can she be pure?'

'She is, Father. You would only have to meet her to see how good and kind she is.'

'I do not think this...'

'Please. All I ask is you agree to meet her.'

Samuel walked to the window and looked out. Edward knew his father was struggling with his decision but he also knew he rarely denied him anything—eventually. He waited. He jumped when his father quickly turned around to face him.

'You may invite her to the house, but that is all. If I do not find her suitable, will you promise to pursue it no further?'

Edward knew he was taking a risk but he needed his father's agreement to any marriage. A vision of Rachel came to his mind. He wanted her, despite her strangeness. More than anything else, he wanted her to be his wife. He did not care how she had lived her life before they met. He would trust in her and his father's fairness. Rachel would charm his father as she had done him.

'I agree, Father. I know you will like her.'

At dinner that evening, Edward announced to his mother and sister that his father had agreed to receive Rachel in their home.

'She is coming here!' Margaret shouted. 'Father, how could you allow this?'

'You have met the girl, Margaret?'

'Yes. When Sarah and I went riding with Edward. But how could you invite her here, Father? She is just a common villager.'

'Do not speak of Rachel in that way.'

'She is a peasant girl with probably no education or manners. Why do you invite her here?'

'Heed my words, Margaret, I will not have this. She is my friend.'

'Friend. Huh! I am sure she gives you more than friendship when you meet her in the woods.'

'Margaret!' Both Samuel and Elizabeth spoke at the same time. 'You were not brought up to speak like that,' Samuel said. 'I am ashamed of you.'

'I am only trying to say, the girl will feel out of place here. Sarah will be most displeased to hear that girl if being invited to our home.'

'Sarah! What has she to do with this?' Edward said.

'Well, Sarah thought, we both thought, you and she had an understanding.'

'What understanding?' Elizabeth asked.

'The understanding that perhaps one day she and Edward would ...'

'This is nonsense.' Edward walked over to his sister. 'There is no understanding between us. How could she think that? I have never expressed any interest in her other than a friend of the family. Where did this idea come from?'

'She is very fond of you, Edward, you know that. Our families are close and of the same class. We just thought ...'

'You just thought! You two decided for me who I should wed. You decided my future. What right have you to interfere in my life like this?'

Margaret shrank back from him.

'Children,' Elizabeth said calmly, 'it is not necessary to shout at each other. Margaret, you must realize Edward has to make his own decisions on these matters. You have no right to interfere. And Edward, your sister has only love in her heart for you. She might have been misguided but she meant no harm.'

Seeing the tears clouding Margaret's eyes, Edward released his anger. 'I am sorry for having shouted at you but I will not have you speak disrespectfully of Rachel. I want you to make her welcome in our home.'

Margaret looked at her parents and then back at Edward. 'I apologize also. I will do what is expected of me.'

Without a word, Samuel walked out of the room. Edward saw the anger on his face and his heart sank.

8

Rachel stood under the giant oak tree and looked up at the sky. The moonlight filtered through the canopy of branches. The stars shone brightly and she wanted to reach out to them. She sensed his presence and turned to him.

'Michael.'

'Rachel.' He said her name so gently that the word seemed to float in the air. She walked towards him and took his outstretched hands. Love radiated through her and she trembled as it totally engulfed her.

'You read my heart well, Michael. I need your strength.'

'You have strength, Rachel.'

'I need to feel your love.'

'But do you not feel my love every moment?' He smiled, holding her hands a little tighter.

'It seems different this time, Michael. The tie that binds me to his heart is strong.'

'You do not lack courage, Rachel. A cord that connects two hearts can never be severed. You know this to be true.'

'You are right. Perhaps it is my eyes that will miss the sight of him.'

'See with your heart, Rachel. You do not need your eyes to behold him.'

'You tell me truths I know.'

'Then why did you call me?'

'I can hide nothing from you. I wanted to see you. I know you will always be there to help me on my journey. I feel your love each time you stop the world and take me home. When it is time to return, it is the love in your heart and the strength in your arms as you carry me back that removes any fear I have of the journey ahead.' She took a moment to bask in the radiance of his light until it expanded and she could no longer see his face.

'Grace, Edward has invited me to visit his home.'

'What!'

'Tomorrow.'

'It will not be safe for you. What if they find out who you are?' Grace walked over to Rachel and placed her arm gently on her arm. She saw the sadness in her eyes. 'You must be very fond of him to take such a risk.'

'How did I allow this to happen, Grace? I thought I could control it but I cannot. I try to push him from my mind but his face appears every time I close my eyes. What have I done?'

Grace put her arms around her. 'You have fallen in love. Has this never happened to you before?'

'No.'

'Never?'

'When I felt my heart being pulled to a man, I stepped back. There have been moments of loneliness when I weakened but I always found the courage to walk away.'

'Why do you do this, Rachel?'

'You know why. I have to follow the path set out for me. It was not the time.'

'How will you know when it is?'

She stared at Grace. No-one had ever asked her that question. She had not even asked it of herself.

Elizabeth watched from the window as Edward approached from the stable with the girl by his side. She noticed how he hardly took his eyes from her face. She was wearing a simple brown dress with a cream shawl around her shoulders. Suddenly the girl looked straight at her through the window and smiled. A pleasant rush of warmth engulfed Elizabeth's body and she felt light-headed. She recovered enough to reach the door as they entered.

'Rachel, this is my dear mother. Mother, this is Rachel.'

There was a familiarity about this girl and yet as Elizabeth had no recollection of ever having seen her before.

'I am pleased to make your acquaintance, Rachel. You are welcome in our home.'

'Thank you, Madame.'

'Please come through to the garden. I thought we might sit outside as the weather is so fine.' Elizabeth noticed how gently Edward laid his hand on Rachel's arm to guide her through the house.

Margaret's back was turned to them as they approached. She was throwing an old piece of rope for Pedro to chase. She turned when she heard them, smoothed down her dress and walked towards them.

'Rachel. You remember my sister, Margaret.'

'It is good to see you again, Margaret.'

A smile skirted Margaret's lips but did not reach her eyes.

Suddenly the little dog raced towards Rachel. He ran up her body and was ensconced in her arms. He licked her face in delight, all the time making an excited whimpering sound.

'And who are you, my beauty?' Rachel allowed the dog to continue his licking.

'Pedro, come here. Down, Pedro.' Margaret walked up to Rachel and tried to grab the dog who had no intention of being distracted from his task. 'He has never done that before to strangers. My apologies. He has marked your dress.' Still the little dog persisted.

'Please do not worry. He is such a beautiful creature.' Rachel put her hand on the back of the dog's neck. Suddenly he stopped licking and just gazed into Rachel's eyes. 'Thank you for the welcome, my sweet.' Rachel stroked the dog's back and laid him gently on the ground where he sat perfectly still, gazing up at her.

'Pedro usually does nothing he is told,' Elizabeth said. 'You must have a way with animals. Where are my manners? Please, have a seat and refresh yourself with some wine.'

As Rachel walked towards the chairs, Pedro made to follow. Rachel bent down and put her hand on his head. The dog stopped immediately and then quietly walked over to Margaret and sat by her feet. Margaret watched the scene intently.

'Edward told us you have come recently to England, and you are well travelled.' Elizabeth said.

'Yes, Madame, I have been fortunate.'

'How is it that you have travelled so much?' Margaret asked. 'Edward said you are an orphan.'

Both Elizabeth and Edward looked at her sharply. Rachel fixed her eyes on Margaret and smiled.

'None of us ever travels alone, Margaret. It is true my mother and father have both passed but I have some dear friends who travel with me.'

'How long are you staying in England? Do your friends not miss you?'

'Margaret!' Elizabeth glared at her daughter.

'I am happy to answer, Madame. I do not know how long I will be here. My friends always have my love and we know we will see each other again.'

'Perhaps they will visit you here in England?'

'I am sure they will,' Rachel said.

They all turned at the sound of footsteps on the pathway.

'Samuel, you have arrived.' Elizabeth rose and smiled fondly at her husband. 'I was hoping business would not keep you from meeting our guest.'

'Father, may I present Rachel.'

Samuel watched the girl slowly stand up and turn towards him. He was a little taken aback by her direct gaze and the smile on her face as she curtsied.

'I am honored to meet you, Sir.'

'I see you have been made welcome. Please sit down. How are Tom and your aunt?'

'They are in good health. It is kind of you to ask.'

'Tom is a good man,' Samuel said. 'I have always found him to be honest and hardworking.'

'Please, let us all sit down,' Elizabeth said. 'Samuel, would you like some wine?'

'Thank you.' Samuel took the glass from Elizabeth and sat down opposite Rachel. She was a pretty thing and Samuel could see why his son was captivated by her. There was also a gentleness, a dignity about her, which surprised him.

Margaret stayed silent during the conversation that ensued. It was about the garden and the local area and Margaret waited patiently for her father to ask more probing questions of Rachel.

Suddenly everyone's attention was directed to Elizabeth who had let out a cry of pain and held her hands to the sides of her face.

'Elizabeth! Is it one of your headaches?'

'I am sorry, but it is.'

'You must lie down.' Samuel got up to help his wife.

Rachel too stood up and walked towards Elizabeth. 'I am familiar with headaches, Madame. Do you feel sick when they occur?'

'Yes.' Elizabeth still held her head in her hands, the pain obviously increasing.

'Does your mother have these often, Edward?'

'They seem to be worsening. Sometimes she takes to her bed for a whole day. She lies in the darkness and takes no food until the pain subsides. Dr. Brown has been unable to help her in any way.'

'Please, Madame, will you allow me to be of assistance?'

'I would be grateful if you could.'

'I think my wife needs to lie down, she...'

'Please Samuel, let her try.' Elizabeth said.

Rachel moved to stand behind Elizabeth and gently removed her hands from her face before easing her back onto her chair.

'Madame, please relax and close your eyes. Try to breathe slowly.'

Rachel put her hands together and closed her eyes. The others saw her mouth form silent words. She put her hands above Elizabeth's head and then moved them slowly from the top of her head down her sides, not touching her body. When she had done this a couple of times she moved to Elizabeth's side, placed one hand on her forehead and cupped the back of her head with the other.

After about five minutes Rachel began to rub Elizabeth's shoulders gently. She then moved and knelt down in front of her, taking her hands gently.

'You feel better, Madame?'

Elizabeth slowly opened her eyes. She looked around her and then at Rachel.

'The pain has gone! Samuel, the pain has gone. What did you do, Rachel?'

'It is a simple thing. I am glad you are well.'

'Thank you, my dear, thank you. I feel wonderful.'

'The pain will not return in this manner.'

'You mean I will not get these headaches again?'

'Not these ones, Madame. You might experience a slight headache now and then but it will not be serious.'

'You are a blessing. I still cannot believe it. Samuel, the pain has truly gone.'

'So it would seem. My wife has suffered a long time with this malady.'

'I am happy to be of assistance,' Rachel said. 'Now I must go. Thank you for making me welcome in your home.'

'I will get the carriage and take you home.'

'Thank you, Edward, but I will walk. I have some herbs to gather on the way.'

'It will take you a long time to walk home,' Elizabeth said. 'Let Edward escort you.'

'Thank you but I would prefer to walk. It is such a beautiful day.'

'You are always welcome in our home, my dear.' Elizabeth kissed Rachel on the cheek.

'We owe you our thanks,' Samuel said. His gratitude that his wife was no longer suffering did not affect his determination that his son would not wed this woman.

Rachel walked up to Margaret. 'It has been a pleasure to meet you again, Margaret.'

This time Margaret's smile reached her eyes.

'And you little one,' Rachel said, bending down to stroke the dog, 'thank you for your welcome.'

'I will walk a way with you,' Edward said.

'No, Edward, I will be less distracted from my task on my own. Thank you.'

They all watched her for a while as she made her way towards the trees. Her visit had not gone as any of them had expected.

Sarah arrived the next day with her mother for a visit. 'Well, tell me all.' Sarah jumped onto Margaret's bed, her legs swinging impatiently. 'What did she wear? What did you talk about?'

'She stayed only a short time.' Margaret had avoided any discussion of Rachel's visit since Sarah's arrival, but she knew that once they were alone she would want to know everything.

'Margaret, tell me. What did your father say to her? Surely he would not have wanted a girl like her as a guest in your home?'

'My father is a good man. He would not treat a guest with disrespect.'

Sarah frowned as she watched Margaret avoid her eyes and her questions. Margaret sat down on the bed next to her and took her hand. 'Sarah, you are my dearest friend. I love you very much and I want you to be my brother's wife more than anything, but I cannot lie to you. Rachel is not a bad person. She was polite and respectful and she cured my mother's headaches.'

'She did what?'

'You know those bad ones she suffers from that make her take to her bed. Rachel laid her hands on her and the pain disappeared. She said they would not return.'

'She is not a doctor. How could she do that?' Sarah's jealousy was now overtaken momentarily by curiosity.

'She said it was simple.'

'She laid her hands on your mother and cured her. She must have done something else.'

'No, just put her hands on my mother's head and shoulders. I think she was praying too.'

'You did not hear what she was saying?' Sarah asked.

'No, but it looked like she was praying.'

'And the pain went immediately?'

'Almost. It took a few minutes. And you should have seen Pedro. You know how he disobeys me constantly and is only quiet when there are strangers around, well he took an immediate liking to Rachel but she was able to control him when he got excited.'

'Mm.' Sarah was deep in thought.

'What are you thinking?'

'Nothing,' Sarah said, 'nothing. So you think your father will approve of her. Will he allow a marriage?'

'There was no talk of marriage. They have not known each other long. Besides, she talked of friends and travelling. It did not seem she intended to stay here forever.'

This news raised Sarah's spirits a little but she would have preferred the girl to just leave the district so Edward could then concentrate on her.

9

Elizabeth was in the drawing room, her needlework lying idly on her lap. Samuel and Edward were off somewhere and Margaret was with Sarah at her home. The servants were busy in other parts of the house.

Much as she loved Samuel and the children, Elizabeth enjoyed these moments of quiet. Usually she would allow her thoughts to wander. Sometimes they would rest on memories of her childhood or her early years of motherhood. She drew strength from the love that radiated from them. Recently she had been unable to linger long on those joyous memories. In her quiet times she now felt a restlessness, a longing. For what, she did not know. Her mind turned to Rachel. Since her visit to their home, there had been no recurrence of her headaches. In fact the feeling of wellbeing and lightness excited her. She felt an energy which had no direction. She put down her work and walked to the window. She felt no surprise at the sight of Rachel walking across the garden towards the house. She smiled and went outside to wait for her.

'It is good to see you again, Rachel. You were in my thoughts.'

'You look well, Madame.'

'Yes, I am very well. Come. Let us sit by the roses.' She called for one of the servants to bring some wine. 'I knew I would see you again.'

'And I you.'

'You helped me once, Rachel, and I would ask for your assistance again.'

'What can I do for you?'

'I have felt so well since you laid your hands on me. I have so much energy. It has left me with a need to do something worthwhile with my time. The children are grown and have little need of me. I want to do something more than just needlework and oversee the household. I would like to help people but I do not know how to take the first step.'

'By being willing, you are already on the path.'

'I do not know if I can make a difference.'

'We all make a difference in this world. Sometimes it is easy to lose sight of that. You have already made a difference. You nurture and protect your children, give them comfort and understanding. You affect how they regard the world and others in it. You instill in them integrity and acceptance of others. You give them someone to come to when the process of growing up is too much for them. You provide them with a safe haven where they can feel loved and important. Making a difference comes from giving of ourselves to others.'

'I never thought of it like that. How can I continue to make a difference—to help others?' Elizabeth asked.

'What do you enjoy doing, Madame? Something just for yourself that gives you pleasure.'

'I enjoy reading. I have many books. Yes, reading. That gives me great pleasure. I do not know how I would manage without my books.'

'There are many people in the villages around your home, both adults and children, who do not know how to read. The only book some of them own is their Bible and they cannot read it.'

'That is indeed sad, to be denied the pleasure of reading,' Elizabeth said. 'I am ashamed. I have thought about those unfortunate people but I always pushed the thought away as I knew I could not change their circumstances.'

'As I said, I believe we can all make a difference, Madame. We receive inspiration throughout our lives on how we can do this. Inspiration is a feeling of the soul. It is a way of guiding us, of helping us to reach a higher place. When inspired we see the things around us differently. Our senses are intensified and we get a chance to see what we are capable of. Inspiration comes from the part of us that knows who we really are, and is trying to get us to remember what we are here to do. Without it we would stand still. With it we can do anything.'

Elizabeth was silent for a long time. Suddenly she laughed and clapped her hands. 'I can teach people how to read. I can do that. Do you think I could do this?' How would I go about it? Perhaps they would not want me to help them. Perhaps they do not have the time or need. And Samuel. He would object most strongly I am sure. Oh Rachel, I could do it. I am sure it would give them great joy to be able to read and great pleasure to me to teach them.'

'I think you would be a good teacher, Madame.'

'How would I begin?'

'You know Mary Booth, the wife of John Booth?'

'Yes. Well, I have met her on occasions in the village but I do not know her. I know my husband and Edward think highly of John.'

'When Mary was ill and unable to leave her bed, I read the Bible to her. She said one of the things she regretted about her life was she was unable to read the book herself. Perhaps you could visit her and discuss the matter. She is a gentle woman with a kind heart. I am sure she would welcome any offer of assistance.'

'An excellent idea. I will go tomorrow.' Elizabeth kissed Rachel on both cheeks and held her hands tightly. 'Thank you, Rachel. You have helped me again and I am truly grateful. I will do this. I will make a difference. Samuel will just have to accept it.'

10

Rachel and Grace were in the vegetable garden by the side of the house. The sun was warm on their backs but they were enjoying the work and the talk.

'I wonder who this can be. It is too early for Tom.' Grace said.

Rachel looked up from her task to see a carriage approaching from the distance. It was not until it had almost reached the house that they recognized Elizabeth Mills. Grace quickly dusted the dirt from her hands and smoothed her hair.

Elizabeth's face was beaming as she got out of the carriage and tied the horse's rein to the post. 'Rachel. Mistress Clarke. I wish you good day. I hope you do not mind my coming unannounced to your home?'

'No, Mistress Mills. You are always welcome here,' Grace said.

'I have interrupted your work,' Elizabeth said.

'No, not at all. We will be glad of the rest,' Grace said. 'Please come and sit in the shade and I will fetch some ale.'

'You have caught the sun, Mistress Clarke.'

'Please call me Grace.'

'And you must call me Elizabeth. My reason for calling unannounced is that I have just visited with Mistress Booth and I could not go home without telling you the good news. Rachel has been so kind to me, Grace. Did she tell you of my request for assistance?'

'No, she did not mention it.' Elizabeth seemed pleased Rachel had held their conversation in confidence and proceeded to tell Grace herself of their discussion.

'I was nervous as I did not know how Mary would take my offer of help, but she showed me great courtesy. We shared stories of our children and soon we seemed like dear friends. I like her very much. When finally I spoke of the purpose of my visit, she seemed delighted at my proposal. She told me how much it would mean to her to be able to read her Bible and to help her children read. In fact she said there were women of her acquaintance who were also unable to read and asked if I was agreeable to her speaking to them and perhaps I could be of help to them also.'

'That is wonderful, Madame,' Rachel said. 'You will bring much joy to them, I am sure.'

'And I have the blackboards the children used. And books. I have many books I can give them. I have so much to organize. I said I would visit Mary again in two weeks to give her time to fully recover from her illness and to speak to the others.'

Eventually Elizabeth stopped talking and laughed, her enthusiasm bringing a glow to her face.

'She seems filled with the joy of life,' Grace said when Elizabeth had left.

'She has a good heart and has the ability to help many.'

'You have that way with you also, Rachel.'

'I only help people to recognize what they already know.'

The afternoon was late and they left the vegetable garden to prepare the evening meal. Each was touched by Elizabeth, a woman on the verge of a new adventure.

After the evening meal was over, Elizabeth rose from the table and walked to her husband's side.

'Samuel, will you walk with me in the garden?' He looked up at her and the remembrance of those early days of their courtship returned to him.

Neither saw the surprised glances of their children as he stood up, held out his arm to his wife and led her out into the garden.

'It is a beautiful night, Samuel.'

'Indeed it is.' He enjoyed the touch of his wife's arm through his. They walked in the fading light, in silence, in contentment.

'You are as lovely as the day I first saw you,' he said, 'and my heart belongs to you more now than then. We have a good life together, Elizabeth. I think so. I often wonder if I fulfilled your dreams of what a husband should be.'

'I did not love you the day we wed, Samuel. I did not know you then. I know you now and my heart brims over with the love I feel for you.'

He stopped and faced his wife. 'You are a wonder to me, Elizabeth. I have not been the husband you deserved. I have not always shown you sufficient affection.'

'You have given me what your heart was able to give. You are who you are.'

'Has my love been sufficient for you, my dear?'

'We have grown together, Samuel. I would be no other place than by your side. It has been more than I ever needed. Until now.'

Samuel looked deep into her eyes. A coldness passed through him.

'I do not understand.'

'I have a need in my life, Samuel. A need to be more useful. A need to help others.'

'You are not content?'

'With you, our children and our life together, I am more than content. This need I have is not part of our life together. It is something I want for me, just for me.'

'What is it you need? I will give it to you.'

'It is not something you can give me, unless it is the freedom to do what I need to do. I wish to be of use in this world, Samuel. I wish to be of help where I can. Do you know there are many of our neighbors, people who live in our community, who do not know how to read?'

'I have not thought about it but I would say there are many men who do not enjoy the benefits of an education.'

'I am talking about women. Women like me who have brought up their children and tried to surround their families with love and security. Women who have suffered, as I have, when a child is sick or cried in the night. Mothers are the same whether they have more than enough of what they need or have so little they despair about how they will feed them.'

'I do not understand what it is you want.'

'I want to teach. I want to give women the gift of being able to read a book. To be able to read the Bible, the word of God.'

'You want to teach?'

'Yes.'

'Where? How?'

'I have met with Mistress Booth. She has been ill.'

'Yes, I know. Edward told me.'

'When she was ill she did not have the comfort of reading from the Word of God.'

'You want to teach her to read?'

'Yes. Her and others like her.'

'They are agreeable to this?'

'Yes.'

'How would you do this,' Samuel asked.

'There is the hall next to the Church. It has two rooms. I could use one to teach and the other could be for the younger children to play.'

'How often would you do this?'

'Perhaps two times a week. I want to do this, Samuel.'

He looked at his wife, this vision of loveliness, this woman who had given him so many years of joy and companionship. He saw the depth of her desire to take on this task. How could he refuse? 'My dear, if this is what you want to do, I will support you.'

She kissed him gently on the cheek. 'Thank you, Samuel, thank you.'

'How long have you been thinking about this, Elizabeth? I have never heard you mention it.'

'I have felt a restlessness for a long time. It was only when I spoke to Rachel that I put words to the feeling.'

'Rachel!'

'Yes. I talked to her about how I was feeling and it became clear to me what I could to do help. She has a gift of healing what it is that needs to be healed.'

Samuel said nothing but knowing Rachel was able to influence his family left him feeling extremely uncomfortable.

11

The vision had come as she knew it would—a moving scene showing what lay ahead. It filled her with fear. She had been there before and had no wish to return. Memories flashed before her—the pain, the filth, the hopelessness of it all. There was also the guilt, for in the midst of the darkness she had questioned why a loving God would allow it to happen. But she knew she could not walk away and wondered if her courage would endure. When she awoke the tears still dampened her face. In the late morning, with a deepening sadness, she made her way to the pool.

She watched him, hidden. She sensed his impatience, or was it her own. She ached to be near him, to look into his beautiful eyes and rest for a while from the doubts that plagued her. She had never felt such conflict. Always her choice had been to do what she must. Each decision she made came from the conviction she could not stray from her pre-ordained path. Perhaps that was the problem. She had been doing this for so long, her strength the only bridge between hope and despair. Was she weakening? She hoped not, for she knew not when her journey would end.

Edward ran his fingers through his hair. Hers stretched out, jealous. The sun sparked like liquid flames through her tear-filled eyes. How she despised herself for the pain she would inflict. She should have been stronger. She should have fought the urge to be near him, to dream for a while of what could have been.

Memories of those she had loved, in whose arms she had sought comfort and release, moved across her memory. Why was it different this time? She always held something back because she knew what lay ahead. She did not expect their understanding or their acceptance. Was that the reason? The answer came from her heart, not her mind—she had not given them the choice. In her selfishness she thought her destiny so great that she was unwilling to allow another set of footprints to leave their mark. That was not completely true either. Despite her love for them she had known they were not the one—but how did she know? Perhaps if she had given them the chance they could have been. And what of Edward? She closed her mind and threw her thoughts as far away as she could. There was no point in considering the possibility. He could not be the one or the vision would not have shown her where she needed to be, shown her that it was not here.

She could not deny her love for him because her heart would not allow it. She knew they could not be together and yet he was part of her journey, part of her destiny. As she walked towards him she saw his love radiate from his being. She could not stop this.

'Rachel.' Gently he put his hand on her arm.

She lifted her eyes to his.

'I love you, Rachel.'

She turned away from him.

'Oh Rachel, I am sorry. I did not mean to say what was in my heart. Not yet. I wanted us to become more acquainted. I wanted to give you time to love me. It is too soon to talk words of love. Please, Rachel, pretend you did not hear those words of my heart. Let us spend time together and become friends.' He reached out and touched her arm again. She turned to face him and he saw the tears.

'What have I done? I did not mean to make you sad. Please do not cry. Forgive me for my foolishness.'

She wiped her tears with her hand. 'There is nothing to forgive. You offer words of love. Love is all that matters in this world. You are offering me the only thing that is important.'

'But you do not understand how I can speak of love after our short acquaintance?'

'I understand. I too have love for you. Time has no meaning when one heart reaches to another.'

'You love me?'

'Yes.' She knew it would have been easier if she had denied it, but she owed him the truth.

She heard not the sounds of the birds nor saw the trees surrounding them. She heard only her heartbeat and her eyes saw only him. He lifted his hand to her cheek and wiped away the remainder of her tears. He lifted his other hand and cupped her face. Slowly he bent his head to hers and closed his eyes just as their lips touched. She trembled with the exquisiteness of the contact. He put his arms around her and held her close. She rested her head on his chest as her resistance gave way. How long they stood like that she did not know.

Eventually he withdrew a little and looked at her face. 'Let us sit and talk.' He slid his arm around her waist and led her to a fallen log. They sat side by side, his hand cupping hers.

'Rachel. I want you to be my wife. I want to be with you forever.'

'You do not know what you are asking.'

'I love you. It is all that matters.'

'You do not know who I am or how I have spent my life. I cannot marry you.'

'I do not understand what you are saying.'

'There are things I have to do with my life. If I become your wife I would not be able to do these things easily. I would have other commitments. I would be your wife first. It is the way things are.'

'What is it you want to do that being my wife would prevent?'

'It is not easy to explain. I have to be free. I have to come and go and make my own decisions. I cannot be bound by the ties of marriage.'

'I would not make our marriage a thing that binds.'

'There would be boundaries set. I would not be free.'

He stood up and turned from her. 'You say you love me.'

'It is because I love you I would not have you enter a marriage that would destroy that love. Edward, I cannot bear children.'

He stared at her. 'It does not matter.'

'It will matter. Please accept that I cannot marry you.'

'Listen to me. I will not let it matter.' She knew that it did.

'We will not meet again like this,' she said. 'No use will come of it. I did not mean to cause you pain. I want only what it best for you.'

'You are what is best for me. We can be together. I love you too much to let you go.'

'It is not our time. We cannot change the ways things are.'

'Please do not say goodbye. I will not live without you.' He held her hands tightly.

'Let me go. I do not wish to cause you further pain. I will not marry you but I promise you we will meet again.'

'Meet again?' Suddenly he was angry. 'I do not understand what you mean. When will we meet again?'

'I do not know. All I know is that we will always be part of each other's lives.'

'You talk in riddles. I want us to be together now. Now! I do not want to wait. What good would waiting do?'

'Forgive me.' She took her hands from his and started to walk away. Her resolve weakened with each step, her mind battling her heart. This time she did not turn when she reached the edge of the clearing.

12

The cool evening air was a relief after the heat of the day. Tom and Grace sat on the bench against the outside wall of the house watching Rachel separating the small piles of herbs on the ground.

'You are sure he is not the one, Rachel?' Tom asked. There had been only sadness in her eyes since she told them what had happened.

'Yes. Perhaps we will get our chance again.' She had not told them of her vision. They would know soon enough what was to come. 'I have explained this to him but he did not understand. He was angry. I do not think he will seek me out again.'

'You may be wrong,' Grace said. 'If he loves you as he says he does then he will not let you go so easily.'

Rachel sighed. She would have to be strong. She wanted to see the love in his eyes and seek comfort in his arms but she knew it was not possible. She was tired. Her time in France still lay tender on her mind. She closed her eyes and saw Jean Paul's smiling face. After all this time she still found it difficult to live in the now. Sometimes her body just needed the comfort of the memories.

Suddenly the calmness of the evening was disturbed by the pounding of a horse's hooves on the ground.

Edward jumped off his horse almost before it had stopped moving. She had to stop herself from rushing into his arms.

'Tom, Mistress Clarke. I apologize for the late intrusion. Rachel, it is Margaret. She is very ill. My mother asked me to fetch you. Dr. Brown can do nothing it seems. She said you would know what to do. Please, can you come with me?'

'Of course. Let me fetch my pouch.'

'Thank you. Tom, I will see her home safe.' Edward jumped back on his horse and waited for her to return. He reached down for her and pulled her up onto the horse. She slid her arms around him and every cell of her body quivered with the joy of it. There was no time for further talk as they galloped towards his home. He dismounted at the front of the house, helped Rachel off the horse, and threw the reins to a waiting stable boy.

He led the way through the house. Rachel stopped outside the open door of the drawing room. She did not look at the others in the room. She saw only the man standing by the fireplace. Her body turned to ice. She remembered another time, another place. They held each other's gaze for a moment until she looked away. She knew his conscious mind did not recognize her. She had faced her fear and in a single moment knew he could no longer hurt her.

Once up the staircase Edward opened the door to one of the rooms.

'Rachel, thank you for coming.' Elizabeth rushed from Margaret's bedside and took Rachel's hand. 'She has a fever and keeps rolling around on the bed in pain. Come, please look at her.'

'I do not see how this girl can help your daughter.' The short, rotund man standing by the bed gently put down Margaret's hand and glared at Rachel.

'This is Dr. Brown,' Elizabeth said.

Rachel glanced at Samuel Mills who was standing by the window. The worry on his face made him seem so much older than she remembered on her visit to this house.

'I will do what I can.' She walked over to the bed. Margaret's face was flushed and beads of sweat covered her skin. She was moaning softly and every now and then her body convulsed.

'How long has she been like this?' She put her hand on Margaret's forehead.

'She said she felt unwell late this afternoon. She would eat nothing and retired early. I visited her room during the early evening and found her in this state. I sent one of the men to fetch Dr. Brown. He thinks it is the fever. She seems to be getting worse so I thought of you and how you helped me.'

Rachel placed her hands, palms downward, above Margaret's body. Slowly she lowered them and stopped about a hand's distance from her face. She started to move them over Margaret's body, stopping for a while longer in different areas and then continuing down until she reached her feet. She then moved them back up the way she had come. She stopped above the area around Margaret's waist. She stayed like that for a few minutes and then opened her eyes. She put her hands by her side and walked over to Elizabeth.

'Madame, Margaret has an infection in her womb and it is causing her blood to poison.'

'No, please no. She is too young. She is only a child. How can she have something wrong with her womb?' Elizabeth began to cry.

Dr. Brown rushed to Elizabeth. 'It is not possible. Do not listen to the girl. How can she tell that when she has not even touched Margaret.'

Elizabeth ignored the doctor. 'You are sure, Rachel?'

'Yes, Madame.'

'Can you help her?'

'I will try.'

'Samuel, do not let this girl near your daughter.' Dr. Brown rushed to the window where Samuel still stood in silence. 'I have heard about her. She uses plants taken from the woods. She boils them up and feeds them to the villagers. She lays hands on them and speaks words in a foreign language. She is not a doctor. She is more likely a witch.' He spat the words in Rachel's direction.

Rachel closed her eyes. It had begun.

Samuel walked over to Rachel and stared at her. 'Let her at least try,' he said and returned to the window.

Rachel returned to Margaret's side. She put her hands together in prayer, and then got up to onto the bed and knelt beside her. She saw Edward standing silently by the door and felt his pain.

'I will not be part of this,' Dr. Brown said. 'I will wait downstairs in the event you need my assistance.'

'How is the child?' Charles Griffin asked as Dr. Brown strode into the room.

'The same. I cannot understand Samuel. He is allowing that peasant girl to administer to his daughter. What can she do? She is not a doctor. Huh. With all her strange ways, how can she help the sick child? She is a witch. I am sure of it. She will be of no help. In fact I think she will do more harm than good. I do not know why I am even here. To allow a mere girl to deal with such matters is abhorrent. I wash my hands of this.'

'A witch you say?' Richard Newman asked. He walked over to Dr. Brown.

'What else can she be? She puts her hands, not even on the child but above her, and says it is an infection in the womb. She did not even touch the child but says the infection is poisoning her blood. A witch I tell you.'

'Dr. Brown, please take a glass of wine and calm yourself.' Richard Newman smiled.

The family did not measure time as they watched Rachel. There was a stillness in the air. They could not take their eyes from her as she moved her hands over Margaret's body. They watched her, not Margaret. They directed their hope, their faith to her.

'Michael, Michael. I am lost.'

'Lost. No, Rachel. You are not lost.'

'It has begun. I can feel it. I do not know if I have the strength.'

He stood before her. 'When have you ever lacked strength? What you are feeling is only momentary. You know who you are. You know your destiny. Why do you question? Look within Rachel. Your strength can move mountains. You have moved mountains. Feel the love. Do not despair. Remember who you are. Here, take my hand. I am always with you. Take my hand.'

She reached out her arm and connected with him. Slowly she uncurled herself and stood up, still clutching his hand. She looked into his face.

'Have I not always been here for you?'

She raised his hand to her lips and kissed it gently. 'Thank you.'

He put his other hand on her head and stroked it tenderly.

'Will I be able to help her?'

'It is both your choice and hers. Remember, your destinies are entwined.'

'There have been moments when I have doubted myself and you,' *she whispered.*

'I know this,' *he said.*

'It has been but for a moment.' *She reached up and touched his cheek.*

He smiled. 'I know this also.'

When Rachel opened her eyes everyone's gaze fell to Margaret. Her face was still flushed and beads of sweat still lingered on her face, but she was no longer stirring. She seemed to be resting. Rachel stepped down from the bed.

'Will she be well, Rachel?' Elizabeth was the first to speak.

'I do not know.'

'She seems calmer,' Samuel said.

'Will she li…recover?' Elizabeth asked again.

'It is not in my power to decide.'

Elizabeth walked over to Rachel. 'I understand. You did what you could. Thank you.' She kissed Rachel on the cheek and went to her daughter.

Rachel picked up her pouch and walked to the door without looking at Samuel or Edward.

'I will get the carriage and take you home,' Edward said.

She followed him down the stairs. He stopped when they reached the drawing room.

'Edward.' Sarah rushed to his side. 'How is Margaret?'

'She is resting.'

Sarah became aware of Rachel standing behind him. Her jealousy overwhelmed her concern for her friend.

'I am taking Rachel home.' Rachel stopped in front of Sarah and looked into her eyes. She bowed her head to the girl and then to Richard Newman.

'Namaste,' she whispered, and then followed Edward out of the door.

The stars shone brightly in the clear night sky. Edward held the reins lightly as the horse slowly made its way along the road. Words were hard to find. Silence was more comfortable.

'Why do you not love me?' he said.

'I do love you. Never doubt that I love you.'

'But you will not marry me.'

'This is not our time. I have things I must do. And I cannot give you a son.'

'You either love me or you do not. You want to be my wife or you do not love me. I would not restrict you in what you have to do. And I do not need a son. I need you.'

'Edward, you do not understand and I have no other words to explain to you. Perhaps we will have another chance. Perhaps in the future we will meet again. Our love will bind us forever.'

'What do I care for forever?' He was angry again. 'I want you now. I want your love now. I want you. Now!'

The horse stopped. The air was still. Edward jumped from the carriage and paced back and forth. Then he stopped and came back to the side of the carriage. He gazed up at Rachel. He saw the tears on her cheeks and reached out his hands, and she let him help her to the ground. Her eyes were drawn to his as a moth to a candle. She was overtaken by the yearning to touch his beautiful face. Even if she closed her eyes she knew she would still see him—the way the skin crinkled around his mouth when he smiled. She was afraid of the depth of her feelings, or perhaps it was her lack of control over them. A warm, sweet sensation filled her. She knew she could not stop this. She did not want to. He brushed her tears. He took her hand and she followed him to the trees. The grass was soft under their feet and the scent of the day lingered in the night air. Beside an old, tall oak tree he turned to her. She looked into his eyes, his heart, and felt an overwhelming feeling of love, of destiny. This moment in time was all that mattered. No past, no future, just this moment. The instant she thought of reaching for him he moved towards her. He put his arms around her and she rested her face on his shoulder.

'I love you, Rachel. I will always love you.'

'I know.'

The house was quiet when Edward returned. On his way to Margaret's room he looked into the drawing room. Charles and Agnes Griffin were dozing in their chairs. Richard Newman was seated by the fire with Sarah. She jumped up when she saw him.

'Is there any more news?' he asked.

'No. Your parents are still with her.'

Sarah stared at Edward. He had been gone a long time. Something was different about him. She walked over to him and looked into his eyes. She knew then. Her heart exploded with jealousy and hatred for Rachel. She was unable to move, even after Edward had walked away. Finally she turned and walked over to Richard Newman.

'She is indeed a witch.' She spat the words. 'A whore and a witch.'

13

When Rachel heard Edward approach, she picked up her shawl and medicine pouch. She kissed her aunt on the cheek and smiled. She knew Grace was worried for her. Rachel was outside waiting by the time Edward reached the house. The warmth of his smile engulfed her. He reached down his arm to help her up onto the horse. She put her arms around him as they set off towards his home. They did not talk. Both were content with the touch. She savored the feel of him, the scent of him. She knew it would have to last her a lifetime.

Elizabeth met them at the door. Her hair had loosened from its clasp and her eyes were red. 'Rachel, my dear, thank you for coming. Margaret is quiet but the fever is still there.'

Rachel followed her to Margaret's bedroom. She stopped outside the open door of the drawing room. Samuel Mills was alone, slumped in a chair by the fire. He got up and followed them up the staircase.

The drapes were drawn and a single candle lit the room. Rachel went over and drew back the drapes, letting the sunshine flood in. 'She needs to feel the light.' She handed her pouch to Elizabeth. 'Madame. I would ask you take these, cover them with this much water,' indicating the amount with her fingers, 'and boil them for five minutes. Drain the water and bring it to me.'

Elizabeth took the pouch and headed to the door. Meanwhile Rachel did as she had the previous day. When her hands reached the spot where she had felt the fire before, she looked up at Samuel.

'The infection is still bad.' She again knelt on the bed, closed her eyes and touched Margaret. She was still doing her work when Elizabeth slipped back into the room with the mixture. She put it on the table and joined her husband and son as they watched Rachel in her stillness. It seemed a long time before she opened her eyes and climbed off the bed.

'How is she?' Elizabeth asked anxiously.

'No better, but no worse. She has to decide her path now.'

'What do you mean, decide her path?' Samuel asked. 'She is ill. How can she decide anything? I do not understand you, girl. Either you can help her or you cannot. If you cannot then I will fetch Dr. Brown.'

'Samuel.' Elizabeth touched his arm.

'I have gone along with this but it seems she is unable to help Margaret. I will not just stand by and do nothing. I will send someone for Brown.'

'Father, please, give Rachel a chance.'

'She has had her chance. I will not gamble my daughter's life on this girl's strange ways. I do not understand what she is doing.' He stormed out of the room.

'Oh Rachel,' Elizabeth said, 'can you help her?'

'I am trying, but as I said it is not my decision. Margaret herself must decide.'

'You helped me.'

'I helped you to help yourself. You made the decision to stop the pain.'

Elizabeth sighed and slumped down in the chair, 'I too do not understand you.'

'Let us give her this broth,' Rachel said. 'Edward, please help me sit her up.' Edward held Margaret while Rachel tried to get her to sip some of the liquid. When she was finished he gently laid her down on the pillow.

'Try to get her to sip a few drops whenever you can, Madame. It will give her strength to fight her battle. I will go home now. If you wish me to return please come for me. I will understand if you do not.' She walked towards door.

'I will take Rachel home, Mother.' Elizabeth did not answer. She sat dazed in the chair.

They rode in silence as the horse carried them along the road.

'You are not able to help her?' There was sadness in his voice. She was glad she could not see his face.

'I have helped her. She now knows she will have to decide.'

'I do not understand what you mean but I know you are doing the best you can. You will come again?'

'If I am asked.'

'We need to talk about us. What happened between us? We cannot let that go. We belong together.'

'I have told you it will not be possible.' She sensed his body stiffen.

'You do not mean that, Rachel. You cannot mean that, not after what we shared. I love you with all of my heart. Please tell me you will marry me.'

'I will not change my mind.'

When they reached her home she did not wait for him to help her from the horse. She jumped down and walked to the door without a backward glance. She could not allow him to see her tears.

14

The Griffins, Samuel, Richard Newman and Dr. Brown were gathered in the drawing room. They watched in silence as the servants cleared away the refreshments.

'There can only be one explanation,' Richard Newman stated with authority. 'The girl is a witch.'

'What are you talking about?' Samuel said.

'Let us look at the facts, Samuel. This girl has enchanted your son. He is totally under her spell. He wants to marry the girl. I have spoken to Sarah. She said when they were out riding with Edward they came across her. Sarah said Edward could not take his eyes from her. She had him bewitched. Is this not true?' Everyone turned to Sarah.'

'Well, my dear, speak up,' her father said. 'Is this true?'

'I...I...well, that is how it looked to me,' she whispered.

'And did you not say she looked into your eyes and you felt sick?'

'Mmm...yes. I felt I was being pulled into them. I felt dizzy and sick.'

'That could be anything,' Samuel said. Jealousy more like, he thought.

'Perhaps in isolation, but not when taken with the other occurrences. Dr. Brown has been telling me about her dealings with the villagers.'

'I hear she helps them.' Samuel remembered what Edward had said about Mary Booth.

'So it would seem. No-one knows what concoction she gives them. I heard she lays her hands on them and is able to diagnose their illness and then cure it. She is heard to mutter strange words.'

'This is nonsense,' Samuel said.

'Sarah said Margaret told her the girl laid hands on your wife and cured her of a headache. Apparently she suffers from these regularly but the girl said they would not return.'

'Yes. Elizabeth was in pain and Rachel stopped it. How does that make her a witch?'

'Think about it, Samuel. Elizabeth was well the day before the girl came to your home. Within a short time she became ill. Rachel laid hands on her and stopped her pain. You told me yourself you would not accept the girl but after she helped your wife you were not so adamant. Is this not true?'

'I did soften my opinion of her but I certainly did not agree to any marriage.'

'The ways of a witch are subtle. That is how they work.' Richard Newman was warming nicely to this course of events and trying to keep his excitement in check. 'A witch would know you were against her and do all in her power to change that. Think of the power she would have if she married Edward.'

'You are wrong. Edward told me she turned down his offer of marriage,' Samuel said.

'This is but a ploy. Has her refusal lessened Edward's desire for her? No. He no doubt wants her more than ever and is totally bewitched by her.'

'I have seen that also,' Sarah said. 'He was gone a long time when he took her home and when he came back his eyes were glazed. He looked strange.'

'And what about Margaret? Has she been a sickly child?' Richard Newman asked.

'To the contrary. She is extremely healthy. I do not remember her being ill.'

'And look at her now. Margaret comes into contact with this Rachel and she becomes sick. Again the girl is there to help. I think she made Margaret ill so she can pretend to cure her.'

'But she is not curing her. Margaret is still sick. No-one seems to be able to help her.' Samuel glared at Dr. Brown.

'Samuel, I am unable to help her while she is under the influence of that witch,' Dr. Brown said.

'But surely if what you say is true then she would be helping my daughter. What is she waiting for? Why has she not helped Margaret?'

'Perhaps it is too soon. She wants to put you through the agony of fearing for her life and then she will cure her. Would you not be eternally grateful to her? Would you not then be willing to welcome her into your family? Samuel, she has bewitched your wife, your son, your daughter and now she is trying to bewitch you. She needs to be sure you are under her spell'

In Samuel's distress Richard Newman's explanations of Rachel's behavior seemed logical and yet he considered himself a sensible man. He had thought all that witch nonsense had been the product of the wild imagination of the peasants. When they had been hanging witches he had thought it the foolishness of those wanting to blame others for their misfortunes. That was what his friends were now asking him to do. He thought about every event since his son had mentioned the girl's name. Each member of his family had indeed been affected by her. Even he had softened slightly when she had helped Elizabeth. Despite that he had still been determined not to allow his son to marry her. Perhaps this was her way of ingratiating herself with him. If she cured Margaret he could refuse her nothing. His head ached. He was very tired. He had slept hardly at all since Margaret became ill. If they were right, what could he do? If Rachel had indeed caused Margaret to be ill then confronting her would not help. If she had not caused her illness then he either had to trust her to help or put Margaret back under the care of Dr. Brown.

'I am going to see my daughter.' Samuel strode out of the room without a glance at the others.

He slipped quietly into the room. Rachel was kneeling on the bed with her hands on Margaret's stomach. He had given in to Elizabeth's pleadings and allowed her to try once again. Elizabeth sat on the chair at the other side of the bed. She smiled briefly at him and returned her gaze to Margaret. Edward was on the window seat, his elbows resting on his knees and his hands cradling his head.

Samuel stood watching his family for a long time. His eyes came to rest on Elizabeth and he was overwhelmed with love for her. From the first moment he saw her, he knew he wanted to spend his life with her. It was not only her beauty, because she was indeed the most beautiful creature he had ever seen, but she had a quality of peace and harmony about her. Just being in her presence calmed his soul. She reached out with her eyes and engulfed him in warmth. Her tender and giving nature during the first weeks of their marriage had continued throughout their life together. He had always found it hard to put into words his feeling for her. It was not in his nature. Elizabeth never pressed him for words she knew he could not utter. When Edward was born, he was overjoyed. A son. He had a son. He wanted to be a loving and caring parent, something his own father had not been to him. He wanted Edward to know how much he loved him but the words never came. It shamed him that he could not hold his son close and feel the beat of his tiny heart. His love grew stronger with each passing day, but he found it impossible to reach out with his arms or his words to show that love. He knew Elizabeth was disappointed but she accepted that it was his way without making him feel less of a man. She taught Edward some of the gentler ways in life and he allowed her to do that.

He delighted in watching Elizabeth play with Edward as a child. She would chase him round the garden and Edward's screeches of excitement brought joy to his heart. He was content to watch her engulf him in the love and affection he was unable to show.

Margaret's birth was yet another wonder. He could not resist the little hands that reached out to him and tugged at his heart. For the first time he let go. Elizabeth found him one night sitting by Margaret's cradle. She saw his tears, kissed him gently on the head and left the room. Each day his bond with Margaret strengthened and his heart continued to soften. He would grant her any wish and she knew how to make him laugh. He considered that a fair trade.

He thought things would be different with Edward but no matter how hard he tried, he was never as open and affectionate with him as he was with Margaret. It hurt him that this was so. He often saw Edward watching from a distance as he sat with Margaret on his lap. He appeared to hold no resentment. In his children's years of growing Samuel no longer questioned his relationship with them. He accepted that this was the way of things.

Now, as he stood in the doorway watching his daughter lying ill on the bed and his son waiting anxiously by the window, Samuel came to a realization. His love for his son merged with his love for his daughter and he could no longer distinguish between them. They were his children and his love for them both overwhelmed him. This realization brought also a return of his guilt about Edward. How could he have done that to his son? Emotion caught in his throat at the thought of the years he had wasted. Why had he acted like that? Perhaps it was his own experience of being a son that set the pattern. What did it matter? All that mattered was he now knew the truth. He felt as if a heavy weight had been lifted from his heart. He was unaware Elizabeth had been watching him as his eyes had gone from Margaret to Edward and had then rested on his son. He knew she saw into his heart.

Rachel came off the bed. She stood silently for a moment with her hands in prayer. She bowed her head and put her hand on Margaret's heart.

'Namaste,' she whispered softly.

'What is happening?' Elizabeth was alarmed at the sadness in Rachel's eyes.

'She is not yet ready to return,' Rachel whispered.

Samuel strode to stand in front of Rachel. 'Not ready to return. Return from where? Tell me, girl. What is happening to my daughter?'

'She has her reasons for being where she is.'

'You talk in riddles. Tell me. Is she getting well? Are you helping her?'

'She has accepted my healing but is not ready to return from the place she is now.'

'I have had enough of this nonsense.'

'Samuel.' Elizabeth rushed to his side. She stared at Rachel. 'Please Rachel, tell us what is happening.'

Rachel looked over at Edward. She saw the same confusion in his eyes. She only had the truth to offer them but her strength faltered. She closed her eyes and felt the familiar arms enclose her. 'I am with you,' the words echoed in her head. She opened her eyes.

'The infection is subsiding. Margaret is in a healing place. She knows where she is. She said it is not yet time for her to return. She asks you to have courage and to look to your hearts.'

'Did she speak when I was not here?' Samuel asked. Elizabeth looked sadly from Rachel to Samuel.

'No. She said not a word.'

Edward walked over to Rachel and put his arms gently on her shoulder. 'Rachel. We do not understand. We have been here all the time. Margaret did not speak. How is it that you heard her?'

'Her spirit spoke to mine.' She had offered these words of explanation so many times and so few times had she been understood.

'Rachel, please.'

'Edward, it is who I am. I see things that are not visible to your eyes because you do not know how to look. I hear the voices of spirits you do not hear because you do not know how to listen.'

'Are you mad, girl?' Samuel shouted.

'Our bodies die but our spirits are eternal. I can see and hear those who have passed from this life. They are not strangers to me. Margaret's spirit has not passed but she is in another place. Her spirit has a purpose. It is her choice whether to allow her spirit to live once more in this body or to move on.'

Elizabeth's hand covered her face, trying to shut out this moment. Samuel's anger flashed in his eyes. Edward was looking at her as if she were a stranger.

'I want you out of my house,' Samuel shouted. 'Richard is right—you are a witch and I will not have you near my family.'

'Father, no.'

'Edward.' Rachel put her hand on his arm. 'Do not concern yourself. This is the way it must be.'

Suddenly the door opened and Richard Newman and Dr. Brown rushed in. 'We heard shouting,' Richard Newman said. 'What is happening?'

Rachel ignored them and turned to look at Samuel. 'I have been asked to give you a message.'

'Get out of my house before I throw you out.'

'Your father is standing beside you. He is a tall man with pure white hair. His brow is wrinkled and his face reddened by the sun. His eyes are dark as night. He is wearing a blue overcoat with silver stitching. He is showing me a lion's head. He said ...'

'Stop these tricks. You saw the portrait in the hallway. You will fool us no longer. Richard, I would appreciate if you would remove this girl from my house immediately.'

'First I must give you the message from your father,' Rachel said calmly.

'My father is dead. He can give you no message.' Samuel's face was red with anger.

Elizabeth was sobbing uncontrollably as Edward tried to comfort her.

'Get her out of my house now.'

'Father, please,' Edward begged. He was confused and in great pain. He saw now that Rachel was indeed insane. His heart was broken.

Dr. Brown and Richard Newman gripped Rachel by the arms and led her roughly out of the room and down the corridor.

The small cell was foul smelling and the stone walls radiated the cold and dampness. Fear clung to the air like a perpetual haze. This was a place of darkness, where the light of love had never shone. She did not struggle as the jailor put on her chains. She watched Richard Newman and her gaze reached to his soul.

'I know you, witch. I know what you are. You would make this world a place of lawlessness with your lies. You have spent so long trying to destroy something that cannot, will not, be destroyed. I will not allow it.'

'After all this time you still do not understand me.'

'Oh I do. I understand you well. You are a witch and a servant of the devil. You would have people believe you can heal like the Christ; that you can talk directly to Him when in fact you serve only your dark master.'

'Why will you not believe I serve God?'

'Only God can heal. Only God can lift the veil between the dead and the living. God would not give a mere girl these powers. If I had my way you would burn.' He dismissed the jailor.

'Richard.' She said his name so gently. 'Open your heart. Your hate and fear take up so much room that love cannot reside there. Allow truth to enter. Allow your spirit to be free. I will help you.'

He felt a heat begin to radiate from within but his fear turned it to ice. 'Do not use your tricks on me, witch. I will not rest until I see you destroyed.'

He left her there in the dark. He saw not the shadows that followed him.

15

Edward stood by the pool, looking up at the clouds moving quickly across the sky. He could sense a storm coming. It would bring rain and quench the thirst of the land. But what would quench his thirst? Not a storm, not the water of life, only one thing.

He felt his blood run hot as it swept through his veins. His stomach churned and his head ached. He wished he had never met her. If this was love, he wanted no part of it. He wanted to be in control of his life, master of his own destiny. She had come along and torn his heart from his body and trampled on it as it lay bleeding on the ground. Why did she let him love her? He knew she could not have stopped it. A fire engulfed him, the flames of desire licking his body, caressing his lips, engulfing his mind. Perhaps they were right; she was in league with the Devil. How else could she blind him to everything except his need for her? How else could he lose all sense of himself and be filled with a yearning so great that it threatened to drive him to madness.

Samuel sat with Elizabeth by Margaret's bedside. They did not ask where Richard Newman had taken Rachel. Edward had rushed out of the room shortly after they had taken her away, his eyes filled with pain. He looked lost and confused. Samuel did not try to stop him for Margaret was their concern.

As darkness fell, Samuel left Elizabeth asleep over Margaret's bed. He had to get away for a while. His head felt as if it would explode. He could not bear to lose his daughter. He blamed himself for allowing Rachel to try to help her when he should have had Brown attend to her. Perhaps precious time had been lost. He did not join the others in the dining room but instead walked the hallways. He had lived all his life here and knew every corner, every hidden place. It had been his playground as a child—a place where he could imagine a mother he never got to know. He would whisper to her in hidden corners and laugh as he imagined her playing games with him and holding him tight, taking away his loneliness. As he grew to be a man— before he met Elizabeth—his memories of his imaginings were all he had to comfort him. He needed the stillness of those hidden corners now to calm his aching head and heart. How could things have gone so wrong in such a short period of time? Before that girl had come, life had been good. Now it was in complete disarray. He wondered how he had managed to be taken in by her. She was either a witch or insane. There was no other explanation. Why did he not immediately see her for what she was? She talked of seeing the spirits of the dead. She said she had seen his father. Samuel shook his head. She must have thought him a fool. She had been very clever. She had described him exactly as he appeared in the portrait in the upper hallway. Rachel must have seen it when she came to visit Elizabeth. And the lion's head. In the portrait his father was holding his favorite walking stick topped with a carved silver lion's head. Yes. She must have thought him a complete fool.

He found himself drawn to where his father's portrait hung. But the portrait was not there. He stared at the empty space on the wall and then remembered it was in London. He had taken it there over a month ago for cleaning. Rachel could not have seen it.

The cell was dark and the smell made him catch his breath. He still did not know why he was here. He needed to talk to the girl. If she was insane then perhaps she could not have helped her behavior. He had to be sure. He saw her as his eyes adjusted. She was chained by the arms to the wall.

'Rachel.'

'Samuel. I am pleased you have come.'

'I felt the need to talk to you. You have caused great distress to my family but I do not think you are a witch. I think perhaps you have lost your sanity. I need to find out for myself.'

'I am not insane. I think you know that.'

'You could not have seen the portrait in the hallway. It has not been there for many weeks. There is no other portrait of my father in the house. I want to know how you were able to describe him. Did Edward tell you about him?'

'Edward never mentioned his grandfather. Will I give you his message now?'

He shook his head and walked to the door. He was the insane one. He was encouraging the girl's craziness by being here.

'He said to tell you how proud he was of you when you first rode the black stallion. He knew you were afraid but you did it despite your fear. He said he was hard on you because he thought it was the way to make you a man. It was the way his father had been with him. You were to him a precious gift. He thanks you for the tears you shed when you were alone with him the night he passed. You thought he could not see you. He saw you and heard your words. You asked him why he had never loved you. He tells you now he has always loved you and always will. His regret is he was never able to show you how much. He felt your lips on his forehead. He felt your love. He knew you hesitated to take the gold ring from his finger. Your hands shook. He willed you to take it. You gently took it from his finger, kissed it and put it on your finger. He thanks you for honoring him. He knows your heart has opened towards Edward. Do not let it close again. Do not regret leaving this life without having made him aware of your love. Do not make his mistake. Edward will need you in the time to come.'

Samuel did not try to wipe the tears from his eyes. 'Is he still here?'

'Yes. He is standing by your side. He has his hand on your shoulder.'

'Will you tell him I love him?'

'He can hear you, Samuel. He knows.'

He looked at her for a long time. For the first time he noticed the bruise on her cheek. He knelt beside her. He saw the redness on her wrists where the chains held her bound to the wall. He saw her dignity, her acceptance.

'I have hurt you deeply,' he said.

'It is of no matter.'

'I will get you out of here. I will demand Newman release you immediately. I will take you home and keep you safe. You can marry Edward and I will protect you.'

'No, Samuel.'

'What! I thought you loved my son.'

'I do, but it is not our time.'

'Why not? No-one would dare lay a hand on you while you are under my protection.'

'I have work to do. There is a time of great sadness ahead. It is coming soon and I must go where I will be of most help.'

'Rachel, I want you to stay.' He looked down at her. She was chained and battered. Her face was dirty and bruised. She seemed such a tiny helpless creature. When he looked into her eyes her outward appearance disappeared and he saw only the depth of her courage.

'I will get you out of here and we can talk more.' He marched over to the door. 'Jailor. Open this door at once.'

'Had enough?' The toothless old man winked. Samuel's stare soon wiped the grin off his face.

'Send someone for the Magistrate. Ask him to come here immediately.'

'Sir, it's late.'

'I care not. Get him here now. And bring me a cloth and some clean water. Now.' He shouted the last word and the old man scurried away.

By the time Richard Newman appeared at the door, Samuel had done the best he could to tend to Rachel. Her face was now clean and he had gently bathed her bruises.

'What is the meaning of this, Samuel?'

'I want you to get these chains off now. The girl is innocent. She is no witch.'

'That has not yet been proved.'

'I do not care. I know she is not a witch. I want her released into my care immediately.'

'I cannot do that. There are procedures to be followed.'

Samuel walked up to Richard Newman. 'Let her go. I will not be pressing any charges against her. I will be responsible for her.'

'Does this mean your daughter is now recovered?'

'No. But this girl is innocent of any crime. She is not responsible for Margaret's sickness. Order the chains removed.'

'I do not like this but if you insist. Come with me. You will have to sign the necessary papers.'

'Anything. Just get these chains off.'

'As soon as you sign the papers. Jailor, come with us. I want a witness.'

Before he followed them out the door, he turned to her.

'All will be well.'

Richard Newman indicated where he wanted Samuel to sign. 'You are certain about this. She will be your responsibility.'

Samuel merely looked at Richard Newman and signed the paper. 'Jailor, bring the key to the chains.'

Samuel was the first to enter the cell, followed by the jailor and then Richard Newman. They stared at the empty space where Rachel had been.

'She has gone. What trick is this?'

'I do not know.' Samuel continued to stare.

The pounding of hooves could be heard outside in the courtyard. They all rushed out to find a soldier dismounting from his horse.

'I need to speak to the Magistrate. Where can I find the Magistrate?'

'I am he. What's happened?'

'It is the plague. The plague is in London.'

'Where have you been? You have been gone a long time.' Elizabeth looked up only briefly as Samuel came into the bedroom and then continued to wipe Margaret's forehead. 'Edward has not returned. I am worried about him. He was very distraught.'

'I went to see Rachel.'

Elizabeth stopped what she was doing and went to him. 'Oh Samuel, how is she? We must stop what is happening to her. She does not deserve this.'

'I know, my dear. I know she did what she could to help Margaret.'

Elizabeth no longer saw the fury in his eyes. 'What has happened?'

'I will explain later but ...'

The door flew open and Edward rushed in. His hair fell across his face and his clothes were dirty.

'Edward. What has happened to you?'

'I have been foolish, Father. I have allowed my pain to cloud my senses. I love Rachel. I know in my heart she is not responsible for this. I will have her released. I will go with her wherever she needs to go. I will put no demands on her. I love her and I will not let this happen to her. Please come with me to see the Magistrate.'

'It is too late, son.'

'Too late! Dear God, what has happened?'

'I have spoken to Rachel. I too know she is not to blame for this. She has gone, Edward.'

'Gone?'

'She somehow escaped from the cell. I went there to demand her release. I spoke to her and when we came back to unlock her chains she was gone.'

'I will go to her aunt's house.'

'I went there on my way back. She was not there. Grace said she came with two men. They told her Rachel would be safe with them and they would care for her. She collected some of her belongings and left with them. Grace said they were not expecting her to return.'

'She cannot have gone,' Edward said. 'Who were the strangers? You spoke to her, Father. Where would she go?'

'She is safe.'

All eyes turned to the bed where Margaret was lying. Her eyes were open and she was trying to push herself upright.

'Margaret, Margaret.' Elizabeth rushed to her side. She cupped her face with her hands and smothered it with kisses. 'Oh, Margaret, you are well again.'

'Yes, Mother.'

'This is a miracle. We thought we had lost you.' Edward picked up his sister's hand and kissed it. 'I am happy you are well. But Rachel. She said she spoke to you. Do you know where she might have gone?'

Margaret looked at her father who was standing at the foot of the bed. He nodded and smiled. They both knew where Rachel had gone. To London. To the plague.

'I know only she has gone to where she needs to be.'

Edward walked over to the window and gazed out. His pain radiated to those who loved him.

'She said we would be together some day. Will I see her again?'

'I think you will, Edward,' Margaret said. 'Rachel would not make empty words of a promise.'

16

His power was such a physical force; it surrounded her but did not engulf her. His face was wrinkled and aged and his long white hair hung thinly around his shoulders. His right hand clutched his long staff, the wood worn where his hand had held it for centuries. He wore a long brown cloak which seemed too heavy for his frame. His body might have betrayed his years but his eyes were bright and ageless. They sparkled with humor and knowledge, and above all, love.

'*I feel as if I can see the whole world from here,*' *she said.*

They stood together on the mountaintop where the air was crisp and clear. Below them the valley, green and abundant, followed the path of the river to the distant sea. On either side other mountains protected the land below.

'*The world,*' *he said.* '*Ah, now I know what troubles you, my child.*'

'*I feel I am learning nothing, Master.*' *She almost shouted the words.* '*I sometimes think I am not worthy of the destiny allocated to me.*'

'*You expect too much of yourself. Not all lessons can be learned at once. You have had many experiences, made many choices, and you* have learned from them and moved forward. Why do you feel like this, child?'

'Because there is still a place for hate in my heart. I think I have overcome the darkness but it is still there, hiding deep inside me. How can I be learning if I cannot learn to love unconditionally? It seemed worse this time, Master. I saw the pain and the weariness in their lost eyes. They were without hope and it seemed they had long given up faith in their God.'

'Tell me child.' He touched her cheek and wiped away her tears.

'I tried to ease their suffering but it did not seem enough. I saw a man kicking a dog. Such a beautiful creature. It did not run away. It just let the man kick it. I rushed to the man and I know he felt the depth of my anger for he stepped back. I truly felt hate for him, that he could do this to a starving dog. I tried to feel love but I could not. I let the darkness remain. I felt a stranger to myself. I was afraid. That day I had seen so much suffering, so much destruction, and gave only love, but when I saw this man's cruelty I grasped the hand of hate. I took away the dog's pain but could not eradicate the hate I felt for his abuser. Master, I wanted to feel this hate. I did not want to feel love for such a man.'

'You are weary child. You need to rest.'

'I have had so many chances, so much time to learn but still I cannot.' She walked away from him and moved closer to the edge of the mountain. 'When will it end, Master? How long must I go on like this, waiting for the world to be ready? Sometimes I think I do not have the strength. I have journeyed so far but I feel what I have accomplished is not enough. When will it be enough?'

He walked slowly to her and rested his hand on her shoulder. 'My child, I cannot answer that question for you. You are the only one who can decide.'

She turned to him. 'Me? You know it is not my decision.'

'Why is it not?'

'I do not understand what you are saying. How can I decide? It is not in my power to do so.'

'One of your strengths has always been your determination to fulfill your destiny. This determination has also been one of your weaknesses. You have let nothing stand in your way. You have clouded your natural intuition by binding it to what you see as something that is outside of your reach. You wait for its fulfillment to come from everywhere but from within yourself.'

She stared into his eyes. His love for her shone from his soul and she had never doubted the depth of his wisdom.

'You are saying I can stop this if I want to?'

'I am saying you have the wisdom to know when the time is right, the power to do something about it, and the strength to see it through.'

She smiled at him and shook her head. 'You are very clever, Master. You do not give me an answer, only more questions to ask myself.'

'My dear child, I have never given you answers. You know I can never tell you anything you do not already know. I am here to guide you, to help you connect to your own wisdom. In all the time we have been together you have always made decisions based on your own truth. I have just cleared some of the stones from your path to make it smoother. If I was not here to clear the stones you would go around them and still reach your destination.'

'I am grateful for your presence. In my times of need you are there for me. You always re-light the candle when the flame is almost gone.'

'You bring joy to my spirit with your words.'

17

And if our hands should meet in another dream,
we shall build another tower in the sky.
The Prophet, Kahlil Gibran

Rome, November 1991

The man in the black suit opened the door and indicated for him to enter. There was no sound as he closed it behind him. The room was rich in its furnishings and heavy drapes, lit only by a single lamp and the flames from the fire. He knew the room well.

'Patrick. Come, sit down.' The voice of Cardinal Ricardo came from behind one of the winged chairs by the fire.

Patrick shivered despite the heat of the room. He sat down and stared at the fire. He did not look at the old man whose appearance was already etched in his mind; the wrinkled face, the gaunt features and a body that had the smell of decay. Whenever Patrick looked into the Cardinal's eyes he felt a coldness touch his heart. He had felt an instant dislike for him the first time they met all those years ago and that dislike transformed into loathing as time passed. Despite the Cardinal's smile and soft voice, Patrick felt this was a man of pure evil. His gut told him. Many times Patrick thought of telling the

Cardinal where to put his money, but he stayed. He often wondered why.

'You have news for me, Patrick?'

'She's in Australia.'

'Ah. She did not linger long in the Sudan. Are those Guardians with her?'

'Only the three. I've seen no sign of the others. She looked tired. Perhaps she's gone there to rest.'

'Tired! Do I detect sympathy in your voice?'

'No. I was merely making an observation.'

'I hope that is all it is. I thought perhaps for a moment her influence had infected you. We both know that would be unwise and extremely dangerous. It is how she works. Little by little she contaminates the world. Her evil knows no bounds.'

'Why did you call me here?' Patrick had heard the Cardinal's speech before. Many times.

'I feel the time is near when her evil plan will come to fruition. If I am right then we need to discuss what action to take.'

Patrick had always known this day would come. He had followed the girl for 20 years. When the Cardinal first hired him to watch her, he had been a Bishop then, Patrick thought little of why the Vatican would be paying someone like him so much money for this kind of job. The girl was about four years old and living with a couple and a boy child about the same age in a small village in southern France. Patrick had been at a low point in his life. His wife had left him, he had no children or family and he was nearly broke. He trained as a Navy Seal and had worked for 10 years for the CIA. Although he worked hard at keeping his six foot frame lean and in shape, civilian life held few opportunities for a man with his skills.

At their first meeting, the Cardinal explained the girl was a threat to the stability of the Church. He did not use the word 'witch' until their second meeting and after that it was the only name he used for her. Patrick did not understand how a child could be such a threat to anyone but the money was good and he got to travel. When it looked like she would stay in one place for a while, he would hire reliable people to do the job for him while he took a break at some expensive resort and spent some of the money he had accumulated.

Every now and then the Cardinal asked him to come to Rome to give him a personal report. Despite his loathing for the man and the fact he had more money in the bank than he could ever spend, Patrick continued doing his job. He watched the girl, took notes of where she went, what she did, and who she spent time with. He became fascinated with her. He watched her grow from a pretty child into a beautiful woman. During his time working for the government he had learned to be inconspicuous—a master of disguise, a shadow—and these skills made it easier for him to spy on her. He followed her to places of poverty and disaster. He had seen her walk into villages of starving people. She brought no food or water with her but the eyes of the dying shone with gratitude. She would talk quietly to them in whatever language they spoke and they understood her and seemed comforted.

Although his false identity was that of a journalist, he was unable to follow her to some of the places she went. He remembered the time he attempted to follow her to a village in Afghanistan. She and two companions managed to get access to an area of heavy fighting but the authorities were reluctant to let him through. Finally he bribed some soldiers to take him. The guns had fallen silent by the time they reached the area and as he stepped out of the Jeep he saw her walking slightly ahead of her companions in a clearing. Her clothes were bloodstained and she looked sad and weary. A trick of sunlight had made it appear that a bright glow emanated from her and that image stayed with him. Often in his dreams he saw her in the clearing, surrounded by the white light.

His seemed a surreal world. He had known her almost all her life and yet they had never spoken. As far as he was aware she did not know of his existence. There were occasions when he thought she sensed him watching, but he was never sure.

'What should I be looking for?' he asked the Cardinal.

Thirty minutes later Patrick slowly got up from his chair, a feeling of dread weighing down his heart. He walked through the door, closing it quietly behind him.

18

Frankston, Victoria, Australia

David loosened his tie as he made his way from the air conditioned car to the house. It had been a long day and he was glad to be home. He felt the warmth of the sun on his back and thought he might have a swim before dinner. He unlocked the door and waited for the inevitable sound of Robbie's scurrying paws as he made his way from wherever he was to greet him as he always did, with excited little whimpers while bouncing up and down on the same spot. The bounces were not quite as high as they used to be ten years ago but the enthusiasm of the little terrier never waned.

Robbie had not appeared by the time David had put down his briefcase so he followed the aroma of freshly baked biscuits coming from the kitchen.

'They smell yummy Mummy,' he said as he planted a kiss on his mother's cheek.

Jenny laughed. 'You haven't said that since you were a wee boy.'

David tried to take one of the biscuits off the tray but was gently smacked across the hand. 'They're too hot, and besides, they're for the hospice fete tomorrow.'

'Where's Robbie?'

'He's probably managed to get into Andrew's garden. For some reason he's started doing it again. Could you be a dear and retrieve him? I don't think anyone's home but you never know what he'll get up to.'

'No problem.' David headed for the back door, grabbing a biscuit from the tray on the way, as his mother knew he would.

David called Robbie's name as he made his way across the lawn to the bottom of the garden but he knew if the little dog was chasing a bird or burying something, he would not heed the call. Many years ago part of the fence separating their garden from next door had broken away. Andrew and Helen Graham had been their neighbors and friends for twenty years and Jenny and Helen took advantage of the gap in the fence as a quick way to visit to each other's houses rather than use the long way around the front. The fence was never fixed even after Helen's death from cancer 18 months ago.

David pulled back some of the bushes which partially grew across the gap and carefully stepped through into Andrew's garden. He walked across the lawn, dusting his trousers as he went, regretting he had not changed his clothes before going in search of Robbie. As he looked up, David became aware of two things at the same time. A woman was sitting in the gazebo in the center of the garden, her face hidden by shadow, and a man was striding across the lawn towards him.

'Can I help you?' His voice was polite but his dark eyes hostile. The stranger was about David's age with dark brown hair. He was a little taller than David and broader in build. He had positioned himself so that the person in the gazebo was completely obscured.

'Hi, I'm David Morgan. I live next door. I was looking for our dog. I didn't mean to disturb you. I didn't know anyone was staying with Andrew.' David smiled, hoping to somehow break the stare of the other man.

'I know who you are.'

'Oh! Well I'll just have a look around. Andrew won't mind.'

'That will not be possible.' The man turned as the woman began walking towards them, her face still hidden as she clutched Robbie in her arms.

David would always remember the first time he saw Rachel, but in recalling it he was never be able to find the right words to describe how he felt. Her eyes, an incredible color of blue, were fringed by long lashes and her dark hair framed a face, flawless and beautiful. Her simple lilac dress revealed slim arms and legs. The smile on her lips reached all the way to her eyes, but then suddenly it disappeared and she swayed. The man quickly put his arm to steady her and the two stared at each other. Unsure what was happening, David waited. He saw her take a deep breath, and as she slowly exhaled, her smile returned. Matt let go of her arm as she looked back at David. She slowly lowered Robbie to the ground and the dog sat at her feet gazing up at her.

'Good evening, my name is Rachel.' She held out her hand in greeting.

'Hi, I'm David Morgan. Pleased to meet you.' Her hand was cool and soft but he did not give in to the urge to keep holding it and reluctantly let it go.

'This is Matt. We are visiting with Andrew.' Matt did not offer his hand.

'Sorry to have barged in but Robbie used to spend of lot of time here when Helen was alive. He thinks of this garden as part of his territory. Andrew's never minded.'

'It is not a bother. He is a lovely little dog.'

'You're not from around here, are you?' David could not even guess at their accents.

'No.' Matt answered.

'Andrew is out at the moment but we were just going to have a cold drink. Would you like to join us? Let us sit in the shade,' she said pointing to the gazebo.

As David moved to follow her, he noticed Matt look back at the house and following the direction of his eyes, he could see someone standing in the doorway. A man dressed in black stepped outside onto the covered decking as they approached the gazebo but his face was obscured by shadow. David saw Rachel slightly lift her hand towards him as she walked.

'David, please sit down. Matt, keep our guest company while I get some juice.' Rachel smiled at him and walked to the house. The man on the decking did not move until she was inside and then he followed her.

'How long have you been in Australia, Matt?' David wondered what his relationship was to Rachel.

'Not long.'

'What do you think of the place?' he asked.

'Rachel likes it. Yes, we like it.'

David was unsure how to progress the conversation, and was relieved to see Rachel approaching with a tray of glasses. He stood up with the intention of helping her.

'Stay,' Matt put out his hand to prevent him. David was so taken aback he stopped dead and sat down again. Matt went to meet Rachel and took the tray from her.

'This is weird,' David thought as he watched them approach, but then the sight of Rachel put all thoughts out of his head, except that she was the most beautiful woman he had ever seen. He realized that for a moment he had stopped breathing. Matt left his glass on the tray and sat down immediately across from him. David watched Rachel sip from her glass. Her hands were delicate and she wore no rings, which pleased him.

'This is great, thanks. How long are you visiting Andrew?'

'We do not know yet,' she said.

'Have you seen much of the area? There are some great places to visit and you've come at the perfect time of the year. Lots of sunshine and not much rain.'

'Andrew has shown us a few of the sights. We are enjoying our visit.'

'You'll have to get Andrew to bring you over to meet my parents. I'll get Mum to arrange something, that's if you'd like to.'

David noticed Andrew come out of the back door and speak to the man in black. When he reached the gazebo, he shook David's hand, and sat down beside Rachel.

'It's good to see you, David. When I spoke to John last month he said you're staying at home while your apartment's being renovated. Jenny will be happy about that no doubt.'

'It was supposed to take two months but I think Mum's paying them to go slow so I can stay longer. She spoils me, but I'm not complaining. I was just saying to Rachel you should all come over some time. My folks would love to see you.'

'I'm not sure if ... I mean, it might not be possible,' Andrew said, looking at Matt.

'We would enjoy that, Andrew,' Rachel said.

'Good. Then I'll phone David's mother and arrange it. What about, um, what about the others?' Andrew asked.

'We have another two friends with us, David, would that be too many for your mother?' Rachel asked.

'Oh no, she loves entertaining. I know Mum's busy tomorrow, but perhaps Sunday afternoon. It's going to be hot so bring your stuff and have a swim if you like.'

Rachel sharply sucked in her breath and then let out a deep sigh. She continued to stare at him and David saw the others looking at each other. Then she smiled. 'We look forward to it.'

'Well, I'd better be off. We'll see you all on Sunday then.'

That night David lay on his back with his hands behind his head. He was staring at the ceiling but seeing Rachel's smile. He seemed to sense everything so acutely; the smell of the flowers from the garden wafting in through the open window, the path of moonlight shining across the room. He could feel his heart beating and sensed the movement of his breath. 'Rachel.' He whispered the name. He loved the sound of it, the feeling he got when he said it. He would try, in the years that followed, to recapture the events that had taken place. He would question if they had been real, their sequence, and their accuracy, but always he would be able to clearly picture that first time he saw her.

19

'Are you feeling okay, David, you seem away with the fairies?' Jenny Morgan asked her son.

'I'm fine, Mum, just thinking. What time are they coming tomorrow?'

'That's the third time you've asked that. Around one. So what does this Rachel look like?' Jenny's curiosity was fuelled by David's obvious interest in Andrew's visitor.

'About my age, I reckon, she has long dark hair and blue eyes. She's slim and she has this sm...' David looked up to find his mother with a big grin on her face. 'You'll get to meet her tomorrow. When's Dad due back from golf? I thought I might tidy up round the garden today.'

'About two. He's staying for lunch at the club. I'll be leaving about one for the hospice fete.'

'Well, I might just give the pool a clean and make sure the barbecue is ready for firing up. Do you think the lawns need a cut? I might just give them the once over.'

'You're going out tonight aren't you, to some party with Jack?' Jenny asked.

'I was going but I don't think I will. I'll see how I feel later.'

'I forgot to tell you, Paula called round on Thursday night before you got home to ask if you were going. I told her I wasn't sure.' Jenny tried not to interfere with David's life but she was curious about how things were between him and Paula. She knew the girl was besotted with him and although their relationship lasted only a couple of months, she still called him and seemed to always be where he ended up at the weekends. Jenny knew David was upset by her persistence. It wasn't in his nature to hurt anyone but he knew he could never have a long term relationship with her. He told her that although she was fun to be with, her jealously over the time he spent with his friends and her constant phone calls, made him realize his feelings for her were not as strong as her feelings for him, and never could be. Apparently there had been tears and tantrums and he assumed she had always been the one to do the breaking up. Although Paula made it hard for him, he never wavered.

'I wish she wouldn't phone. I might not go. I hadn't really confirmed I would anyway. I'll phone Jack and let him know.'

Jenny hated to hear the annoyance in David's voice and wished Paula would just leave him alone.

'Hey, this looks great,' John Morgan said as he came out into the garden. 'We wouldn't happen to be having visitors tomorrow, would we?' he asked with a smile.

'I just thought I'd tidy up a bit.' David accepted the beer from his father. 'It does look good though, doesn't it?'

'It's obvious that one of the friends Andrew is bringing over tomorrow is a pretty young woman.'

'Dad, you'd think I never help around here.'

'Yep, that's what I was thinking.'

They both sat down on the plush garden chairs, relaxed in each other's company. Since John had sold his real estate company and worked only part time as a consultant, he had much more time to spend in his beloved garden. As he sipped his cold drink he thought how lucky he was in his life. He and Jenny had been married for 33 years and he still loved her with all his heart. He had come to Australia from the States nearly 35 years ago and Jenny from Scotland around the same time. Both strangers in a new land they struck up a friendship that developed into love after only a few weeks. Her Scottish lilt and easy smile gave him great joy. Since his semi-retirement he had been able to spend more time with her. They went for trips all over the country, sometimes just on the spur of the moment, went for long walks on the beach and visited their favorite restaurants. They played golf together and even went cycling. He also had time for his other favorite hobby—reading. He was trying to catch up with all the books he had wanted to read but never had time for during the years of running his business and looking after his family. He saw other couples of their age, even friends they had known for years, whose relationships seemed distant, and he often wondered why he and Jenny remained so close. He found the answer when he read the section on marriage in a book called 'The Prophet.' He memorized the passage because the words were so beautiful to him. "Let there be spaces in your togetherness. And let the winds of the heavens dance between you. Love one another, but make not a bond of love". He felt that was how he lived his life with Jenny. He recited the words to her one night a few weeks ago when they were enjoying a glass of wine in the garden. The air was warm and still, and the stars sparkled in the dark sky. She looked at him with love, took his hand and gently raised it to her mouth. She kissed it gently, her eyes never leaving his. That night their lovemaking was the most beautiful he could remember, full of gentleness and sharing.

John smiled at his son, hoping that one day David too would share such a love. David was 32 and showed no signs of finding that person. John was glad he had not continued the relationship with that pretty young blonde, Paula. She would never have let the "winds of the heavens" dance between them.

John's thoughts went to the forthcoming barbecue tomorrow. He remembered with fondness the easy, caring friendship he and Jenny had shared with their neighbors. All through Helen's year long fight with cancer, they all shared tears and laughter and the emptiness that resulted from her death. He watched Andrew close down inside, the grief overwhelming him, the emptiness filling his every moment. He and Jenny tried to comfort him but they were unable to reach through his grief. Andrew threw himself into his work and spent even longer hours than usual at his general practice and with his hospital work. John worried about him but never seemed to be able to find the words to help him. Over the last year they saw less and less of him. He travelled overseas frequently and they only caught up with him on his return.

'Are you going out tonight?' John asked.

'I was, but now I don't think so. Jack said he'd pop over later.'

'It's been a while since we've seen him. Why don't we order in pizza?'

'Great idea.'

20

David was fishing some leaves out of the pool when he saw Rachel, Andrew, Matt and two others approaching from the bottom of the garden. Just for a moment he thought he saw Helen with them but realized it was just his imagination. He quickly put away the net and headed down the garden. Robbie too had seen them and bounded by him to get there first. The sound of Rachel's laughter as she bent down to pick up the excited dog made him smile. They met halfway. He thought how beautiful she looked in her long red floral skirt and white tee-shirt. Her silky hair was tied in a ponytail with a red ribbon. Rachel gently put Robbie on the ground and he instantly sat down at her feet.

'Welcome. It's good to see you again.' He tried to encompass all the visitors but his eyes lingered on Rachel. She put her arm around one of the strangers.

'David, this is Anna, you know Matt, and this is Joe.'

'Pleased to meet you.' David shook hands with them. Anna's long auburn hair was piled in a bun at the back of her head. Her smile went all the way to her green sparking eyes which perfectly matched the color of her dress. She appeared to be a woman comfortable with her natural beauty. Joe was wearing black jeans and a black shirt and David realized this was the person he had seen watching from the doorway when he was talking to Rachel.

His parents were already outside by the time they all reached the house.

David made the introductions. When his father held out his hand to Rachel, David noticed she did not take it immediately. Finally she took it in both of hers, holding it for a moment or two longer than David thought necessary.

'It is good to see you, John,' she said, before turning to Jenny and kissing her on both cheeks.

'It's nice to meet Andrew's friends,' Jenny said. She hugged Andrew affectionately. 'How are you, stranger?'

'I know, Jenny, I know.' She was pleased to see their friend looked well and fit. The sadness seemed to have gone from his eyes and there was a lightness about him that hadn't been there in a long time. 'I brought some wine from my cellar. A particular favorite of yours I remember, Jenny.'

'Thank you,' she said, kissing him on the cheek.

'Please, have a seat,' John said. 'What can I get you to drink? Anna, a glass of wine?'

'White would be lovely, thank you.'

David helped his father with the drinks and then sat down on one of the single chairs.

'And how long have you folks been visiting Andrew?' John asked.

'We've been in the country for just over a week,' Joe said.

'Your first time?'

'Yes, as far as we're aware.'

The oddness of the reply made John think he had misheard it. 'You're obviously from Europe somewhere but I can't quite place the accent.'

'We come from different places,' Joe answered. 'We travel a fair bit and haven't really had a base for a while.'

'Travelling can get under your skin, can't it?' John said. 'Jenny and I went on a trip to Europe about five years ago and we loved it so much we felt we could have gone on forever.'

'Oh yes,' Jenny said, 'there were so many places to go and things to see, but being on holiday we didn't get to experience the places as much as we would have liked. My favorite was Italy. The history, the atmosphere, the people. We loved everything about it. Have you been there?' Jenny directed her question at Rachel.

'Yes, we have spent time there.'

'John loved Scotland best, didn't you, Sweetheart?'

'It was my first visit to Jenny's homeland but I really felt I'd been there before, especially when we went up north. Sometimes I seemed to know what was around a bend in the road. It was strange, but a good strange.'

'So, are you all related?' Jenny asked.

'We are family. Anna has looked after me since I was born. Joe and Matt joined us when I was only a baby.' Without taking her eyes from Jenny, Rachel reached out and put her hand on Matt's arm.

David was hoping Matt was her brother, or her cousin at least.

The conversation shifted to the weather and how the visitors liked Australia. By the time they fired up the barbecue, the conversation was flowing easily.

'Now Andrew told us you all don't eat meat, so I've made some vegetable burgers and there are salads and lots of bread. I also made a cold pasta dish and we are cooking fish. I wasn't sure if you ate fish.'

When the food was ready, Jenny directed her guests to the table and lifted the covers of the various dishes. David deliberately took a seat opposite Rachel.

All of the guests, except Matt, accepted a glass of wine and they settled down to enjoy the meal. David went through the motions of eating his food but his eyes never strayed far from Rachel. He was fascinated by everything about her, from the delicate way she ate her food and lifted her glass to her lips with her slender hands, to the sound of her laughter. He was also aware that Matt kept glancing his way. His expression never changed and when he caught David looking back at him he didn't look away. David realized that most of the conversation was centered on his family and general topics. He learned little about Rachel and her companions. Anna and Rachel helped Jenny clear away the dishes before they had coffee.

'Robbie seems to have taken a shine to you, Rachel.' The little dog was lying quietly by Rachel's feet, one paw over her foot. 'He hasn't left your side since you arrived and he usually isn't this quiet either. You must have a way with animals.'

'He is beautiful.' Rachel put her hand down to stroke Robbie's head.

'Are you planning to do some sightseeing while you're here?' John asked.

'We hope to and are definitely going to visit Uluru. It is a sacred place and we could not come this far and not see it. Have you been there, Mrs. Morgan?'

'Jenny, please. Yes, when we went on a trip to Darwin. I'd seen so many pictures of it but to be up close was just fantastic.'

'We are looking forward to it,' Rachel said. 'Just to touch it will be special.'

'There are some very nice art galleries up that way. Some of the landscape paintings are wonderful.'

'Joe is an artist, a very good one. We travel to sacred sites around the world. He gets his inspiration from these places.'

Joe smiled back and David saw the same look on his face as Andrew had when he looked at Rachel; the same look Robbie gave her. Adoration was the only word he could use to describe it. It seemed everyone who met Rachel adored her and it hit him that he too had become like them.

'Anna also is an excellent artist,' Rachel said.

'Well, when I get some help I am.'

'What do you do, Rachel?' asked Jenny.

'I am a healer and I teach others how to connect to Spirit,' Rachel said, 'and I write whenever I get a chance.'

David noticed that for once his mother was at a loss for words, but she recovered quickly.

'Really! Are you some sort of preacher?'

Jenny caught a glimpse of John trying to catch her attention. She knew him well enough to know it would be one of those 'stop being so nosey' looks. 'I'm sorry, I ask too many questions.'

'I am happy to answer. I am pleased you are kind enough to be interested.' Rachel's smile seemed genuine. 'I speak to anyone who wants to hear what I say. I communicate with Spirit and this helps others to accept that there is more to life than this existence.'

'By Spirit, do you mean people who have died?' John asked

'I am able to do this and also connect to those who have never lived in this reality. But mainly I help people to understand who they really are.'

David stared at Rachel. He did not expect this.

'Are you a psychic?' Jenny was curious and John knew better than to stop the conversation now.

Rachel laughed. 'We are all psychic in different ways. My main work involves healing. I will be meeting with a few groups while I am here. You are welcome to join us if you would like. Please do not feel obliged to do so, just if you want to.'

'We've known you all these years, Andrew, and we've never discussed religion.' John had to admit he was curious about Andrew's involvement with Rachel.

'Helen and I were both brought up Catholics but we never attended church or anything. Rachel's teachings are, well, something that touched my heart. Helen and I owe her a great deal.'

'You knew Helen?' Jenny asked.

'We first met some time ago.'

John noticed how uncomfortable Andrew was looking. 'Well, my dear wife, if you've stopped interrogating our guests, perhaps we can get them something else to drink.' John got up and started to walk towards the door. 'I might take you up on that offer to attend one of gatherings.'

'That's great, John,' Andrew said, 'I'll let you know the details.'

Jenny and David stared after him.

The conversation flowed easily for the next hour, although David realized he still knew very little about these people. They were very good at turning a conversation away from themselves.

'If anyone would like a dip in the pool, I'll get some towels,' John said. Although they were in the shade, the afternoon heat was building up.

'No, thank you,' Rachel said, 'but Matt, it has been a while since you had the chance.'

'It's safe, Matt,' Joe said. 'Have a swim.'

"I didn't bring anything.'

Rachel took out a pair of black shorts from her bag and handed them to Matt. 'I did not think you would bring them. No excuses. Enjoy.'

David felt uncomfortable—he was loathe to use the word jealous—with the smile Rachel and Matt shared.

Soon Matt was swimming up and down the pool. David noticed how fit he looked. He obviously worked out as there was no excess fat on this body.

His father, Andrew and Joe were having a conversation about sports and his mother and Anna were discussing recipes. David saw his chance.

'Rachel, would you like to have a look around the garden? Mum has loads of native plants.'

Both Anna and Joe turned to Rachel. She smiled at them and then at David. 'Yes, I would like that.'

They walked in silence for a while, Rachel stopping now and then to touch a flower and smell it. 'You have a lovely garden. Everything seems to grow so easily in this beautiful country.'

'I suppose we take it for granted. We get to spend a lot of the year outside. I'd hate to live in a cold climate.'

'I have lived in many places that are cold and it has not seemed too bad but to feel the warmth of the sun, this is something special. I feel more at one with the earth when I feel a warm breeze caress my body.'

David's breath stopped in his throat. He felt a strangeness, as if he had been here before, but the feeling quickly faded. 'What sort of things do you write about?'

'Many things.'

'Have you had anything published?'

'Many people have read my words. I keep journals but these have not been published yet.'

'Do you write any fiction?'

She laughed. 'Some would think so, but no, it is not fiction.'

'The reason I ask is I've a friend who works for a publisher. Perhaps he could have a look at it.'

'Thank you, but it is not yet time for wider circulation. I will remember your offer to help when the time comes.'

'Good. That means you'll have to keep in touch.'

'You would like this?' She stopped and turned to him. She took a step back and stared at him although her eyes did not seem to be focused.

'Yes, I would.' David wanted to reach out and put his arms around her. He'd met her only two days ago and yet she seemed to touch a place inside of him that he didn't know existed.

'And you, David, do you enjoy working with computers?'

'I love it. The technology changes all the time and it's a challenge to keep up with it. I work for a big firm with offices all over the world so there's an opportunity to travel if I want.'

'It is good to enjoy one's work.'

'And you enjoy yours?'

'Yes. It too challenges me.'

'Rachel, it's time.' It took Rachel's glance over his shoulder for him to realize someone else had spoken.

'Yes, I will come.'

David turned around to find Matt standing behind him at some distance. He was wearing his shorts and tee-shirt again. Rachel gently touched David's arm.

'We have to go now. I have some things I must do. I enjoyed myself today.'

'So have I. I hope we can do it again sometime.'

'I hope so too.' Rachel took her hand away and walked towards Matt who waited until she had gone past him before following her.

Back on the decking, their guests were standing up, making ready to leave. Rachel shook hands with John and gave Jenny a kiss on the cheek. 'Thank you for making us feel so welcome.'

'It's been a pleasure,' Jenny smiled 'and we'd love to have you back again.'

'We'd like that,' Joe said, shaking John's hand.

They all walked slowly to the bottom of the garden, chatting away like old friends.

'Thanks again, John,' Andrew said, 'I'll let you know about the gathering.'

'I look forward to it.'

Rachel stopped and turned back before she walked through the fence. 'Thank you for showing me the garden, David.' Then she was gone.

John poured them each a glass of wine and they settled down to enjoy the evening warmth. 'A very pleasant afternoon,' Jenny said. 'Such lovely people. I really like them. What about you two?'

'I feel as if I've known them a long time,' John said. 'I don't know about this religious thing though. It certainly was the last thing I expected them to be involved in.'

'Why did you mention about attending one of their gatherings then?' Jenny asked.

'I don't really know to be honest. I just heard myself saying it.'

'Rachel's such a lovely girl. They all seem so close. It's obvious our David's taken a shine to the young lady.'

'Mum, she's a nice girl. I hardly know her but, yes, I do like her. Anyway, she isn't going to be around for long so don't look for anything else in it.' David suddenly felt an emptiness. Logically it would seem the best thing not to get involved but he had a feeling it was probably too late.

21

As he stood by the river and watched the clouds obscure the light of the moon, he felt the first drops of rain on his face. With each burst of thunder the rain became a heavier torrent. He wanted to move but his legs wouldn't obey him. He wanted to run for shelter but he knew in his heart there was no shelter, not from the storm in the night or the storm within. Then he heard her voice, calling to him. He looked around searching for her but he couldn't see anything except the rain and the darkness.

'Please help me.' Her voice was carried on the wind and for a moment brought joy to his heart.

'Where are you?' he shouted.' Tell me where you are and I'll come to you.'

'I am here. I need you. Please do not abandon me.'

The words tore at his heart. He had indeed abandoned her and he thought she had gone but she was here now and he wouldn't let her go again.

'Stay where you are and keep calling. I'll find you.'

'Please do not abandon me.' She said the words over and over again, each time bringing pain to his heart.

At last his legs carried him into the night, following the sound of despair in her voice, but each time he thought he was near, her words seem to come from another direction.

'Please believe in me and do not abandon me,' she continued to call from the darkness.

The rain felt like darts on his body. He rushed in this direction and that, but couldn't see her.

'Keep calling, keep calling, my love.' The rain fell harder.

'Please, do not abandon me. You said you loved me. Please do not abandon me.'

His tears of frustration combined with the rain that ran down his face. He tried to wipe them away but they felt hot and sticky. He opened his eyes to see his hands covered in blood. He screamed into the night, a terrifying scream, and then found he could not stop. He was no longer able to hear her voice.

David felt he had been dropped from a great height as he awoke from sleep, his hands stretched out in front of him. His body was covered in sweat and he felt tears streaming down his face. He looked at his hands, expecting to see blood. He tried to slow his breathing, realizing he had been dreaming. But it was so clear. How could it have been a dream? The voice calling to him was one he knew. He still felt an overwhelming sadness. He sat there in the silence, trying to remember every detail but the memory had already started to fade. Eventually all he was left with was a feeling of loss and the woman's plea still ringing in his ears.

'Sweetheart, you look awful. What's the matter?' Jenny put down the tea towel and went over to him as he sat down at the table. She put a soothing hand on his forehead.

'Nothing, Mum, I just didn't sleep very well. I'm a bit tired, that's all.' He allowed her to hold her hand there, knowing that protesting would do no good.

'Well, you don't appear to have a temperature. Maybe you shouldn't go to work today. You might be coming down with something.'

'I'll be fine. I've got a couple of important meetings. I'll get an early night.'

'If you're sure.'

'I'll be fine, don't worry.'

John Morgan came into the kitchen just as his wife planted a kiss on the top of David's head and went back to the sink.

'Well, if it's a kissing morning, I'd better give you one.' He kissed on her lips and sat down at the table opposite David.

'God, you look awful, son.'

'He didn't sleep well.'

'I'm fine, Mum, honest.'

'Wouldn't be pining a bit would you?' John asked.

'Why would I be pining?'

'Well, it's been a few days since you saw Rachel. I just thought you might be pining.' John laughed and patted David's arm affectionately.

'Dad, I hardly know the girl.'

'Time matters not in the affairs of the heart,' John said. 'I'm so poetic in the mornings aren't I?' David and Jenny both laughed.

'I'm not pining, as you call it. I just didn't sleep well. While we're on the subject, have you been speaking to Andrew recently?'

'I saw him yesterday and he mentioned the others had gone away for a couple of days. He didn't say when they'd be back. Sorry. Did you notice a change in Andrew, Jenny? He seems so much more relaxed and content with life. I think his visitors have a wonderful effect on him. We joked about old times when the four of us spent time together and he didn't have that sad look in his eyes anymore. Maybe there's something about this religious thing they're involved in. It certainly isn't doing Andrew any harm.'

David just loved the sound of Rachel's name and he was glad of any conversation that involved her.

'There is something special about the girl, I grant you that.' Jenny said. 'She has this, oh I don't know how to describe it, this radiance about her. When she's near you, you feel good.'

'Well, I hope they stay a while,' John said. 'I've a feeling it will do us all good.'

For a few moments they stayed deep in their own thoughts. David took a final sip of his coffee and stood up. 'I'd better shower and get going. I probably won't be home until about six thirty tonight.'

'Fine. Your Dad and I are playing golf this afternoon so it'll just be leftovers for dinner.'

David kissed his Mum on the cheek and smiled at his Dad as he headed off to the bathroom. He was glad he hadn't mentioned his dream, his nightmare more like. What bits he remembered, he wanted to keep to himself.

22

John opened the door slowly. Something was wrong. He felt it. The house was too quiet. He knew Jenny was visiting the hospice and wouldn't be back until later in the afternoon. He closed the door behind him and stood for a moment. There was no sign or sound of Robbie. There was rarely a time the little dog did not come to greet whoever entered the house. Even if he was outside he could hear when a car pulled up in the driveway and would be right there before anyone had a chance to reach the front door. Perhaps he was in Andrew's garden again.

'Robbie, where are you, boy. Robbie, Robbie.' John was suddenly filled with dread. He walked to the kitchen and that's when he saw him. He was lying, perfectly still, by the flap that allowed him to come in and out as he pleased. John rushed over to him, calling his name. He knelt down and gently touched his body. He was cold. John knew he was dead. He felt the tears run down his cheeks as he gently lifted Robbie into his arms. He stroked him gently, the loss engulfing him. He realized Robbie must have died alone and that filled him with sadness. Something made him look up and he saw Rachel standing by the glass door. Still holding Robbie he unlocked the door and opened it.

'Rachel, I'm taking Robbie to the vet. I think it's too late. There's no heartbeat. Oh God, what am I going to do? What will I tell Jenny? It'll break her heart.'

Rachel put out her arms. 'Please, may I hold him?'

Without hesitation, John gently handed Robbie to her.

'I will take him into the garden. May I ask that you do not disturb us? We will be back soon.'

John watched her as she slowly walked out to the middle of the lawn, and then sat down with her back to him.

She walked slowly towards the ridge where he stood watching the cluster of tepees by the river, the dog lying still in her arms. His lean body was erect and proud. His coal black hair hung down the front of his left shoulder. He smiled as he always did when he felt her presence, his eyes still fixed on the tepees.

'Welcome.' His voice was deep yet gentle.

She stood beside him and together they watched the scene before them.

'All is well?' She asked the question that formed part of their ritual.

'Yes, all is well.' He turned to her. Rachel placed the dog in his outstretched hands. He gently stroked the little creature and then turned towards the forest. Rachel followed him until they came to the circle of grass, surrounded by tall majestic trees. It was warm and rays of sunlight shone through the canopy. They walked to the center of the circle and sat down cross-legged, facing each other. He put one hand

under the dog, resting the other on his back. The air was still and the only sound was that of the birds. He smiled at her and then closed his eyes. She put the palms of her hand together for a moment and then faced them towards the dog. She too closed her eyes.

John stood by the door, his eyes fixed on Rachel, as she sat perfectly still on the grass. He was unaware of time passing. Suddenly he saw Robbie's head pop around Rachel's arm and then he was bounding towards the house. John's tears ran freely as he reached down and scooped Robbie into his arms. The dog yelped excitedly as he licked his face. John's glance returned to Rachel who was still on the grass. She stood up slowly, turned and walked towards him.

'I thought we'd lost him' He stared at her. 'He was dead.'

'Now was not his time. I have to go now, John.'

'I need to talk to you about this. Can't you stay a little longer?'

'No, but perhaps we can talk about it again.'

'Yes. I'd like that.' John reached out and touched her arm. 'Thank you, Rachel.'

John watched her as she walked to the bottom on the garden. When he could no longer see her, he took Robbie into the kitchen. He set him down and put some food in his bowl. Leaving the dog to his unexpected snack, he wandered back outside and sat down. He felt a stillness, as if the world had just stopped. He knew Robbie had died. He could feel no heartbeat and the heat had left his body. Rachel had brought him back to life. How was that possible?

Up until this last year, John never thought about death. As he grew older and people he knew around his age died, he accepted that one day it would be his turn. The thought made him uncomfortable.

He was drawn to books on life after death, and near death experiences. He hadn't come to any conclusion on whether he believed it or not but now he'd seen something that was forcing him to give it more thought. He felt his body, his mind, had received a tremendous jolt. He needed answers but he didn't seem able to formulate the questions. What had just happened touched a part of him he didn't know existed. He felt a strangeness but he could not define it. He couldn't say it made him feel good or bad. It merely felt strange. The only thing he did know was that he didn't want to lose it. He would talk more to Rachel. Until then, should he tell Jenny and David? Would he be able to find the words to describe what just happened? They'd think he had imagined it.

23

The Vatican, Rome

'Come, sit down, Philippe, sit down.' Cardinal Ricardo pointed to a chair by the fire. 'Let me get you some wine.'

Philippe watched him as he poured the liquid into the fine crystal glasses. Even in the evening, in his own apartments, the Cardinal dressed in his formal attire. Perhaps he wanted to be ready in case he was called to the Pope's side. Philippe neither trusted nor liked the Cardinal but he knew the Cardinal liked him. He was not sure about the trust element though. He could not imagine the Cardinal trusting anyone, not even God. He also knew the Cardinal only liked to look, not touch, and Philippe was fully aware of his own attractiveness. His black hair was just long enough to touch his collar, framing his perfectly proportioned tanned face. His mother had always told him he had the face of a god, although he doubted that was what she was thinking when he slit her throat. He was twelve at the time and caught her in bed with a married neighbor while his father was away on business. Philippe knew she had to be punished.

The Cardinal was a weird weasel of a man, but he had power. Philippe had heard his power came from knowing the secrets of others, and the Vatican held many secrets. It would be an unwise man who got on the wrong side of him. 'I have a mission for you,' he said, 'an important mission.'

It amused Philippe when the Cardinal referred to the tasks he asked him to undertake as "missions", as if they had some holy purpose. Five years ago he had been recommended to the Cardinal by a business associate in Paris. The Cardinal wanted an accident arranged. One of the nuns in the Vatican was pregnant to one of the priests who worked for him. The problem had to be eliminated. Philippe arranged for the young woman to be killed by a hit and run driver on one of the days she left the Holy City to visit her mother. Life in the Cardinal's household returned to normal and during the following five years Philippe eliminated several problems for the Cardinal, for which he was more than adequately compensated. Much as he was repulsed by the man, Philippe recognized a kindred soul. Somewhere deep inside they shared the same thing–an empty space, where love and compassion should have resided.

'What can I do for you, your Eminence?'

'How much do you value your soul, Philippe?'

'My soul? I'm not sure I have one.'

'Everyone has a soul.'

'If you say so. If I have one I put little value on it. What has my mission to do with my soul?'

'The subject of your mission is a woman who steals souls.'

Philippe laughed. 'No-one can steal something I do not want to give.'

'I pray not. She is clever. She is able to make you think you want to give it to her.'

'Tell me what needs to be done.'

'She is being watched over by someone in my employ. This man, Patrick, does his job well but I fear if she tries to take from him his soul, he will not have the strength to resist.'

Philippe was tiring of this talk but he knew the Cardinal's ways.

'She is a danger to the Church and must be destroyed. I have waited a long time for this.'

'You want me to kill her or bring her to you? Either way will be easy.'

'Not as easy as you think. But she is not to be killed. Not yet. There is information that must be extracted from her first. Perhaps you can help me with this also.'

'Whatever I can do to assist Your Eminence.'

'She will know you are coming. She is well guarded by people who will die for her.'

'I always succeed.'

'This is different. It has to do with timing. Certain circumstances must be in place. Patrick will know when it is time.'

'This is important?'

'It is essential.'

24

John rang the doorbell. He was both nervous and excited. Andrew smiled broadly. 'Come in, come in.'

'I haven't picked a bad time?'

'No, no.'

'I just wondered if I could have a chat to Rachel, if she's around.'

'Yes, she's here. Go into the lounge. We're just having a cup of tea.'

They all looked up as he walked in. Their smiles dispersed his awkwardness. Joe came over and shook his hand. 'Good to see you again, John.'

Matt nodded to him and Rachel got up and walked over to him.

'John, welcome. Would you like some tea?'

'No thanks.'

'How are Jenny and David?' she asked.

'Good. They're good.'

'And little Robbie?'

'He's fine. Running around as usual, wanting attention. Actually that's what I wanted to see you about. You said we might talk about it.'

'The others know about Robbie. We are glad you came. Whatever questions you have, please ask. I will answer them truthfully.'

'Rachel!' Matt said.

'Do not worry, John will not betray us. Let us walk in the garden.' Rachel slipped her arm through John's and guided him through the open patio doors.

'You wanted to talk about Robbie?' She said as they sat down in the gazebo.

'He was dead, wasn't he?' You brought him back to life.'

'It is not that simple. Robbie was between worlds. His body was dead but his spirit was waiting. He could have returned or moved on to another life.'

'You really believe there is life after death?'

Rachel smiled at him. 'I know there is. There is so much more to our existence than what we experience in this reality. There is a whole world out there, waiting for us.'

'Even if I believe this, it doesn't explain why or how you brought his body back to life.'

'All things happen for a reason. It was not Robbie's time to leave. He had a purpose, a reason for what he did.'

'I don't follow.'

'Are you perhaps at a point in your life when are wondering about life and death? You are questioning your own mortality or are being drawn in a different direction.'

'As a matter of fact I have. I never used to but lately I've given it more thought. I find myself reading books I wouldn't normally have chosen or ones I've always wanted to read but never got round to it. I've read a book called 'The Prophet' about a dozen times. I find every time I read it I seem to understand more about what the author is saying. The words touch something inside me.'

'Kahlil Gibran.'

'You've read it?'

'Many times. I am very fond of his work. He was a very gifted man. You are continuing your spiritual journey. That book may not have meant anything to you if you had read it many years ago but now it holds meaning for you.'

'I'm leaving my run a bit late,' he said.

'It is never too late. In Gibran's book 'Jesus the Son of Man' there is a line "the Spirit who knocks at our door that we may wake and rise and walk out to meet truth naked and unencumbered". I find that so beautiful. There is always time. That knock on the door can come any time.'

'You said there's a reason for everything.'

'Yes. We learn from everyone we come in contact with. Every situation, everything that happens to us contains a lesson.'

'What has this to do with Robbie?'

'I was drawn to come to you. When you found Robbie I felt your sorrow. Perhaps that happened for that reason. You now have questions that perhaps I can answer for you. I hope to help you on your path. You may not take my words to your heart but that is your choice.'

'So you're saying Robbie died so we could talk like this?'

'Perhaps.'

'It's funny but for some reason that doesn't sound crazy. How can someone so young be so wise?'

'I am not as young as I look,' she said with a smile. 'You will have many questions and I will try to help you. We are having some people over on Friday night. You said perhaps you would be interested in attending. Would you like to join us?'

'Yes, I would.'

'Good.'

That night, as Jenny lay asleep in their bed, John stood by the window staring out at the night sky. What was happening to him was important. He sensed it. He felt the excitement. He couldn't talk to Jenny about it just yet. He would know when the time was right.

25

David sat with Rachel under the old tree. It was warm so they had walked down to the bottom of the garden where the trees offered shade and where they could have some privacy. She said she couldn't go out to dinner with him and instead invited him to go for a walk in the garden with her. He didn't understand why she wouldn't leave the house with him.

'Do you like travelling Rachel? Do you never feel the need to settle down somewhere?'

'I do not think much about it. I move around because I have to. I need to be able to do what I can to help.'

'There are people who need help in Australia too. We have our problems here just like every other country—poor people, homeless kids, drugs.'

'I know there are problems but you are a rich country. There are countries not so rich or free and their problems are greater than you could ever imagine.'

'It seems too difficult to fix,' David said. 'I feel sick to my stomach when I watch the pictures of those starving kids in other countries.'

'Everyone can help.'

'Mum and Dad sponsor a child in Kenya. The first child they sponsored is now a teacher. But there just seems so many of them.'

'Yes there are, but the problem can be overcome. There is no need for a child to die of starvation. People have put boundaries around themselves. They see themselves as being separate, as being British or Asian or African. They think because they look different they are different and they are not. God sees us as being all the same, all part of Him. We are the ones who create the difference.'

'You really believe that?' David asked.

'Yes I do. As long as people think they cannot make something better, they will not, but if we believe we can, we can accomplish anything.'

'I hope I'm wrong but I can't see it happening in my lifetime.'

'You will have other lifetimes, David.'

'You believe in this reincarnation stuff, that we come back again?'

Rachel smiled. 'I know it to be the truth.'

323BC, Babylon

'Why did you not come to me?' He had opened his eyes to find her standing by his bed.

'I am here now, Alexander.'

'I dreamt much. I saw Bucephalus and Hephaestion. We stood all three together again. It was good to see them. I miss them. My heart still aches for them.'

'You will be with them again, Alexander.'

He sat in silence for a long moment, his thoughts with the two great loves of his life.

'The pain has now left you?' she asked.

'It always does when you are by my side. But why am I still in my bedchamber. I need to be with my men. I have much to do.'

'Rest a little, Master.'

'Master! You only call me Master when you are going to lecture me.'

'I never lecture you.'

'You think you do not, but you do. When you call me Master I know you want to tell me something I do not wish to hear.'

She smiled. How little the world knew of him. They saw their general, their king, their god. She saw the little boy who fought a battle which raged inside him and from which he never walked away the victor.

He moved himself to sit on the edge of the bed. *'I feel good. All the old aches and pains have left me. Come, sit here.'*

She sat beside him and he took her hand.

'I often wonder why you stayed with me all these years. Why is it you are never afraid of me? The others, I know they fear me, especially when I have enjoyed too much wine or when things do not go well in battle. But you, you never flinch from my temper or my moods.'

'I do not judge you, Alexander.'

'You do judge me. I know you do. When I come from the battlefield you are no-where to be found. Sometimes I do not see you for days. You are afraid I will see the judgment in your eyes when you look at me, covered in the blood of others and pacing the ground with exhilaration. You know you would judge me if you saw the excitement that fills me, the power that surges through my body. You would ask me how it is I can feel this way when I have caused the deaths of many; when I can still hear their death screams in my head.'

'Perhaps it is only the screams of one you hear,' she said.

He looked away from her. 'You are talking about the child of that whore who took my mother's place? I had no choice. Do you think I bear guilt for the child? It was necessary for me to fulfill my destiny. It was so long ago. There have been many deaths since then. Do you think I should bear guilt for deeds that were necessary?'

'Only your heart can answer that.'

He held her gaze for a moment and then laughed. 'You know me. You see inside my head and my heart. You know it is not the injuries of battle that cause me pain. I cannot change the past. But why is it you never come to me after a battle? That is the time I need you most. That is when the demons appear.'

'I have other work to do, Master.'

'Ah. Master again. What is it you do? Where do you go that you cannot face me?'

'I go to the battlefield.'

'The battlefield! Why? There is nothing left there but the dead.'

'I tend to those who need it.'

'You tend to the dead?'

'I help those who have not accepted their death to walk to the light of their God.'

'Is that why you stay with me, to tend to the people I have killed? I do not understand. Why do you do this?'

'Because I can.'

'The living need you. I need you.'

'I am here now.'

'Will you make my demons go away? Is that why you are here?'

'Alexander,' she gently touched his cheek, *'I am here to help you accept your death and walk to the light of your God.'*

26

John stood in the silence of the house. Jenny had gone to the hospice and David was out with Jack. He was glad to be alone with his thoughts for a few minutes before he left for Andrew's. He knew he was starting on a journey and it excited him. He hoped that along the way Jenny would want to join him. Until then he would take it a step at a time.

Andrew showed him into a room that he remembered had once been a large bedroom. It was lit only by a single large candle and chairs were arranged in a circle. Joe, Matt and Anna were there with the other guests. Rachel greeted him with a warm smile and introduced him to Christine, Ella, Joan, Natalie, Maria, Bridget and Nicky.

'I am happy you could join us, John,' Rachel said.' She turned to the others. If you would like to take a seat we will begin.'

They all sat down and John found himself between Christine and Anna.

'Can we please begin by saying the Lord's Prayer,' Rachel said.

John was amazed he remembered all the words.

'I thank you all for coming tonight,' Rachel said. 'We are gathered here together to form a circle of energy. From this circle we will send healing to various people and parts of the world. A circle of energy is a powerful force and there are many thousands just like this around the world, each with the aim of sending healing to where it is needed. With enough loving energy we can change sickness to wellbeing, war to peace. People do not realize they each have the power to do this. They often think the problems are too big and do not try. If only they could see the healing energy produced by a single thought of love. For this time we need to set aside the workings of our mind. This will be about connecting to our spirit, the part of us that belongs to our Creator. The part of us that is our Creator. We need only to feel, not think. We will go into this with no expectation of an outcome. We will trust.'

John walked home through the garden. He stopped and looked up at the stars. They seemed brighter and closer than he was used to seeing them. The air was still and he heard the gentle sounds of the night. He felt high; high on excitement and energy.

Jenny returned to find him sitting in the garden. 'Hi sweetie, I'm back. I was just going to make a cuppa. You want one?'

John stirred from his thoughts. 'Thanks. Come and join me. It's lovely out here.'

'OK, give me a minute.'

Jenny sipped some of her tea and then let out a long sigh.

'How was your night?' John asked.

'Good. The entertainment went down well. We had them singing along. I wish I had their resilience. What about you? Did you enjoy your meeting?'

'Yes.'

'I'm glad.'

John was surprised, but not ungrateful, Jenny left it at that.

On the street outside, the two men sat in the car, obscured from the outside by tinted windows. They had a good view of the driveways, even in the dark.

'I usually hire my own men,' Patrick said, 'why did he send you?'

'I am just obeying orders, like you,' Philippe said. He turned back to look at the house.

'You know she is there?'

'Yes.'

'And the car they drive?'

'I know how to do my job.' Patrick did not like this man. He guessed he was between 35 and 40 and very handsome. His clothes were expensive, his hair and nails perfectly groomed. He carried himself with confidence and ease. His soft French accent hid what Patrick knew was a man without compassion or fear—a dangerous man. His instincts were normally right about people.

'How many in the other house?'

'It's all in the log,' Patrick answered coldly.

'I will read the log later. How many?'

'The girl and her friends are all inside. The wife has just returned next door but the son hasn't come home yet.'

'And regular visitors?' Philippe asked.

'No-one regular. The recent one was a friend of the son I think. The other was a blond girl. I have still to find out about her.'

'I will do that,' Philippe said. Yes, thought Patrick, it would be right up his alley.

'You have been doing this job for many years, Patrick?'

'Yes.'

'What will you do when it is all over?'

Patrick turned to him. Philippe just smiled. A cold, emotionless smile. He did not wait for an answer. He got out of the car and drove away in his own without a backward glance.

27

Andrew phoned to check how John was doing and happily accepted the invitation to pop over for coffee. As they sat in the garden chatting, John thought how contented his friend seemed.

'How did you get involved in this, Andrew?'

'It was about six months after Helen died. I have to tell you John, I didn't want to live without her. I missed her every second. I went over our life together, over and over. I felt totally lost.

'One Sunday I was on my way to Bentleigh. An old aunt of Helen's had invited me for afternoon tea. I didn't want to go but I knew I was getting more and more dragged down. I thought I should make the effort. Anyway, I got as far as Seaford and suddenly stopped. I decided I just couldn't face it. I couldn't do a U turn so I cut into this street and pulled up. There was a line of traffic waiting to get back onto Beach Road so I just parked. I saw some people going into this hall and then I saw a sign saying "Spiritualist Church". You know how I've always been an admirer of the works of Sir Arthur Conan Doyle. Well, I remembered reading he was a spiritualist. I thought it strange for a man of his intellect to be involved in that kind of thing. Actually I say 'that kind of thing' but I didn't know much about it. It conjured up séances in darkened rooms. Calling up the dead. I recalled he'd gone right into it, did proper research and everything before he came out publicly and said he was a spiritualist. He spent the rest of his life spreading the word of his belief in life after death.

'The backlog of cars seemed to be getting worse—it looked like a car had broken down just at the junction—so I went to check out the hall, just to pass the time until the traffic cleared. It was an old community hall. Ella and Christine who you met the other night are part of the Spiritualist church there. Well, Ella met me at the door, introduced herself and told me a bit about what would happen. They all seemed decent folk. They made me feel welcome. The service included some hymns and some prayers and we did a meditation. I'd never done one before but I tried and it felt good. Then Christine stood up and started talking to people and telling them about spirits she had with her. It seemed to make sense to the people she was talking to. Then she looked at me and said there was a woman with me. John, she described Helen perfectly. She told me things she couldn't have known. She said Helen was saying our two babies were with her. How could she have known about Helen's two miscarriages? She said Helen knew I'd always thought her life had been a little empty without children but that I needed to know she'd had a wonderful life and is still having one.'

'I cried, John. I can't tell you what it meant to hear that. I had no doubt it was Helen. It helped me. After that I could feel her around me sometimes but I still felt this empty space inside. I was so lonely and just couldn't get past missing her. Then I met Rachel. Remember when I went to visit Helen's brother in Italy last year? One day I got up early and went along to the little church in the village where Helen was baptized. I was sitting in one of the pews thinking of her and about what the medium said that day at the Church. I thought I'd feel closer to her there, John, but I truly felt lonelier than I'd ever been in my life. I prayed to God for proof. I actually said 'Show me it's true. Show me she's with you.'

He heard footsteps in the aisle. He turned and saw a young woman standing beside him.

'My name is Rachel. I was passing the church and I heard you ask for help.'

Andrew was sure he hadn't said the words aloud.

'Tell me what it is you want,' *she said as she sat down beside him. He told her about Helen's death and his experience at the church. He thought how odd it was he was talking to this stranger so easily.*

'I thought if I came here I would feel close to her again.'

'You need proof she is still with you?'

'I know it's selfish but I want to know for sure.'

Rachel smiled and closed her eyes. There was total stillness. He noticed how the dust sparkled in the shafts of light coming through the windows. A butterfly caught his attention as it fluttered across the paths of light. The whole church seemed bathed in a warm glow. He could smell lavender. Helen loved lavender.

He looked again at the woman and saw gentleness and beauty in her face. Then, in the blink of his eyes, Helen was standing in the aisle.

'Andrew.' *She said his name so softly, so lovingly.*

'Helen.' *His heart ached with joy.* 'Helen, my love. Is it really you?'

'It is, my darling,' *she said.*

'I've missed you so. You don't know how much I've missed you.'

'I do know, Andrew. Haven't you felt me? When you lie in bed at night and the breeze catches the lace curtain, didn't you smell the scent of lavender as it drifted across you. When you are reading and you think you feel a hand on your shoulder. It wasn't your imagination. I was trying to comfort you. I was so glad when you went to that church. I stood by the medium and whispered my message to her.'

'I knew it was you.'

'Don't cry, my love. Rachel has allowed me to be with you like this because I have something I need to say to you. I'm torn between my love for you and my need to move on. You're in great pain and you cling to me for fear if you don't you'll disappear into a pool of darkness. You get glimpses of the darkness and you don't want to go there. You see no point to your life without me but you're not looking hard enough, Andrew.'

'You were, are, my life, Helen.'

'I was only a part of it. Before we met each other you lived and laughed and learned. You formed bonds and shared your love with others. You coped with the sorrow and the joy and became who you were when I met you. We've had our joys and sorrows too and hopefully we grew stronger because of them and the fact we shared them.'

'I remember every harsh word I ever said to you,' he said. *When I was working too hard and got grumpy. I spent too long away from you. I sometimes put work before you. I wasted so much time.'*

'Let go of the regrets, my darling, and think only of the good times, the adventures and a love and life shared. It's the only way through this for you. When you focus on the things you regret you block the love I'm sending you. If you think of the happy times and remember me with

a smile then you'll be able to feel the love I still have for you. I'll help you through this and rejoice with you when you reach the other side of grief. Say my name and I'll come to you. But don't bind me so tightly to this place. I won't abandon you but I'm anxious to explore this new world. It's truly a wondrous place, Andrew. I feel only peace and love surround me. I'm not dead, Andrew. I'm just somewhere else. Let your memories of me give you feelings of love, not sorrow. Do you understand what I'm saying to you?'

His tears flowed freely. He knew this would be only time his wife would come to him like this. She was telling him to let go of his grief. It hurt him to think he was holding her back. 'I know what you're saying, Helen. I'll love you always and I will try. You'll still visit me sometimes?'

'I promise. Now I have to go. One more thing I want to ask you. Take care of this girl. She's very precious to us all and will need your help.'

'Can't you stay a little longer? Can I touch you?' Helen stretched her right arm across Rachel and reached out to him. He felt its familiar softness and gently kissed it. She smiled at him and then was gone.

'You actually saw her and touched her?' John was overwhelmed by his friend's story.

'Yes. She was real, John, she was real. Since that day my life has changed. Not only do I know she is around me when I need her, I know she'll be there when it's my turn to go.'

John was silent for a moment as he watched Andrew wipe his tears. John wiped his own tears and then they both started to laugh.

'Anyone seeing us like this would think we were a couple of senile old men,' Andrew said.

'But we're not, are we?'

'No, John, we're not.'

28

They were walking in the garden. He had again asked her if she wanted to go out for a meal but she had said she couldn't. She asked him instead to join them at Andrew's for dinner. Anna had sent them out to pick some fresh mint from the herb garden.

'Have you any idea how long you'll be staying in Australia, Rachel?'

'I do not know, David, I still have places to go.'

'You must have a lot of friends,' he said.

'Yes. Friends I know and those I have still to meet.' She delicately picked some mint leaves and put them in a small bowl.

'I got a couple of movies out the other night. I wanted to find out more about what you were talking about, the talking to dead people thing.'

Rachel laughed. 'It is a popular phrase these days. Did you enjoy the movies?'

'I don't know really.' He paused for a moment. He was not comfortable with the subject. 'Is that the way you see the dead people, with their injuries; like they were when they died?' He still couldn't believe she could do what she said she could.

'Sometimes,' she answered. 'The ones who have difficulty in letting go of the physical I see them as they perceive themselves to be. They have not accepted the death of their physical body.'

'And what is it you do exactly?' David asked.

'For those souls I help them to accept the light.'

'How do you do that?'

'I talk to them?'

'In your head?' he asked.

'It does not seem that way to me. My spirit communicates with their spirit.'

'I'm sorry I'm asking so many questions but I don't really understand.'

'Ask me what you will, David.'

'Why do you do it? It must be depressing to deal with dead people all the time.'

'To me they are not dead. Only their bodies have died. I do it because I can. I also try to help those who have not yet passed from this life.'

'Have you cured a lot of people?'

Rachel smiled at him. 'I heal them. It is not about curing. Each of us is responsible for our own sickness. Therefore we can heal ourselves. What I do is help people to remember how to do it. I channel healing energy which allows the sick to recognize the spirit within. Their spirits know how to heal.'

'It sounds complicated and I have to say I'm not sure I believe it all.' David felt he had to be honest. He knew he didn't want to pretend with her.

'We are all capable of doing what I do. The world has changed. Do you know that not so long ago people were burned at the stake and hanged for saying they can communicate with those who were regarded as dead. Now mediums are even on television.

'I caught a bit of one of them once but it's all tricks isn't it? I mean it's a TV show. It's fixed surely?'

'I know there are people who pretend to be what they are not but there are also those whose gifts are great.'

'How do you tell the difference?'

'You open your heart, David. It will tell you. Dismiss what everyone says and find your own truth. Ask with an open mind and heart and feel the answer. Feel what is true for you.'

'Are you saying what's true for one person isn't necessarily true for another? I'm not sure I understand that exactly.'

'What is the most beautiful thing in the world to you? Is it a sunset, or perhaps a flower? For each of us it is a different thing but it is our own truth. What is the most beautiful to you?'

'You.'

She laughed. 'Oh David. I am being serious.'

'So am I.'

'Thank you. But before you met me what was the most beautiful thing you have ever seen?'

'I don't remember before you.'

She looked at him and held his gaze. He didn't want to move. He had said it without thinking but he knew he meant it.

The moment was lost as they heard Anna's voice call them for dinner. They walked silently back to the house. Rachel turned to him just before they reached the door.

'What I was trying to say was we each have our own truth and it does not make one person right and the other wrong. There are those whose truth is I am a witch and I must be destroyed.'

David suddenly felt a chill. For the first time he wondered if Rachel was a little crazy. He quickly dismissed the thought. He wanted so much for her to be normal.

29

David and Jack dropped down onto sand, laughing from the exhilaration of their swim.

'That was great but I think I'm getting old,' David said. He took two bottles of juice from the icebox and passed one to Jack.

'You're not tired are you? Hell, we only just got here,' Jack said, throwing a towel at him.

'I haven't done it in a while. The pool isn't the same.'

'You haven't done much at all recently. I hardly see you.'

'I've been busy. Sorry about that.'

'You've been moping, haven't you? Things not going too well with the neighbor's visitor? Rachel, isn't it?'

'Yes. I really don't know how things are going with Rachel. I hardly get to see her.'

'So you're moping? Why don't you just dump her? There are plenty of unattached girls just hanging around waiting for a stud like you to ask them out.'

David threw the towel back at Jack. 'I've thought about it, believe me, but I just can't seem to get interested in anything else.'

'Sounds like love to me, mate.'

David stared out at the sea. 'I know it is but I don't know what to do about it. It's all happened so fast. I didn't know it could happen like this.'

'It's not just the not seeing her is it? What's holding you up?'

'It's complicated. She's involved in this new age spiritual thing.'

'A cult of some sort you mean?'

'No, not that. Well I don't think it's that. I don't really know. I hope it's not because my Dad's involved.'

'What!'

'Yeh. Who would believe it? He's around there all the time. They have a healing group or something.'

'Doesn't sound too bad.'

'It's more than that though. It's the way he talks about her, the way he says her name.'

'He obviously likes her.'

'I've heard the others do it too. Even Robbie is besotted. It's hard to explain but it's like she's someone really special.'

'You think she is too.'

'Yes, but this is... I don't know really. They treat her like she's a saint or something. I know it sounds crazy.'

'Hell! I can see where you're coming from. Everyone thinks she's a saint and you're the one trying to make her a sinner. Boy, have you got problems.'

'It's not the only problem. The people she's with are always watching her. She won't come out with me. Even when I go over to see her, the most we do is walk in the garden and talk but I feel them watching me.'

'No chance of sneaking a cuddle then?'

'No chance.'

'So why are they watching her all the time?'

"I don't know. There's all this secrecy about where they go and what they do. I hardly know anything about her. Like I said, they seem to treat her like she's really precious.'

Jack shrugged his shoulders. 'Maybe she's some sort of cult leader.'

'You think?'

'I don't know, but it does seem a bit strange. What's she told you?'

'She said she's a healer.'

'She cures sick people?'

'She says she helps people to heal their spirit and their relationship with God, I think that's how she described it.'

'You're not telling me everything, are you? Come on, we're mates. Tell me.'

'Rachel says she can talk to dead people.'

'What!'

'Weird, huh?'

'Okay, I admit it sounds weird, but I work with a woman whose sister does that and some of the girls at work go to her house for readings. It's just one of those new age fad things. Look, it sounds like she can either do what she says she can, or she's one of those cult freaks who con people into believing what they're told, or she's just plain crazy. I can see why you're a bit confused though. Does she seem crazy?'

'Not at all. She's gentle and smiles all the time. I feel really good around her, all peaceful and comfortable, like I've known her forever.'

'Maybe she is a saint.'

'So I'm in love with a girl who's either a saint or some cult leader. On top of that I can't get to spend time with her.'

'And, on top of that your father's become a follower.'

David started laughing first then Jack joined in.

'I can see the funny side of this except for one thing,' David said.

'What's that?'

'I think I really do love her, Jack. She's all I think about.'

'Either way it's not going to be easy for you.'

'I know. I just wish I knew more about her.'

'Can't you go to one of these meetings they have?'

'I don't know. I think you have to be invited.'

'It's up to you. If it was me I'd have to find out. I mean I couldn't live with myself not knowing if my girl was a saint or,' Jack's eyes widened, 'someone in league with the devil.'

David smiled, but an uncomfortable feeling took hold of him. He thought how much easier it would be if Rachel was a secretary or a nurse.

30

'Tomorrow night! Are you going again? You're spending a lot of time there.' Jenny handed John a cup of coffee and sat down beside him on the garden sofa.

'I know, sweetheart, but I really enjoy it,' John said. 'I feel I'm doing something worthwhile.'

'There's plenty you could do at the hospice if you wanted to.' She'd never asked him to help at the hospice and he'd never offered.

'We each do our bit in different ways.'

'What is it you do exactly, this healing group of yours?'

'We sit in a circle. We pray and then we meditate.'

'You meditate!' She stared at him. 'I thought that was for hippies.'

'It's a common thing these days. I've heard some companies have meditation sessions at the office for their staff.' He took a deep breath. 'When we meditate we ask those in Spirit to join us to help with the healing.'

'I've lost you.'

'Rachel says there are those in the spirit world who've chosen to help us. We just have to ask.'

She stared at him. 'John, I can't believe this! It's like I don't know you. You're not the kind of man to get involved in this ... this sort of thing. What's happening to you?'

'I know I've changed Jenny but it's for the better. It does seem strange, talking about it, but when I'm with the others it seems so natural.'

'I thought you were happy with our life. Why are you suddenly searching for something else and why does it have to be something so crazy?'

'It's not crazy.'

'Can't you hear how weird it all sounds? You're sitting in a circle healing people and talking to ghosts. What's it all for?'

'We have to start somewhere, Jenny, if we want to change the way the world is. We're lucky, but there are others who aren't and if I can help in any way I have to try. Since I retired I've felt as if something's been missing in my life. I didn't feel it when I was so busy but even though I love being with you and David and doing all the things I do, I still feel I'm missing out on something, something important. Now I don't feel like that anymore. I feel this is what I should be doing.'

'I don't understand, John, truly I don't.'

'Have you ever thought about dying, Jenny, about what's waiting for us when we die?'

'I see people die all the time at the hospice and I'd like to believe there's something better than this life for them. I don't know what I believe really, whether I believe in God or not. Is this what you're asking me?'

'Yes.'

'Well, I just don't know. I can't understand a God who makes people suffer so much.'

'Are you afraid of death?' He took her hand in his.

'I suppose so. I don't like to think about my own death, or yours or David's.'

'Do you want to know what I believe? That we don't die. I hadn't thought about it either but now I really do believe it. Our body dies but our spirit, our soul doesn't. We move on and this life and everything else becomes clearer to us. I've just read a book about reincarnation and normally I would be skeptical but I instantly felt it to be the truth, that we have lived before and will live again. It's a wonderful feeling, Jenny. I don't just want to believe it, I do believe it and I'm not afraid to die anymore.'

'You really feel like that?'

'Yes. I want you to believe the same but I can't make you. You have to make that decision for yourself.'

'I don't know if I can. But do you really believe Rachel can heal the sick and talk to the dead as she says she does?'

'I do, Jenny. Can I suggest something? What if I asked Rachel to visit the hospice with you? You can see what she does and judge for yourself.'

'I don't know, John. What would she do?'

'Talk to them I would imagine. I'm sure she wouldn't cause any problems or upset people. She might not even agree to do it but I could ask.'

'I suppose it wouldn't do any harm.'

'I'll speak to her.'

Later, Jenny stood at the window, watching John in the garden. He was standing perfectly still, his hands in his pockets. How she loved him. After all the years they had been together the sight of him still gave her such pleasure. He spent a lot of time recently just being still, his thoughts turned inwards. A chill ran through her. Their life together was changing and she didn't want it to. John seemed to be looking for something he didn't already have. Hadn't they always shared everything, talked about everything? Now he seemed to be looking for something she couldn't give him. What tugged at her heart was that what he was searching for seemed to be with Rachel. Jenny knew it wasn't a sexual thing between them but still she was jealous. John was finding a spiritual side to his life. He was embracing it and hungered for more. She could see the pleasure it gave him and she wasn't part of it. He'd bring books home and spent hours reading. She'd feel him get out of bed around 5.00am and he would bring her a cup of tea round seven. She didn't know what he did with those two hours.

If only she could share this with him but something held her back. Did she think it was possible to communicate with the dead? She couldn't believe that. Her beautiful, loving mother died when she was six years old. She adored her. She remembered praying every night for her Mummy to come back. She would have conversations with her and tell her about school and her friends and how much she missed her, but she didn't come back. Her father told her Mummy had gone to heaven to be with God. Jenny thought she hated God for taking her Mummy away and not sending her back when she'd asked Him to.

Jenny realized those memories were probably what made her feel uncomfortable when John spoke of the things he now believed. She hated to see him get involved in something she knew was a fantasy but she couldn't tell him her thoughts. She hoped it was some mid-life crisis thing he was going through.

When her thoughts drifted back to the present she found him looking at her through the window. He smiled and blew her a kiss.

31

'Thank you for inviting me today, Jenny,' Rachel said as they walked up the pathway to the hospice. Matt had insisted on driving them but said he would wait outside.

'John said you might be able to help. We've a couple of ladies who visit and do Reiki and something called energy healing and the patients seem to enjoy it, so the nurses are quite open to alternative methods. Anything that makes them feel better really. Some of them don't have very long.'

'This journey may end for them but another is about to begin,' Rachel said.

Jenny hoped Rachel wasn't going to preach to the patients. She was starting to feel this might be a bad idea.

She introduced Rachel to some of the nursing staff and the volunteers. They were just about to serve afternoon tea in the lounge so she cut up the cakes she'd brought and she and Rachel carried a plate into the lounge.

'Hi Jenny. You brought us a visitor?' Mae Jones called from her wheelchair by the open patio doors.

'Hi Mae. This is Rachel.' A new face ignited interest in a place where the only change in days of sameness was a death.

'And what brings you to God's waiting room?' Mae asked.

'Mae!' Abby, one of the other volunteers, shook a finger at her.

'This is a nice waiting room but not as good as the main part of God's house. You have a lot to look forward to when you get there.'

Even the few who hadn't bothered to look up earlier now lifted their gaze to the stranger.

'Can I interest anyone in a piece of Jenny's lovely cake?' Rachel asked. At least she got their attention, Jenny thought, as she saw the patients watch her walking around.

Rachel served the cups of tea and helped two of the older ladies who didn't have the strength to hold the cup. Jenny watched her when she could but saw only that she touched them all. It was done subtly–a hand on a shoulder or an arm. Rachel helped Mrs. Wilson fix the clasp on her hair and gently rested her hand for a few seconds on her head.

When Jenny returned from washing the dishes in the kitchen she realized Rachel was no longer in the room. It took her a minute to realize what was different. It was the noise; the sound of voices.

Usually the lounge was fairly quiet at this time of day. They would be watching TV or reading or knitting. Today they all seemed to be talking. Mae was having a chat to young Beth Taylor who had hardly said a word to anyone since her arrival the week before. Bev and Irene were discussing a knitting pattern. Loreta, Jane and Mabel were playing cards at the table. Irene, who suffered badly from depression and refused to go outside, was now sitting on the patio laughing at something Jeanette said. Jenny stood there silently, watching them. Something had changed in these sick and dying people.

Cheryl, one of the nurses, came and stood beside her. 'Your friend seems to have put a bit of a spark into this place.'

'Yes. She seems to have done. Do you know where she is?'

'She asked if she could visit the ones confined to bed. I said it was okay. After what she'd done in here she might be able to cheer the others up a bit.'

Jenny found Rachel in Mrs. Wade's room. The old lady had been expected to die the week before and the doctors didn't know what was keeping her alive. She should have been in hospital but nothing could be done for her so the staff at the hospice kept her as comfortable as possible. No-one visited her and Jenny always spent time chatting to her when she could. What upset her most was not seeing the old lady sick but the loneliness in her eyes.

Rachel was sitting on the side of the bed and blocking the view of the patient. Jenny could hear them talking but couldn't make out the words. She saw Rachel holding the old lady's hand. She felt she was somehow intruding and went to walk away.

'Jenny, please come in.' Rachel said without turning around.

She made her way over to the bed just as Rachel stood up. Mrs. Wade was still clutching her hand.

For a moment Jenny thought she was in the wrong room. Mrs. Wade's smile and the sparkle in her eyes, had transformed the sad and lonely face she usually wore.

'Thank you for bringing this sweet girl to see me, Jenny.'

'You're looking much better, Mrs. Wade, much better.'

'I feel it, my dear. Jenny, please do something for me. Get the small wooden box out of my drawer for me.'

Jenny took out the box and handed it to her. It was old and worn and inlaid with pink roses. The old woman stroked it gently and then opened it to reveal faded photographs.

'Ah, here it is.' With a gesture of adoration Mrs. Wade picked out one of the photos, put two fingers to her lips, and then laid them on the photo for a few moments.

'This is my Harold.' She handed the photo to Jenny. 'He was killed in the war. We'd only been married five weeks when he went away. I never saw him again. There was no body to bury, no grave. I've missed him every day of my life since.'

'He was a very handsome man.'

'He certainly was. I was the envy of all my friends. He was also gentle and caring and when he smiled I felt my heart would burst with the love it held for him.'

'I'm sorry you lost him so young.'

'But that's it, Jenny, I didn't lose him. I thought I had but I didn't. I've spent all these years missing him and my misery stopped him coming to me. I've been foolish. I could have had him all this time. But no matter. Rachel made me see I still have time.'

Jenny looked at Rachel, wondering what she had been telling the old lady.

'Oh Jenny, isn't it wonderful?'

'What, Mrs. Wade?'

'My Harold spoke to Rachel. I know it was him. She described him exactly as he was the last time I saw him, so smart in his uniform, and he was even wearing the red scarf I knitted for him.

He's waiting for me. I'll see him again. My precious Harold. I'll see him again.' Mrs. Wade gently stroked the old photo. 'Such a wonderful day but I'm feeling a little tired. I think I'll have a nap. Rachel, will he come to me in my dreams?'

'If you want him to, he will come.'

'Thank you, my dear. Thank you so much. I wondered why I didn't just die but now I know. I was waiting for you. My misery kept Harold away while I was living so maybe it would have kept him away when I died.'

'He would have found a way.'

'Thank you, my dear. Will I see you again?'

'We will meet again.' Rachel bent and kissed her gently on the cheek.

Slowly the old lady's eyelids dropped and she was asleep.

They made their farewells to the others and walked out to the car park. Jenny really didn't know what had happened. Rachel had gone into the hospice, appeared to have done nothing specific but had left behind her people who had changed. They seemed to have found their spirit again.

'You enjoyed your visit, Rachel?' Matt asked.

'Yes. Such lovely people, so open and accepting. I was honored to have met them. Some old souls among them.'

Jenny sat in silence. She knew Rachel had made a difference. She helped the patients to accept life and their fates, and find some joy in both. She knew she should acknowledge it to her but something was stopping her. Why could she find no words to say to her? She felt like crying. She closed her eyes as she recalled the afternoon's events. She realized she was angry. No, not angry. What was it? What was she feeling? Why couldn't she just thank Rachel for helping them? She didn't want to feel this way. She felt resentment. Yes. That was it. Why? Jenny felt sick. She kept her eyes closed and tried to control her breathing.

'Help me please,' she pleaded. Almost instantly, the atmosphere in the car became less oppressive. Somehow it was comforting. It came to her, not in a flash, but as a wave of clarity. She was jealous. She had put a name to the feeling and somehow it made her feel better. Yes, she was jealous. She had been involved with the hospice for years. She visited regularly, she baked cakes for the patients and made them tea, and she talked to them. She was sensitive to their needs, to their frustration at the loss of their health and their dignity and anger at the ending of a life not yet completed. She worked hard to help them. She cried after visits and mourned those who died. All of this and she was unable to stop their feeling of loss and their fear of death. Rachel had spent two hours there and had made a difference. Jenny took a deep breath, then another. Her confusion seemed to dissipate with each breath. She wanted to make a difference and hadn't. Rachel made a difference. She felt the jealousy slowly being released from her body.

'You are such a brave woman, Jenny. You are a light shining in the darkness.' Rachel said.

'What? I didn't do anything. You were the one who made a difference. I don't seem to be able to.'

'Do you not hurt when they hurt? Do you not cry to see their loneliness and their isolation? Do you not ache when you cannot reach them to comfort them? Do you not suffer with them?'

'I suppose I do.'

'And yet you still do it.'

'I've often thought of stopping.'

'But you do not?'

'No.'

'What you do takes much courage. You connect to their spirit in the hope a smile, a touch, a prayer, will help them. You suffer with them and you feel their loneliness and their fear. We are each here in this life to make a difference to the world we are part of. You make a difference. You give of yourself. It is the greatest gift of all. You give it freely and in spite of the pain it causes. That is true courage.'

Jenny took the hand Rachel offered her.

John heard the door open and close and Robbie's excited greeting. When he didn't hear any further noise he put down his book and went towards the front door. He found Jenny standing with her back to the closed door, clutching Robbie in her arms. It took her a moment or two to realize John was there.

'How did it go?'

Jenny put Robbie down, walked slowly to John and put her arms around him. He smiled as he held her close.

32

The room was again lit by a single candle in the corner of the room. They sat on the same chairs in a circle as last time. John felt an excitement pulse through his body. He felt the peace, the lightness of the room, and noticed the others were alert but calm.

'Are you comfortable?' Rachel asked. They all nodded. 'Hawk is anxious to speak to you. Let us sit quietly for a few moments. Try to clear your mind of thought and just be. John felt his body relax as he focused on the path of his breath entering and leaving his body. He was unaware of time passing until he felt a slight breeze in the room. Then it began. A pale light appeared in the center of the circle. Gradually it changed to a white glow which grew until it reached to the ceiling and became a thick white fog. John tried not to be afraid but the anxiety of the unknown began to take hold. He felt a gentle touch on his arm. It was Christine. Her smile told him everything would be fine so he concentrated on the light in front of them. Gradually colors appeared. When it happened he felt the breath catch in his throat and his heart stand still. Before them, in the middle of the circle, was a Native American Indian. His long black hair hung over his left shoulder. He wore only buckskin leggings. Around his neck hung a strand of braided leather from which hung a large blue stone. He was smiling.

'My friends, it is good to meet with you again.'

Hawk turned to John and bowed his head. 'John, it brings joy to my spirit to again be in the company of so great a warrior.'

John could not find his voice.

Hawk smiled. 'I have this effect on people.' Everyone laughed. Hawk stepped towards John and put his right hand on John's shoulder. John felt a warmth pass through his body and his breathing return to normal.

'And how is your little dog? I hope he is fully recovered. He has a strong spirit.'

'He's great thanks.' How did this man know about Robbie?

Hawk stepped back into the center of the circle. 'I hope you will enjoy your time with us, John.'

'Thank you.' John has a passing thought this might be a dream.

'No,' Hawk said,' it is not a dream. Well, my friends, what shall we talk about this evening? Do you have any questions?'

'We are sensing danger,' Joe said. 'How long will we be safe here, Hawk?'

'A little longer. Those who want to destroy you are drawing close. We will be with you, my friends. Do not worry. You will be guided and protected. It is a difficult time for you now. It would be easy for fear and hate to find a place in your heart. Perhaps I will talk about these things.' Hawk closed his eyes for a few moments and then began to speak.

'I am standing on the plain. The sun is warm on my skin. The grass is long because the buffalo have not yet passed this way. I feel the spirit of the earth well up through my body. Such power. I am alone, yet not alone. It is here I feel most alive. There is nothing to distract me from the peace I feel. It is here I have my visions. I still myself. I think only of this moment and feel the connection with all things. I am no more precious than the trees or the mountains. My life is part of the smallest of creatures and their lives part of me. I can see the world that has passed and the world that is to come and I know these worlds are part of this day. I see the river that starts high in the mountains. I am part of it as it flows down to the plains. It makes its mark on the earth. Its path is not always straight but it keeps moving forward. Then the vision begins.

'I watch the river flow and the clouds pass over the mountains. I know man had not yet come to live on the earth. I know no hate, no sadness, no judgment. There is only the Great Father and me. I know this is how we all begin our journey in life. Each of us stands alone with the Great Father. I am at peace with my Creator. There is nothing else.

'Then I see myself an old man. I am lying on the plain as I exhale the last breath my body will take. I see my body become part of the earth and my spirit rise into the heavens. I feel the love of the Great Father and am engulfed in its intensity.

'Time shifts. I have my bow in my hand and my arrows strapped to my back. I am silent as I creep towards the fort filled with the soldiers who have come to destroy my people. I watch myself as I lead my warriors into the fort and we kill our enemies. Then time again stands still for me. I see the dead soldiers lying on the ground. I see their bodies become part of the earth and their spirits rise to the heavens where the Great Father embraces them.

'I understand my vision. We are all children of the Great Father. We begin our journey with him and end it with him and what we do with our life is our choice. The beginning and the end are the same. The Great Father does not judge but loves us all equally. So how should we fill our earthly existence? If we know the Great Father loves every creature on earth equally, no matter how he has lived his life, how can we think we know better than He? How can we justify our judgment and hatred of others? Because of that vision I tried to live my life without judgment and hatred. I tried to love all people equally. It was not always easy but I tried.'

Hawk smiled and bowed his head. 'I hope you will bear this story in mind in the days ahead.'

'Thank you, Hawk,' Joe said. 'As always you found the right words.'

'John, is there anything you would like to ask me?'

David immediately came into John's thoughts. 'I am worried about my son, David. I feel he's a bit lost at the moment.'

'David is on his own path through this life, John. He has chosen this lifetime for the lessons it will teach him. He agreed to be part of this although he is unaware of it. Recognition of his purpose is slow in coming to him. Be not afraid for him. He is always moving towards his destiny and he is protected and guided.'

'Thank you,' John said.

'Rachel has finished her 'meeting' as she would say,' Hawk said. 'I will bid you farewell with the hope we will meet like this again soon.' He laughed. 'I have many more stories to tell.'

The white fog returned and engulfed Hawk and when it faded he was gone. Rachel opened her eyes and smiled 'Did you enjoy Hawk's visit?'

'He was wonderful as usual,' Anna said.

'And you, John?' Rachel asked.

'I don't know what to say, Rachel. I can hardly believe what I just experienced. It was amazing. Thank you for allowing me to be part of this.'

'Hawk will be a good friend to you, John. You will not always see him with your eyes but you will be able to feel when he is around you. Now, let us send some healing.'

An hour later they were all seated outside sipping tea and reliving the evening's events. Joe took Rachel to a spot out of hearing distance from the others.

'Hawk recognized John. They've met before, haven't they?'

Rachel laughed. 'You miss nothing, do you, Joe? John was once a Guardian. I recognized who he was when first met in his garden. He found me when I was a child and took care of me all his life. We met Hawk when we journeyed to his land. They shared a friendship that only warriors can.'

'Will you tell John?'

'When the time is right. Recognition of who he was, and still is, will take its own pace.'

Later that night, when the guests had left, Joe gathered the others together. They were anxious to hear of the connection between John and Hawk.

'How did they come into your life?' Anna asked. She was always surprised that there was still much to learn about Rachel's past lives.

'In America. My friends and I landed there in the year of our Lord 1398. I remember it well, the first time I saw him.'

'In 1398?' Joe said. 'But Christopher Columbus didn't discover American until 1492. We learned that at school.'

Rachel smiled. 'He did not discover America.'

'Sorry, yes. I know the Native Americans lived there for thousands of years before that. I meant the first white people.'

'No, Joe. Brave men travelled there long before then.'

33

Atlantic Ocean, 1398

She stood at the bow of the ship and looked to the horizon. Dawn had yet to embrace the new day. She delighted in the sounds of the night; the ropes tugging against the wood, the shift of the sails against the wind, the voices of the sailors carried on the night air. She could taste the salt on her lips and she let the smell of the ocean fill her lungs. She could see, dotted in the distance, the silhouette of the other ships, their lanterns sparking in the darkness. She pulled her black cloak closely around her body and wondered if this would be the day.

She sensed his approach and smiled as he came to stand beside her. 'Luke.' She said his name softly. At their first meeting when she was but a child, she had thought how handsome he was. Although his body was wearier now and his long dark hair white, his smile shed the years from his face. He was still a man that held the attention of others. He wore with pride his white robe, emblazoned with the red cross of the Knights Templar.

'You could not sleep either I see.'

'No.'

DISTANT WHISPERS

'You think it will be soon, Rachel?'

'Yes. I am sure of it.'

'You should rest then. We do not know what we will find when we land. We will need your strength and your guidance.'

'I am well rested. All this time at sea, I have had more than enough rest. I am prepared. All will be well.'

'They did not all feel it was the right course of action to bring it so far from its home. But they trust you, Rachel. How could they not when you more than anyone has the right to decide.'

'I have no more right than they. It belongs to us all.'

He smiled. 'As you say.'

She pointed across the ocean. 'Prince Henry's ship is drawing close.'

'Yes. He never strays far from our sight. He too is anxious to find the new Scotland.'

'Will he call it that do you think?'

'Perhaps. His family has always fought bravely for Scotland's freedom. As you know his great grandfather and grandfather fought with the Bruce at Bannockburn. They helped gain independence from the English.'

'With more than a little help from the Templars.'

He smiled and put his hand on her shoulder.

'Yes. After our Order was betrayed, King Robert graciously gave the Templars sanctuary. The Order never forgot this. They were happy to train his men and fight alongside him at Bannockburn.'

'I remember you telling me the story when I was a child. The Templars carried no banners but the English knew who they were anyway and were filled with fear.'

'They did indeed.' This was a story Luke himself had heard as a child and it had inspired him to join the Order. It was a decision he never regretted. He had been a Templar for almost 40 years and been witness to great wonders. Perhaps this would be his last adventure, but what an adventure, to sail across the seas to find a new land where all could be free from persecution. When Prince Henry Sinclair had agreed to this venture, Luke felt the excitement surge through him. There was no way he would be refused a place at his friend's side. The Templars' fleet of ships was of the highest order and he felt confident they could carry them around the world and back.

'The journey has not been easy for you, Rachel.'

'Of the many journeys in my life this one is special. Thank you for allowing me to accompany you.'

'How could we not. It was your inspiration to bring what is precious to us and we knew you would not allow it to make the journey without you. And with your gift of tongues we will be able to communicate with any natives we encounter.'

Rachel had told him about the man in her vision. The man wearing the blue stone around his neck.

'My visions showed me I was destined to come here and to bring it to sanctify the new land. When it is done I will return it to its hiding place.'

Luke sighed deeply and gazed again at the horizon. 'I will watch with you this night.'

Two hours later, as the dawn light began to spread across the sky, came the cry from aloft. 'Land ahoy. Land ahoy.'

The preparations were made. The landing parties had gone ashore and when they returned to Luke's ship they brought good news. Fresh water had been found. The land near the shore was heavily wooded so would offer protection until shelters could be built.

'The maps were correct, Rachel.'

'We are fortunate. I am anxious to step on this land.'

'As I am, but you must wait. The men will ensure the area is secured and will need time to erect the shelters before you will be allowed to go.'

She smiled at him. 'Please, Luke, let me go ashore for a short time. I am small. I will not take up much room on the boat and I promise to return before dark. Please let me come with you, for I know you will not wait as you expect me to.'

Luke shook his head. There was nothing she could ask of him that he would not grant.

'Prince Henry's ship has signaled he will go ashore with the next boat. You cannot stay long, not until we know it is safe.'

'Thank you.'

As the boat headed towards the shore, Rachel felt great excitement surge through her. The remembrance of all the dreams, the thoughts, the feelings that led to this day, were awakened inside her. She had seen the future and knew this was part of her destiny. Luke had been her guardian for most of her life but when she had told him of her vision she was uncertain he would believe her. But he had. Dear Luke. How could she have doubted him?

'Prince Henry is ashore. Look! He awaits us.'

Rachel saw the Prince half way up the beach. She hoped he would not be angry she had come ashore early. No. He would not be angry for he knew her well enough to understand her need.

Luke jumped out of the boat as it hit the shore, held out his arms to her and lifted her onto the sand.

'You could not wait, my dear,' the Prince said.

She smiled. He offered her his arm and led her across the soft sand.

'Welcome to this land, Rachel. May it indeed become the land of your visions.'

The men continued to unload the supplies from the boats. From the clearing which had been made among the trees, Rachel stood in silence and looked back out to the ocean. Luke nodded to the Prince and the men walked away, leaving her to her thoughts.

She closed her eyes and almost immediately the pictures flashed before her. Wondrous things. Strange looking animals and men who lived in dwellings covered in animal skins that pointed to the sky. She saw mountains and rivers in a landscape that seemed to go on forever. Then there were buildings reaching to the sky and machines that flew in the air. And people. So many different looking faces. Yes! This was the land of her visions.

Early next morning, just as the dawn light started to flood the sky, they all gathered on the beach; Luke and his fellow Templars, Antonio Zeno, whose maps had brought them to this spot, Sir James Gunn, Prince Henry Sinclair and his Scots. Everyone bowed their heads as Luke said the blessing for this land. But as Rachel stood amongst these brave men, her eyes were fixed on the man watching from the edge of the forest. He was tall and lean. He wore animal skin leggings and his chest was bare. He wore a cord around his neck from which hung a magnificent blue stone. He was staring straight at her. He was the man in her vision.

Luke finished his blessing. 'Peace be upon us and this land. Amen.'

The others raised their eyes to watch Rachel raise the Spear of Destiny and plunge it into the earth.

Everyone worked hard, bringing supplies from the ships and erecting temporary shelters. It would take time to decide where to locate the settlement. Much had to be done before the decision was made.

On the third day Rachel decided she would try to make contact with the people of this land. She was anxious to meet the man with the blue stone. Luke was adamant he and some of the Templars accompany here. She was equally adamant she would go alone.

'It is not necessary. I will be safe. How do you think the natives will react to seeing you and your Templars. Please. We need to make peace with these people. It is their land. We are intruders and we need them to accept us. How can we do that if we go in force?'

'I will not allow this. I have sworn to guard you with my life. I cannot do this if I stay at the camp and let you wander this unknown land by yourself.'

'You must trust me, Luke. I know I will not depart my life here. I have much else to do.'

Luke had no argument for her visions were never wrong. 'Only for a short time. Promise me. You will return before noon or I will come for you.'

'I will return before then, I promise. Now you must ensure the men stay here. No-one must venture far until I return.'

'I promise,' Luke said reluctantly. 'Noon!' he shouted as she headed into the forest.

Rachel felt eyes watching her as she made her way through the trees. She savored the feel of this place. The smell of the leaves, the freshness of the air. If she had woken from a dream and found herself here, she would have known it was not Scotland. She heard the birdsong and the sound of her footsteps on the ground. Nothing else. There was no wind, no movement in the trees. She came across a clearing, almost a perfect circle. It was surrounded by majestic trees and she sensed the sacredness of the place. She walked to the center and stood silently. She saw him almost immediately. He walked slowly towards her. He stopped a short distance from where she stood and sat down cross-legged on the grass. She did the same.

'I am Rachel.'

'You speak our language? I am Hawk. The leader of my people.'

'I have seen you in my dreams.'

'I have seen you, Rachel. I saw this day.'

'We mean you no harm. We have come from our home far away and ask your permission to stay on your land.'

'It is not our land. We are part of it but it does not belong to us.'

'I understand.'

'I have told my people you would come. They are afraid.'

'You need not fear us. Our wish is that we live together in peace. Our ways are not the same but we wish to learn from you.'

'You are shaman?' he stated.

'I do not know what you mean?'

'Those among us who can communicate with the spirits of our ancestors. They know the ways of healing. You are shaman to your people?'

'Yes.'

'The Great Spirit has blessed you.'

'He has.'

'We will talk you and I. We will know each other. Ask me what you wish.'

'These trees that surround this place, are they sacred to your people? They feel as if they can talk. Strength and peace radiate from them.'

'Yes. I come here often to communicate with the Great Spirit. Often do I hear the whispers in the wind. The giant trees sway and their leaves give utterances to those who would listen. The trees have seen many passages of the seasons and been witness to the lives of men. They have enjoyed the games played by children around them and have absorbed the sounds of their laughter. They have smiled at the words of the young men and women who speak of love under their branches. When it is time for the old to depart this existence it is to the trees they reminisce about their lives and share their sorrows and joys.

'When I was a young man I sat under one of the trees and thought about these things. I rested my back against it and felt its strength. I listened to its whispers and the echoes of those whispers in the stillness. It spoke of the deeds of my ancestors, of their lives and their adventures. I knew one day I would be a leader of my people and they would look to me for strength and guidance.

'I learned many things from the trees. I rejoice in the laughter of children and I am a guide to the young ones. I give time to the old ones who want to recall their lives before they end. Like the trees I try to be a shelter, a comfort and a strength to my people. Perhaps when my spirit has passed from this life, an ancient tree will whisper stories of me to some young man who has sought the comfort of its strength. I would be honored.'

Rachel looked at this man and knew in her heart they would be connected forever.

She returned to the camp before noon as she promised. She told Luke and Prince Henry of her encounter with Hawk and his willingness to allow them to share the land. They all knew they had much to learn from these people and were depending on Rachel's guidance.

The next day Hawk arrived at the camp with some of his people. The men were apprehensive because of the strangeness of their appearance. Rachel acted as interpreter and soon they were gathered around the fire. Hawk brought gifts of food which they shared and gradually the tension subsided. All knew the way ahead would not always be like this day but they were willing to try.

The months passed and a mutual respect developed between Hawk's people and the newcomers. The Natives taught them what animals to hunt and what berries to eat. They helped them build shelters and invited them to their village. They learned enough of each other's language to speak together without Rachel. When the first winter was over and spring again graced the land, Prince Henry took some of his ships to explore the coastline. Rachel and Luke, along with 50 of the others, remained with Hawk and his people.

The ships returned in the spring of 1400. All too soon it was time for Prince Henry to return home. He planned to organize another expedition, and bring more people to settle this place. Many of Luke's men would stay with most of the fleet to establish the settlement and to explore further along the coast. Rachel did not want to leave but she knew she must. On her final day she met Hawk in the sacred circle of trees.

'Will you return, Rachel?'

'I do not know. I have not seen it in my visions.'

'I am sad that you go.'

'I am sad also. I will value your friendship all the days of my life.'

Hawk smiled. 'I will tell you a story of friendship.'

Rachel laughed. She had come to know that Hawk had many stories and he took great joy from the telling of them.'

'Elk was a great friend of my grandfather,' he began. 'They were boys together and shared the adventures of youth. One day as they sat on the hill watching the sun descend from the sky, Elk turned to my grandfather and said the time had come for him to leave his youth behind him and learn to become a shaman. My grandfather was surprised and asked Elk why he had not shared these thoughts before. Elk said he had not known before that day. As they sat there together in the evening light Elk had known in a moment what his path in this life must be. My grandfather told me he envied Elk that inspiration but that the envy lasted but a heartbeat. He knew Elk always spoke from a place of love.

'Their friendship grew even deeper than before. My grandfather shared Elk's excitement when he talked with wonder of the things he was learning. They shared a trust and love based on giving what was needed.

'When Elk passed to be with the Great Spirit he continued to be a friend to my grandfather. My grandfather told me how Elk would come to him in dreams and even when he was awake. I remember seeing my grandfather smile for no reason at all. I knew he was talking with Elk. When it was my grandfather's time to make his final journey he had that same smile on his lips as the last breath left his body. I knew Elk was with him.

'I learned about friendship from the stories told to me by my grandfather. I learned true friendship comes from a place of love. It means acceptance of each other's choices, giving each other time when it is needed and honoring always. True friendship lasts beyond this lifetime and is eternal.'

She held out her hands to him. 'I know we have a true friendship, Hawk, and it will last forever.'

'I know it also, Rachel.'

34

Rachel rose before dawn and went out to the gazebo. The stillness embraced her. She closed her eyes. So many memories floated before her. The pain and the joy. She felt weariness sap the edge of her strength. Sadness overcame her. She knew what these feelings meant. She could not hold back the doubts and did not want to feel like this. She moved her awareness to another place.

She sat on the white sand a few paces from where the ocean lapped gently on the shore. The sound of waves always soothed her.
　When she felt his approach she stood up to welcome him.
　'I honor you, my child.'
　'I honor you, Master. I need your wisdom.'
　'You never need my wisdom. You only need to see your own wisdom brought forth. I do nothing but reflect your spirit as it speaks. What is the question in your heart?'
　'Is he really the one, Master?'
　'You already know the answer.'
　'He fills my heart with joy and love as he did before. I hold the thought of him every moment. He has a good heart and I know he loves

me but my confusion is the same as it has always been. I will cause him pain. How can I let him love me knowing he will suffer for it?'

'He already loves you. You cannot stop that. You know his heart. If you were to ask him if it is worth it, loving you for a short time or not loving you at all, what would his answer be?'

'I do not know if he is strong enough.'

'My dear child, you know this is not your choice. It has been ordained. The decision was taken by him and you cannot interfere.'

'I know, but it still hurts me to cause pain even when I know the way was chosen so long ago and I am following my path, and his.'

'In all this time your heart still bears this sorrow.'

She smiled at him. 'Talking with you always brings me comfort. Thank you.'

'I am always here for you.'

The others were sitting at the kitchen table, waiting for her, when she came into the house. Anna poured her a cup of tea and she sat down with them.

'You know what has been troubling me?' she asked.

'Yes,' Joe said. 'Have you found your answers?'

She smiled. 'With help from an old friend. As always he knew what was in my heart and reminded me to look within for my answers. I have waited so long for this that I became unsure if I would know when the waiting would be over. It is now. My soul tells me so.'

Anna started to cry and Joe put his arms around her. Matt just stared at Rachel, his thoughts unfathomable.

'I'm not sure what this means,' Andrew said, looking from Joe to Rachel.

'Andrew, David is the one.' Rachel said.

'Good heavens, I never thought... good heavens.' Andrew shook his head.

'What happens now, Rachel?' Joe asked.

'I do not know. I will trust as I have always done.' Tears welled up in Rachel's eyes. Anna went to her and held her tightly.

35

It had rained all day but now the evening was clear and warm. David picked up Jack and they headed for the local pub. It faced the beach and from their position on the decking the breeze was a relief from the humidity.

'I don't believe this,' Jack said. 'She's here again.'

'Hi David, Jack. Can I buy you a drink?' Paula asked. David sighed and turned round. She was such a pretty young woman, with her long blond hair and blue eyes. She was wearing a tight white skirt that showed off her slim, tanned legs and a skimpy pink halter top accentuating her breasts. David saw how she drew admiring glances from men, young and old. Every one of his friends, except Jack, had told him he had been a fool to turn her down.

'No, that's OK. I'll get them.' Jack headed off to the bar. When he returned Paula had pulled up a seat close to David.

'I was just saying to David I hardly see you two these days.' She ran her long, painted nails up and down her glass of champagne.

'We've been busy,' Jack said.

'Anyway, it's my birthday on the 12th and I'm having a party. You'll both come won't you?'

Jack's look told David it was his call.

'I'm sorry but I can't. I'm busy that weekend. But thanks for asking.'

'Oh David, isn't it something you can get out of. It's my birthday.'

'Aren't you having dinner with Rachel that Saturday night?' Jack asked. Both David and Paula stared at him.

'Rachel? Who's Rachel?' Paula asked.

'David's girlfriend.' Jack took a sip of his beer, not daring to look at his friend.

'Your girlfriend? When did this happen? I've never seen you with anyone.'

'She's a friend of a friend. I haven't known her long.' David realized it might get Paula off his back if he went along with this.

Paula sipped her champagne again, for once at a loss for words. 'Who is she? Do I know her?'

'She's from Europe actually. She's a witch or something.' Jack was warming to the subject. 'Lovely girl. You'd like her Paula. She has this cool accent. You could listen to her for hours. And this incredible sense of humor.'

'She's a witch?'

'Well she's into all this spooky stuff, talking to dead people kind of thing. I think our David's rather smitten, aren't you, mate?'

David shot Jack a look that said 'enough.' Jack just smiled back at him.

'Oh! You can bring her to the party if you want.'

'She's really not into parties,' David said.

'Doesn't she want to meet your friends?' There was a hint of annoyance in her voice.

'It's just that she's really busy.'

'Right! So is she just visiting or does she live here?'

'I think that might depend on our Davey here,' Jack said. 'Anyway, I'll just pop to the gents. Back in a sec.'

'Well, you kept that quiet,' Paula said.

'As I said, I haven't known her long.'

'So you think she might stay here?'

'I don't know. I hope so.' As David looked at Paula, he realized he had been right to end his relationship with her. Jealousy seemed to change her physical beauty and he didn't like what he saw. He might not know Rachel all that well but her inner beauty shone through her smile and her eyes and he realized it was the kind that mattered.

When Jack returned, Paula was gone. 'Well, that seemed to have worked well?' he said. 'I know I've never met Rachel but I thought I did pretty well. You're not mad at me, are you?'

'No. I should've just been honest with her from the start.'

'How was she?'

'Not amused I would say.'

'Hopefully she's taken the hint.'

'I hope so,' David said, 'I hope so.'

When David got home an hour later he found the house empty. He wondered if his Dad was over at Rachel's again but then he saw the note from his Mum saying they had gone to friends for dinner and his meal just needed to be heated. He didn't feel hungry, well not for food anyway. He made himself a coffee and took it outside. He pictured Rachel sitting in the gazebo. She told him she spent a lot of time there alone. Perhaps she was thinking of him. Suddenly David felt the need to see her, to touch her. He knew he should call first but he didn't want to talk to anyone but her. It would do no harm to have a look through the fence and see if she was there. He was sure she wouldn't be offended at him turning up unannounced. He had to see her. As he walked through the door into the garden, Robbie looked up from his bed, wagged his tail and returned to his dreams.

The light was fading and the sky ablaze with streaks of pink. The birds were singing their final song of the day. He made his way to the bottom of the garden and as quietly as he possibly could, went through the break in the fence. His heart pounded with excitement when he saw Rachel sitting alone in the gazebo. He watched her for a few moments, delighting in the sight of her. He hesitated to move towards her, for now that he was here he was not sure if he should interrupt her. Again the need to look into her eyes overcame him and he started to move forward. He stopped abruptly when the back door of the house opened and the veranda light came on. Joe and Matt came outside followed by four other men and they all walked towards Rachel. She stood up and looked towards them. When the strangers reached her she held out her hands to one of them. The tall man with white hair lifted each hand in turn to his lips and kissed them and then Rachel put her arms around his neck and embraced him. Rachel then turned to one of the other men. She held out her hands to him also but instead of taking them he went down on one knee before her. Rachel quickly reached down and brought him back to his feet. She embraced him too and when she released him the man wiped his eyes with his hand. Rachel then embraced the other two men. David could not hear what was being said but he heard her laugh. Her delight at seeing these men was obvious and David could not erase the jealousy in his heart. He could not approach them now. Eventually they all walked back to the house and went inside. Rachel had not mentioned knowing anyone else in Australia other than Andrew. He pictured again the man who had knelt before her. He knew he could never ask her about it without admitting he was spying.

36

John knew there was something about tonight that was special. When Andrew phoned to ask him over he heard the excitement in his voice. He would not tell him any more than that Rachel had asked if he would meet with her.

In the lounge he found Rachel, Anna, Joe and Matt, with four other men.

'Welcome, John.' Rachel greeted him with a warm smile. 'Let me introduce you to our friends. This is Anton.' Rachel rested her hand on the oldest of the group,' and this is Craig, Martin and Christopher.' John shook each of their hands. Their grip was strong and each held his gaze as if assessing him. They were ordinary looking men who you would pass in the street without a second glance but John felt a power, a strength in their touch.

'John, I have something to ask you, but first I would like to talk to you alone. Would you please join me in the garden?'

'Sure.' He followed Rachel to the gazebo.

'I have looked into your heart, John, and found it to be true and honest. You are not aware of this but you and I have met before, a long, long time ago in a different place, a different time.'

'We have?'

'You helped me then and I am hoping you will again, but first I want to tell you a story. It is a true story of my life, of the many journeys of my spirit. The others think it is too soon but I know you. I know you will assess the truth of my words.' Rachel closed her eyes and held her hands as if in prayer.

John watched her all the time she was speaking. He felt a stirring in his body, a feeling of floating, a shifting in his awareness. Eventually she opened her eyes and he took the hands she offered him. He was filled with a joy, an incredible joy, and held no doubt at all of the truth of what she said.

Inside the house, all eyes turned to him when he entered the room. Without having to say a word, they were all smiling at him. Anna came up to him and put her arms around him.

'Let us sit at the table,' Rachel said. Anton carried over a small case and put it in front of Rachel. They all watched as she slowly opened the case and took out something wrapped in a white linen cloth, which she slowly unfolded to reveal a book. It had a worn red hard cover and a smell of roses.

'John, I have told you about the journals and the Guardians who keep them safe. Anton, Craig, Martin and Christopher are Guardians and have brought one of my journals to me at my request. They will bear witness to what I am doing. I want to give this journal to you to keep safe for me. This one is very special to me. Will you keep it for me until the time is right?' Rachel held out the book.

John felt an energy radiating from the book before he touched it. He took it from Rachel and gently moved his hand across it. There were no words to describe his excitement.

'I'm honored, Rachel, and I'll guard it well.'

'I know you will, John. Thank you.'

After John had left, there was a stillness in the room.

'You must have great trust in this man, Rachel' Anton said. Although his hair was white, his sparking blue eyes and lean body belied the fact he had passed his seventieth year. 'Or is it something else?' He had been puzzled when he received Rachel's request to bring one of the journals to Australia, but he had not questioned her. The fact she had given it to someone she had known for only a short time made him extremely uncomfortable. The journals had always stayed under the protection of the Guardians.

They held each other's gaze for a long moment. Suddenly he sharply drew in his breath, held it as he looked at Anna and Joe and then looked back at Rachel. He slowly exhaled and then smiled.

'The time has come, the time has finally come,' he said slowly. He looked at the other Guardians. 'Do you not understand? It is time.'

'Time for what, Anton?' Christopher asked.

'The prophecy to be fulfilled.'

It was almost midnight when Rachel asked Anton to walk with her in the garden. The dark sky accentuated the glow of the full moon and the stars seemed almost close enough to touch. The warmth of the day lingered in the air. Arm in arm they walked to the gazebo.

'Sit beside me, Anton. Let me hold your hand.'

He sat down and took her hand in both of his. 'My heart is full but I cannot find the words. I am elated but yet there is a sadness within me.'

'Dear, dear friend. Do you think I will no longer need you?'

'Perhaps,' he said with a smile. 'I remember when I first sensed your presence. I did not believe it could be possible. I did not expect it in my lifetime, but the feeling was strong and the others came to me and said they too felt it. When our search led us to you in Italy, I thought I would never be as happy again as I was when I lifted you from your crib and held you that first time.'

'I remember.'

'You were only a baby.'

'Yes, but I felt your strength and your love.'

He smiled. 'I'm glad. It was such a special moment for me, and the others of course. What I am trying to say is that the feelings I have now, knowing what is to come, are so overwhelming. I am honored, Rachel, and I will protect you until I pass from this life.'

She squeezed his hands and kissed him gently on the cheek.

'Anton, the honor is mine.'

'Can you tell me, will this body, these eyes, be witness to what is to come? I cannot see it for myself. When I try to look, the path is hazy.'

She closed her eyes for a moment. 'Anton, I promise, you will witness the fulfillment of the prophecy.'

He sighed and tears slipped from his eyes. 'Thank you, Rachel, thank you.'

37

'I won't disturb you if you're busy,' John said.

'No, come in,' Joe said. 'The others have gone out for a while. I'll make coffee. Just leave the books on the table.'

'I know Andrew said to keep them as long as I wanted but I've finished them already and I was hoping he would lend me some more. He's got quite a library.'

'Yes. I've come across some I hadn't heard of before and really enjoyed. The authors have insights which are pretty spot on. You can tell there is a shift taking place. What was regarded as crazy not that long ago is quite acceptable to such a large audience now.'

'I just wish I'd been aware of all this earlier,' John said.

'The timing is different for everyone.'

'Rachel said that too, and that there's always enough time. I hope she's right.'

'She usually is. Have you read the journal she gave you yet?'

'I did—twice already. So much makes sense now. I wish I could show it to David but Rachel's right—he isn't ready. You've been with her a long time, Joe. How did you meet?'

Joe took a sip of his coffee and smiled. 'I was 25. I had no family to speak of. I had this dream of travelling the world and just stopping wherever I wanted and painting. I saw myself in years to come having an exhibition of all the paintings I had done around the world and being recognized as a great artist. One day I was sitting on the Spanish Steps in Rome, just enjoying the sun and thinking how life doesn't get much better than this. I saw this girl cradling a baby. She was crying and so I went over to see if she was okay. It was Anna and the baby was Rachel. She told me she worked in a fashion house as a model. She was stunning woman, John, still is. Her best friend got pregnant by a married man who just dumped her. Anna gave her a home but she died during childbirth and Anna adopted the child. I asked her why she'd been crying. She said it was because she was so happy. She was a bit apprehensive about telling me but I think she just decided she could trust me. She'd had a dream the night before and in it an Angel was holding Rachel and he told Anna who Rachel was and why she'd been born. When Anna woke up she said she just knew what she'd been told was the truth. At this point I thought I was dealing with this crazy woman and then it happened. Anna handed me the baby. I took her but I was a bit nervous as I hadn't had much to do with babies, but once she was settled in my arms I was fine. I looked down at her and she opened her eyes and looked straight at me. I felt the world around me just melt away. There was only me and this child. It felt like my heart had just jumped out of my body and into her. I knew who she was. I knew. By then I was in tears as well. I have to tell you it was the most emotional experience I'd ever had. We've been together ever since.'

'It didn't take us long to realize there were others who knew who Rachel was too; people who wanted to destroy her. Fortunately Anton and some of the other Guardians found us and moved us to a safe place in France. They'd like to be around to protect her all the time but Rachel doesn't want that. She's happy just being with the four of us. The Guardians take care of us in other ways. There are many of them throughout the world and they make sure we get where we're going safely and provide protection when we need it, and of course they protect the journals.'

'Have you ever seen the first ones?' John asked.

'Only once, but once is enough. To touch them—that feeling stays with you forever. Even talking about it sends shivers through me.' Joe closed his eyes for a moment. 'Well, back to the story. We moved to a little village in France until Rachel was about seven and we've been moving around ever since. I developed certain skills so I could keep her from harm. It's been a wonderful journey. Despite the horrors we've seen and the danger, I wouldn't trade my life for anything. I still get to paint and I have a wonderful family. Now I'm sure life doesn't get any better than this.'

'What about Matt?'

'We found Matt a couple of days before Anton showed up and moved us to France. We'd gone for a trip to the countryside and on our way home we saw this little church in the distance. There was nothing else around it, no houses or farms. We said how pretty it looked and thought we might stop for a look but we were tired so we decided to go straight home. Just then Rachel started to cry. She never cried. Anyway, she seemed really distressed so we stopped the car at the church. We tried everything but she just kept crying so we went inside, thinking it might be cooler. Still she cried. We walked her up and down the aisle and then when we reached a certain pew at the front she just stopped. But every time we moved away from that pew she started crying again. So we sat down. It was then I noticed a basket under the seat. I pulled it out and this beautiful little baby was just lying there, smiling up at me. There was a note attached to his shawl which said 'God please take care of my baby.' We took it as a sign we should take him. We called him Matthew because it means Gift of God. He and Rachel were inseparable, still are. They know what each other is thinking most of the time. They have a real telepathic connection. When he was about 12 he came to me and said he wanted to learn the skills to protect her like I did. He is now her main protector although we all watch out for her.

'What kind of skills?' John asked.

Joe smiled. He looked around the room and his eyes came to rest on the fruit bowl on the bench. He stared at it for a while and then put his hand out towards it. Slowly an apple lifted up in the air and moved towards him. It came to rest in his hand. John stared at him.

'Nice trick eh?' Joe laughed. 'I'm sorry, I'm just showing off. Our skills are also our weapons. We only use them to guard Rachel.'

'It's amazing. You learned all this stuff?'

'Anyone can do it under the right guidance and if you're open enough. We had the best teacher of course.'

'I could do it?'

'You could but maybe that's not what you're supposed to learn.'

'I don't understand.'

'We're all here for a reason, John. You might be headed in a different direction. There might be different skills you need to learn to complete your destiny.'

'I just need to find out what my destiny is.'

'That's the interesting part.'

'I wonder what David's part in all this is. I think he really loves Rachel.'

'I can't tell you how things will turn out, John. We all have to find our own path.'

'I know. I think he's a little jealous of Matt.'

'Rachel and Matt have loved each other all their lives. That will never change.'

'He'll work it out, I'm sure. I wanted to ask you, what's happening to Rachel when Hawk comes through? That's just the most amazing thing. If only everyone could see him, experience him, there would be no-one who wouldn't believe in life after death.'

'Oh, there would still be those who wouldn't believe. They'd say they were being hypnotized, given drugs in the water, or that it was just a trick. If they don't want to believe it's real, they won't.'

'I suppose you're right. I don't even know if I would have believed it a couple of years ago. But where does she go Joe? What's happening to her?'

'I don't really know. Hawk comes through for our benefit, to teach us. He loves telling his stories but you'll find they all give us something to think about. Even when Rachel's meditating or just goes off somewhere when we're not in the circle, I can still feel him around. He protects her on the other side, just like Matt and I protect her on this side. Rachel says he guards the way for her. The fact Hawk comes through to us means wherever she is, she's safe.'

'You know, Joe, I can't believe all this has happened to me in such a short time. My whole life has changed. It's like I have two lives—the one I've always had with Jenny and David and normal things, and this new life where I feel ... I can't explain it. It's like I'm living my life at two different levels.'

'It's just an adjustment time for you. It'll all come together. This isn't new for you, it's always been there. It's just that you've become aware of it.'

'I suppose so. I feel I've found a piece of myself that's always been missing but I hadn't realized it wasn't there until I found it. Hell, this sounds crazy.'

'I know exactly what you mean.'

'It's such an adventure, isn't it?' John said.

'It sure is.'

38

John found Jenny sitting at the kitchen table. She had not acknowledged his presence and he was concerned. He went over to her and rested his hand on her shoulder.

'Sweetheart, are you okay?'

'Sorry, I didn't hear you come in.'

'What's the matter? Has something happened?'

She started to cry and he pulled her up and held her tightly. He let her cry and then he drew back and held her face with both his hands. 'What's upset you?'

'Mrs. Wade died today. She was the old lady Rachel spoke to when we went to the hospice.'

'You were expecting it though, weren't you? You said she didn't have long.'

'I know, but that's not why I'm crying. I was with her when she died. She was semi-conscious but she seemed so content. I couldn't make out exactly what she was saying but she kept saying Rachel's name. At first I thought she was hallucinating but then I realized in her mind she was actually talking to her. I knew that wasn't possible but it seemed so real. She asked if it was time and then I heard her say "Thank you, Rachel." Oh John, it seemed so real. In her mind Rachel was talking to her but how can that be. Rachel wasn't there.'

'Let's sit down. I've something to share with you that might help you understand nothing is impossible.'

Jenny sat transfixed as John told her about Hawk. He knew in his heart it was not yet the time to tell her the full truth about Rachel.

'This Hawk was real? You could touch him?'

'He put his hand on my shoulder. I felt it.'

'Why didn't you tell me before?'

'I didn't know how. I didn't know if you'd believe me.'

'You've never lied to me. Why would I think you'd be lying now?'

'I thought you might think I was crazy.'

'John, if you say it's true, I believe you.'

"Jenny.' John laid his hand over hers. 'Would you like me to ask if you could come to the next gathering?' Jenny closed her eyes and pressed his hand.

'John, I'm not ready for that yet. Don't ask me how I know but I don't need to see him to believe it can happen. Since that day when Rachel came to the hospice, I'm coming to terms with how I now feel about things, about life and death. I'm taking little steps. Going to one the gatherings would be a big step. Too big for me right now. Do you understand?'

'Of course I do.' He lifted her hand and kissed it. 'I love you very much. You know I can't explain to you how important it is to me to go with this as far as it takes me. I just know I have to do this.'

'Rachel was right when she said she was a teacher,' Jenny said. 'She has taught us both something. We may be moving forward at different speeds but I feel we're heading the same way.'

'But you understand I don't know where this will lead?'

'I know. I'll be with you every step of the way. I want you to always talk to me about everything. Even if I don't understand, I want to hear about it. Whatever you feel you need to do, I'll support you.'

'Have I told you how much I love you, Jenny?' He gently pulled her to him and held her tightly.

'You have, but tell me again.'

39

'Going out tonight?' Jenny asked.

'I suppose I'll go to the pub with Jack,' David said.

'You don't sound too happy about it?'

'I'd asked Rachel out tonight but she's busy again. I suppose you're going over there for one of your gatherings, Dad?'

'Mm, yes. Andrew invited me this morning.'

'I'll see if she'll come out with me on Sunday. It's really odd. She doesn't seem to want to leave the house. I think it's that Matt. She won't go out without him and even those few times I've been over there I feel him around. He watches her like a hawk.'

John laughed.

'What's so funny?' David asked him, a hint of annoyance in his voice.

'Nothing, son, nothing at all. Look David, he's just protecting her.'

'From what? I'm not going to hurt her. I only want a date for God's sake. She's old enough to go out on her own surely. Anyway, I'm going for a shower. Have a good time.' David smiled half-heartedly at his father and left the room. When he came back, Jenny was folding clothes from the washing basket.

'I'll get going. I won't be late, Mum. If you'd rather I stayed home I can phone Jack. I'm not that fussed about going out.'

'Heavens no. An Affair to Remember is on. I'm going to iron while I watch. I'm looking forward to it and I know you won't want to watch it. Say hello to Jack for me.'

'Mum. Doesn't it annoy you Dad's spending so much time with Rachel?'

'No, David, it doesn't. It's just something he has to do now.'

'What is it he has to do? I don't really understand all of this. I looked up this stuff on the web. There are hundreds of mediums around and people who do what Rachel says she does. Jack works with someone whose sister does it for a living. I just can't believe Dad wanting to get involved with something like this. It's not like him.'

'You see him as your father, David. I see him as my husband. But he's someone else besides a father and a husband. He doesn't fully understand why he wants to find out more about these things. It's something he wants to pursue in his life; something that's important to him. We shouldn't judge him. We should be supporting him.'

'But why with Rachel.'

'You're jealous?'

'Yes I am. He can find someone else that does this thing and she would have more time to spend with me. I know how selfish it sounds but it's how I feel.'

'What can I say to you? Rachel has a choice in this too. What she does is important to her. That doesn't mean you aren't important to her but your Dad has nothing to do with what Rachel wants. She makes her own choices. You've seen the connection between them all and you must see she seems to know what she's doing. I know there's something strange about the way she's protected and that maybe she isn't safe here, but it's still her decision what she does. Don't worry about the future, David. Live for the moment and see where it takes you. If she leaves, would you rather not have known her at all?'

'I suppose not. I'm sorry, Mum. I know you're right. I don't have a choice really. If I want to spend time with her I'll have to do it on her terms. She is special though, isn't she?'

'Yes. She's very special.'

David and Jack took their beers out to the garden. They had gone to the pub but left early because Paula had turned up with two of her friends and joined them. Jack, being the good friend that he was, saw that David was trying hard not to be rude so suggested they leave early.

'What are you going to do about Paula?' Jack said. 'She's being a real pain. I guess she doesn't understand the meaning of over.'

'I know. I just wish she'd leave me alone. It seems everywhere we go she's there. I don't know how to get the message across. Even telling her about Rachel doesn't seem to have made a difference. She probably doesn't believe me. It's not as if she's seen us out on a date. At least if she saw us together she might give up.'

'Did you find out what they get up to at those meetings?'

'No. Even Dad won't tell me much other than they meditate and talk about spiritual things. He seems to be over there all the time.'

'Did you find out who those men were you saw her with in the garden?'

'No, and I can't very well ask her either. I was hoping she'd tell me. Mum doesn't seem bothered about it all. In fact she seems happy about Dad spending the time with Rachel. He just seems different these days. He seems to be off in his own little world most of the time.'

'Do you think there's something going on with him and Rachel?' Jack asked.

'My Dad! Jeez he's old enough to be her father. There can't be.'

'It's not unknown. It's always in the women's magazines, about men having a mid-life crisis. Not that I read those things of course. I just noticed a few of Mum's lying around.'

'Come on, Jack, not my Dad.

'Yeh, you're right. At least your Mum isn't jealous.'

'She knows my Dad adores her. She can see that. Hell, I'm the one that's jealous. He gets to see her more often than I do. I don't know why I couldn't fall for a normal person. Someone with a normal job who likes the things I do. Getting time alone with her is still almost impossible. Each time I see her I come away happy. I think she feels the same but when I call her for a date she says she can't but then she asks me if I want to come over for a walk in the garden. I don't understand why she just won't go out with me. It can't be she doesn't want to because she seems to enjoy the times we spend together. What's holding her back? I don't think I've ever really been alone with her. When I'm round there I can feel they're watching us. Surely they don't think I'll harm her? I can't understand why they guard her so much. This is Australia.'

Jack and David looked up as they saw John come out of the darkness at the bottom of the garden.

'Hi boys. Jack, how you doing?'

'Good thanks, John. Yourself?'

'Good. Well, I'll leave you to it. See ya.'

'Where did he come from?' Jack asked.

'There's a shortcut to Andrew's house through the bottom of the garden.'

'Oh.'

40

David pulled up in the driveway just as his mother was retrieving shopping from the boot of her car.

'Perfect timing,' she said. They heard the voices before they reached the kitchen and found Rachel sitting at the table with his father.

'Good afternoon, Jenny, David,' she said.

'Hi,' David beamed. Through the window he saw Matt throwing a stick for Robbie in the garden.

'It is good to see you both again. I called to ask you all if you would like to come to dinner on Saturday night. It's Andrew's birthday and Anna and I thought we would cook something special.'

'I didn't think we had any plans for this weekend but I thought I'd check with you first,' John said.

'No plans, and thanks, we'd love to come,' Jenny said. 'David, what about you?'

'Thanks, that'd be great.'

'Can I bring anything?'

'No, thank you. Just yourselves. Anna has it all planned. She does the cooking and I do what she tells me. It works well.'

The doorbell rang and David noticed Rachel tense. John excused himself to answer it.

'Would six be a good time?' Rachel asked, glancing through the window to the back garden.

'Great. I must ...' Jenny stopped when she saw John return with Paula by his side.

'Hi. I was just passing and thought I'd pop in and say hello.' Paula fixed her gaze on Rachel.

David introduced them. Suddenly the door opened. Matt walked quickly to where Rachel was standing. He looked round the room and then stared directly at Paula who took a quick step backwards. The others stared at Matt. Rachel put her hand on his arm for a few seconds and then seemed to stare past Paula before focusing on her face.

'I am pleased to meet you,' Rachel said. Paula held her hand for barely a second.

'David's told me about you. I hope you're enjoying your stay here?'

'I am, thank you. It is a beautiful country.'

Paula looked at Matt, expecting to be introduced. When it did not happen she directed her attention back to Rachel. 'I'm glad you're here actually. I'd invited David to my birthday party on Saturday. He said you had other plans but I thought I'd drop in and remind you just in case your plans changed. It'll be a good night.'

'Actually we're all going to a friend's house for dinner on Saturday,' David said. He was relieved the excuse he had given Paula earlier was now fact.

'Feel free to come after the dinner. It'll probably go on all night.' Paula smiled at Rachel. 'As you're new to the place, would you like to come out with me and my friends one day? We could go shopping, have lunch somewhere. What was the name of that cute little bistro in Prahran we went to David? You know, the one with those lovely desserts.'

'I can't remember. Jack booked it so you could ask him.'

'Yeh, I'll do that. What do you think Rachel? Would you like to come with us?'

'It is kind of you to offer but it will not be possible.'

'Oh. Well, the offer's there if you change your mind. David has my number. I'd better get going. Nice to meet you.'

While John walked Paula to the door, silence reigned in the kitchen. Rachel returned to Matt's side.

'So we will see you Saturday at about six.' For the first time her smile did not reach her eyes.

As they watched Matt and Rachel walk down the garden they saw Matt put his arm around Rachel's shoulder as she moved closer to him.

41

David took one last look in the mirror. He had changed clothes three times and finally settled for light blue jeans and a short sleeved white linen shirt. He was both nervous and excited at the thought of seeing Rachel again. He wished it could have been just the two of them but he would settle for a crowd as long as she was part of it.

'David, are you ready, it's time to go,' Jenny called from the hallway.

'My, don't you look handsome,' Jenny said when he walked into the kitchen.

'You don't look so bad yourself, Mum.'

'Okay you two,' John laughed, 'admit it, we're a gorgeous family. Now let's go. David, grab the wine, I'll get the beer, and you've got the present, Jenny. No, I haven't forgotten you, Robbie,' he said to the little dog sitting patiently by the door. 'We know you received a personal invitation. Right, let's be off.'

Andrew and Joe waved to them as they approached the house from the back garden. Robbie had bounded ahead of them and was already sitting beside Andrew, his tail wagging furiously. The large paved entertaining area was lit by many candles and although it was still daylight, their glow added an extra festive look to the place. This was the first time they had been to Andrew's house for a meal since Helen's death.

'Happy birthday, Andrew,' Jenny said, hugging him. Both John and David shook hands with him and then Jenny handed him a box wrapped in shiny red paper and tied with white ribbon. 'A little something for you.'

'You're very kind, thank you. I wasn't expecting anything.'

David saw Rachel coming out of the screen door carrying a plate. He rushed to hold the door, as Robbie bounced up and down on the one spot at the sight of her.

'Thank you, David.' Her smile sent his pulse racing. She was wearing a flowery pink skirt that stopped just above her bare feet and a sleeveless pink cotton tee-shirt. Her hair was shining and loose and her ears decorated with dangly pink earrings. Soon they were all sipping their drinks and again the talk was easy and light-hearted. Robbie, of course, was curled up at Rachel's feet.

'I might open my present before dinner,' Andrew said, as he carefully unwrapped the box, pulling out a collection of CDs.

'Dean Martin. This is very kind of you.'

'I know your old record player gave up the ghost and we didn't think you'd have replaced your collection with CDs yet. If you have, we can change them.'

'Oh no, you're right. I got the new system but I've hardly used it. This is just perfect.'

'I thought it would be nice for when you have company.' David saw his father exchange a strange look with Andrew, who smiled and nodded his head.

'Thank you, it's a wonderful idea.'

The evening was relaxed and the conversation covered many topics, but again they talked very little about Rachel and her friends.

'I'm having such a lovely time tonight,' Andrew said. 'I do thank you all very much. It's been too long since this house hosted a party. If you don't mind I think I'll put on my new CDs. I'll be back in a minute.' He got up and headed off into the house.

Soon the sound of Dean Martin's voice came through the speakers.

'This was one of Helen's favorites, wasn't it, Andrew?' John said.

'Yes. Remember the nights the four of us used to dance to this. Such happy times.'

'Now, isn't that a good idea,' Anna said. 'Matt, Joe, help me move a few things.' Between them they moved the table and chairs to make a space in the middle of the decking.

'Andrew, may I have this dance?' Anna asked.

'It would be my pleasure,' he replied, getting up from his chair.

John took Jenny's hand and joined them. Just as he decided to ask Rachel, he saw Joe put out his hand to her and take her to join the others. He watched the easy way they were with each other. Joe had his hand on the small of her back and was holding her hand firmly. Her other hand rested lightly on his shoulder. He saw him whisper something in her ear and she laughed and kissed him on the cheek. He could not pull his eyes away from her. As one song ended, Joe stopped in front of Matt and whirled Rachel around in a circle. She laughed and held out her hands to Matt. Soon they were dancing slowly to the music but David was distracted from watching them as Anna invited him to dance.

Although he tried not to, he watched Rachel and Matt and, as with Joe, saw the easy affection they shared. He was jealous; there was no other word for it.

Eventually they were all sitting down again, sipping their drinks and talking about dance crazes through the years. Rachel had come to sit between David and his mother. Suddenly Jenny jumped up.

'Oh, I just love this song. Come on, Andrew,' she said, holding out her hand to him.

David did not hesitate this time. 'Rachel, would you like to dance?'

She smiled at him and got up. He felt a tingling sensation as he slipped his hand around her waist and she took his hand. It felt so natural to be holding her. He loved the smell of her, the softness of her hand, her breath on his face. He barely heard the music as the beating of his heart filled his being. He looked into her eyes and realized she had already been watching him. Her gaze was penetrating, as if she wanted to see into his soul. He did not look away, but allowed her to look for whatever it was she was searching. Everything around him seemed to disappear and he saw only her beautiful eyes. Then she smiled and broke the spell. As one song ended, he continued to hold her as the next song started. Eventually the music stopped completely and he was forced to let her go. He felt an emptiness the second she walked away from him.

At the end of the evening, when they were all saying their goodbyes, Rachel kissed him lightly on the cheek, as she did with his parents.

As he lay on his bed in the stillness of the night, he still felt her gentle kiss and the feel of her hand on his. What was happening to him? He felt such a need for her and she was all he thought about. It even affected his work. He missed an important meeting on Thursday and his boss asked him if he was ill. Maybe he was in too deep. After all, she did say she would not be staying. It was not like him to feel this much out of control. But he would worry tomorrow—tonight he would just remember her smiling face.

42

Philippe sat at the bar sipping a glass of white wine. He saw Paula come in with two other girls. She was very pretty. Not beautiful. She was a little too slim for his liking and she dressed like a whore. Her skirt was too short and her makeup too heavy but she was eye-catching. He saw other heads turn as she walked by. She looked his way as she headed for a table. He knew she would be discussing him with her friends. After all, he was immaculately dressed in black casual slacks and an open-necked white silk shirt which showed off both his physique and tan. It took only a few minutes and she was standing beside him at the bar. He pretended not to know she was there until she had ordered three glasses of champagne. As she waited, he casually turned to her and smiled. He saw her eyes dilate in appreciation as she returned his smile.

'Good evening, Mademoiselle.'

'Good evening,' she said.

'It is a most beautiful evening, is it not?'

'Yes it is. You're French aren't you? I haven't seen you here before. Are on holiday?'

'No, Mademoiselle, I have business in the area. It is my first visit. I do not wish to bother you but I would be most grateful if you could recommend a restaurant where I might dine tonight.'

'Oh. Well there are quite a few good ones around here. What kind of restaurants do you like?'

'Any kind as long as the food is good and the wine list is interesting.'

She gave him detailed descriptions of a couple nearby, every now and then resting her hand on his arm and smiling.

'Thank you for your assistance and for the pleasure of your company for a few moments.'

She beamed. The barman put the three glasses of champagne on the bar.

'Please allow me to pay for these in return for your kindness,' he said.

'Thank you. If you're on your own, would you like to join us?'

'This is most kind, Mademoiselle. I would like that. My name is Philippe. And yours?'

'Paula.'

'A beautiful name. Please, allow me to carry these to the table.'

The girls were immediately captivated by him as he knew they would be. They wanted to know everything about him. He enjoyed this part of the game. He liked to create a whole new persona on the spot. He was good at it.

'I base myself in the South of France, but as I have varied business interests in the rest of Europe and the US, I have to travel a great deal. Now I am looking for an opportunity here in Australia. It is such a beautiful country. I am looking for a house with a view of the ocean but the difficulty is finding one with space for a helipad.'

'Is your wife with you?' Megan asked. Philippe smiled. He had been asked that question a hundred times and in many different languages.

'Unfortunately I have never married. I have always been too busy but once I have established a business here I have promised myself I will allow others to run my companies and I will relax—perhaps find myself a wife.'

'Where are you staying now?' Paula asked.

'In the apartment of a business colleague in the city. I intend to keep returning to this area until I find what I am looking for.' The girls all smiled and looked at each other. They talked about the local area and the countries he had visited. Eventually he excused himself and went to the bar, returning with a bottle of champagne.

'A little thank you for allowing me the pleasure of your company. Paula, may I impose on your kindness once more. Would you do me the honor of dining with me this evening?'

'I would love to, Philippe.'

'Thank you. Then we will bid you two beautiful ladies goodnight. I am sure we will meet again.' He held out his arm for Paula to take and then guided her to the door.

'You made a good choice, Paula. This is delightful.' Philippe poured more wine—the most expensive on the wine list. He also chose the intimate table for two by the window.

'I'm glad you like it.'

'You would dine here often with your boyfriend, I am sure.'

'I don't have a boyfriend at the moment. I was in a relationship but it didn't work out.'

'He must have been a fool. Is there not still a chance?'

'I thought there might be but he has a new girlfriend now. I didn't know about her but I met her last week.'

'Tell me?'

'You don't want hear about it surely?'

'I do, Paula.' He reached out and covered her hand with his. 'I want to know everything about you.'

'His name's David. He's really good looking and I thought we got on well but he didn't want to go out any more.'

'I find that so hard to believe.'

'I invited him to my birthday party last week. It's a shame I hadn't met you then. I would have invited you. Anyway, he said he was busy and he had a new girlfriend called Rachel.'

'And you met her?'

'Yes.'

'What did you think of her?'

'She was pretty enough. She had this accent but I'm not sure where she comes from. David's friend said she was a witch but I think he was having me on.'

'A witch?'

'That's what Jack said. Said she's into spooky things and talks to dead people. Very creepy if you ask me.'

Philippe stared out of the window and appeared preoccupied.

'What's wrong?'

'Tell me, is this Rachel slim, with long dark hair and blue eyes? You said you did not recognize her accent.'

'Yes. Do you know her?'

'Do you believe in fate, Paula?'

'I don't know. Probably. I like to think it's fate we met.'

'This might sound fantastic but two weeks ago I was having dinner in Paris with a friend of mine who is a police inspector. He told me about a girl called Rachel. He didn't have a photograph but described her to me. The police all over Europe were looking for her but she seemed to have just disappeared. There was a rumor she was headed for Melbourne.'

'What did she do?'

'She swindles people out of money. She pretends she can communicate with their dead relatives. She is supposed to be very accurate. The police say she is a fraud and is very clever at finding out things about people. She pretends to be caring and preys on those who have lost someone. He said she has an amazing power over people. Once she has them hooked, she talks about building a sanctuary where they can go to spend time on spiritual matters and communicate with their deceased family and friends. She makes it sound normal. She has such a way with her that people line up to give her money for this place. When she has what she wants she disappears. My friend said they suspect she even killed someone who got in her way. She is so full of arrogance and no matter where she goes she does not change her name. She seems to think she is unstoppable.'

'It can't be her. David's family wouldn't get involved with someone like that.'

'Many respectable people have succumbed to her lies, my friend said. She has caused a lot of heartache.'

'This is incredible. How would I know if it's the same person?'

'She is said to travel with three companions, two men and a woman and she is closely guarded. One of the men, her bodyguard, is called Matt and he never lets her out of his sight.'

'Actually something very strange happened when I met her. This guy rushed in from the garden and stood beside her. I have to say I was a bit scared. He just stared at me and nobody introduced us. Still, I can't believe this. I'm sure David wouldn't get involved with someone like her.'

'I'm not trying to alarm you but wouldn't you like to know? After all, this David is still your friend.'

'I don't think I should get involved. I mean, I really don't believe it could be her.'

'Can I tell you something, Paula? Can I trust you?'

'Yes, yes of course you can.'

'I told you I was trying to establish a business in Australia so I can live here.'

'Yes.' Her smile told him the idea appealed to her.

'What I did not tell you is I am having problems with your government. For some reason they are making it difficult for me to get things off the ground. I think they are uncomfortable with my wealth and power.'

'Really!'

'They do not like that I have such influential friends around the world and so many varied business interests.'

'But what's this to do with Rachel?'

'If this woman is who I think she is, it would go down well with your government if I could give them proof this criminal is here.'

'It would?'

'Yes. No government would want its people to know they had allowed someone like her into their country when she is on Interpol's list of criminals.'

'Do you really think it could be her?'

'It is possible. It is unfortunate you do not know more about her and we could be sure.'

'This would help you? I mean if I could find out more about her?'

'You do not realize how much. I cannot say how grateful I would be to someone who eased my dealings with your government. But I could not ask this of you. It might put you in danger.' Philippe covered her hand with his. 'In the short time I have known you, Paula, I feel there is a connection between us. I would not want to jeopardize that. I feel, and I hope I am not being, how you say, forward, but I feel I could become very fond of you. You are so beautiful and I would really like to get to know you better.' Philippe delighted in the power he knew he had over women. Paula had been an easy subject for his charms. He knew he had her just by the look in her eyes. It was funny now the combination of money, power and a little danger, dragged them in.

'Just tell me what you need. I'll help you.'

'You are so sweet, my dear. Is there no limit to your kindness to a stranger?'

'I hope we won't be strangers,' she said. 'What can I do?'

'If you could find out more about her, her friends, her movements. Perhaps the depth of her relationship with this David, although that might be painful for you.'

'No. I don't think it would be, now.'

'Good. This way I could confirm if it is her and then I could tell the appropriate people. I am sure this would assist me in being allowed to live here.'

'If it turns out to be her, this could get David and his family into trouble couldn't it?'

'I would ensure it does not.'

'I'll do what I can.'

'Thank you, dear Paula. Now let us talk of other things. Would you do me the honor of having dinner with me again tomorrow night?'

'I'd love to.'

He walked her to his car, saying he would drop her at her home on the way back to the city. It was a black BMW, an elegant but discreet sports model with darkened windows. He had rented it using one of his many identities. When they reached her home he turned off the engine and turned to her. Slowly and deliberately, his eyes never leaving hers, he kissed her gently on the lips. He could feel her hunger for him, her excitement, but he left her wanting. As he drove off he thought again how much he enjoyed his job.

43

Jenny had just finished unpacking the shopping and was enjoying a cup of tea at the kitchen table, when she heard the front door bell ring. She sighed and for a moment thought of not answering it. She was tired and was enjoying the peace. Robbie bounded across the room, heading for the door. She reluctantly put down her cup and went to see who would be calling at this time of the day.

'Jenny, how are you?'

'Paula. I'm fine thanks.'

'I was just passing and thought I would pop in and say hello.'

'Come in. I was just having some tea. Would you like some?'

'Thanks.' Paula followed her into the kitchen.

'David is working late tonight so I'm not expecting him back for a while.'

'That's okay. As I said I was just passing.'

'Everything fine with you?'

'Great thanks. I have a new boyfriend now and he's really wonderful.'

'I'm so glad to hear that. I mean, I'm glad to know you're happy.'

'Oh yes. I think David and I made the right decision in parting. We both seem to be getting on with our lives. Me with my new boyfriend, and David, well he has Rachel. She seems a really nice person.'

'Yes, she is. We're all very fond of her.'

'So she'll be staying around then? David said he didn't know how long she would be here.'

'We still don't know but we hope it's for a while.'

'Does she have family here? That would give her more incentive to stay.'

'Not in Australia, but she travels with three of her family.'

'Was that one of them who came in when I was here the last time?'

'Matt. Yes. They're all very close.'

Paula's heart jumped. The same name Philippe had mentioned. 'Jack said she's a witch, and she talks to dead people.'

'Jack said that?'

'Yes, but I think he was kidding. I mean she isn't a witch, is she?'

'Of course not. She's a loving and caring person. She helps people who need it. She's a very spiritual person. As I said we're very fond of her.' Jenny wondered why Paula was asking so many questions about Rachel. In fact she wondered why she was here at all.

'I didn't mean to pry. It's just that I realize I've been a bit of a pest since David and I split. It took me while to get over it but now I've found someone else, I just want to know he's happy.'

'He is Paula. He's very fond of Rachel. I don't think you have to worry about him.'

'Good. Well, I'd better be going. Thanks for the tea. I'm sure we'll bump into each other now and then.'

'I wish you all the very best, Paula. I'm glad to hear everything is going well for you.'

'Thanks. Things couldn't be better.'

Later that day Paula drove to the wine bar where she had arranged to meet Philippe. He greeted her warmly, holding her hands and kissing her on both cheeks.

'I have missed you,' he said passionately. 'Come, sit down. I have already ordered some wine.'

'I went to David's house this afternoon.' She took a couple of sips from her glass.

'Did you speak to him? I am jealous. I do not want you to speak to any other man but me.'

'Oh Philippe, I feel nothing for David now. He wasn't there. I spoke to his mother. I found out Rachel is travelling with three companions, just like you said. Wait till you hear this. One of them is called Matt. He's the one who rushed in when I met her the first time. You said one of them was called Matt. David's mum said they're like family. I tried to find out more but she seemed to get a bit embarrassed when I told her David's friend said she was a witch. She did say David was very fond of her; that they all were. I think the relationship is definitely serious.'

'My dearest Paula. It does sound as if this Rachel is the one. She travels with three companions, one of them called Matt, she is guarded and she claims to be able to talk to dead people. She fits the description physically. I think there is little doubt she is the one.'

'What are you going to do about it?'

'Do not worry your pretty head about that. I will take it from here.'

'Did I help?'

'My dear, I will be eternally grateful to you. If everything works out then I owe you a great deal.'

'You know I'd do anything for you.'

He took her hands and kissed each of them tenderly.

'I have taken a room at a hotel for the night. I have some champagne on ice. Would you do me the honor of returning with me so I can show my gratitude in private?' Philippe thought he should show her some form of thanks and after all, he deserved a little relaxation.

'I'd like that very much.'

44

They had just finished their evening meal and were gathered in the lounge room drinking tea. Rachel had been quiet most of the day. No-one asked her if anything was wrong. They waited until she was ready to tell them what was on her mind.

'I would like to go out to a restaurant with David,' Rachel said quietly.

Matt and Joe looked from each other to Rachel.' I know what you are both thinking but please listen.'

'Rachel, you know you can't ...'

'Joe, please hear what she has to say,' Anna said.

'I will not go unless you agree but I really want to do this. I want to feel like normal person for a while. Just to go out to dinner and talk to him.'

'You talk to him. We leave you alone in the garden. You talk for hours.' Joe went over and sat beside her.

'I know, Joe, but it is not the same. I just thought it would be fun to get to know him in his environment, not just mine. To go on a date. I've never been on a date.'

They were all aware of how hard Rachel worked. She had lived in a totally guarded space all her days, with them.

'I do not want you to think I am ungrateful. You all sacrifice much to keep me safe. I do not take that for granted but this is important to me. I will not do it without your blessing but is there a way it could be possible?'

'Andrew, will she be safe with him?' Joe asked.

'Safe. Yes, I think so. He's a good boy, always has been. He's never been involved in drugs or loose behavior as far as I know. He's always shown respect for his parents and I've met some of his friends. All respectable people. I'm sure he'd take care of her.'

'But he doesn't know who you are. There's a risk in that. He could put you in danger without meaning to.'

'I know, Matt, but his heart is good. He would look out for me.'

'Will you tell him?' Anna asked.

'The time is not right. He would not accept the truth.'

'They will know where you are now,' Joe said. 'If they suspect the journey is nearing the end they will come for you.'

'I know,' Rachel whispered.

They sat in silence for a while, each in their own thoughts. They were part of a wonderful adventure. They chose to walk with her on this part of Rachel's journey and that carried a great responsibility. They did it out of love for her.

Matt's feelings were churning inside him. He loved her with all his heart. His jealousy of David had been hard to control but he had succeeded in facing it and letting it go. She loved him, he knew, and that was enough for him. His duty was to protect her and be her friend. 'We'll find a way,' he said.

'Did I tell you how beautiful you look tonight?' David said.

Rachel laughed. 'About three times but it is nice to hear again. Thank you. This is a lovely place.'

'I'm glad you like it.' David had chosen the venue with care. After all it was their first real date and he wanted it to be perfect. It was an intimate little restaurant and their table by the window gave them a view of the bay. David had been surprised when Rachel finally accepted his invitation and even more surprised when she had come alone. He picked her up from Andrew's and there had been no sign of Matt or Joe. Because Rachel had asked for the name and address of the restaurant he thought perhaps they might be parked in the car outside but he did not care. He would pretend he had her all to himself now.

'Have you always lived around here, David?'

'All my life. I've travelled about a bit though. When we were younger Jack and I went up to Cairns. We thought we'd work and see the sights up there. It was good fun but we only lasted five months. On our weekends we explored the beaches and the rainforests. We took a four wheel drive and went up to Cape York which is about as far as you can go up north. It's just so beautiful there we thought we'd stay forever. Anyway, the wet season that year was one of the worst. We worked on a building site. It was real hard work. We came home at night and it took us ages to cool down. We'd sit in front of the air conditioner with a cold beer and try to work up the energy to go out. Everyone was praying for a storm to clear the air. We were in bed one night when there was a power cut. The air conditioners went off. We both found it hard to breathe and boy was it hot.

Anyway, that's when we decided we might head off home. It was a great experience though and I can't say I didn't enjoy it. Mum was glad to see me back. We've been to Perth and the Gold Coast but we always ended up coming home. I like the seasons. Then four years ago I got this great job and I realized I should be concentrating on a career. Jack and I always head off somewhere new for our breaks. What about you? I know I've asked you this before but don't you miss having a home base? Wouldn't you like to stay in same place for a while?'

'It would be good but I would always have to move on. We have much work still to do.'

'You can't do it from one place?'

'No.' Rachel reached over and put her hand over David's. 'That is not what you wanted to hear?'

'No, it's not. I hoped we'd get the time to know each better.'

'We know each other, David.'

The meal came and their conversation returned to lighter matters but again he realized they talked mostly about him.

'Would you like to go for a walk on the beach?' he asked when they left the restaurant.

She hesitated for a moment only. 'I would like that.'

They crossed the road and he helped her over the wall onto the sand. The light had begun to fade but there were still people lingering there.

'It is so peaceful here,' she said. 'It will be hard to leave.'

David could hear the sadness in her voice. He held her hand as they walked along the water's edge. For now he had her to himself.

'Leave, you only just got here, surely you don't have to go yet?'

'Perhaps not immediately, but as I told you, we cannot stay here for long.'

'How can you leave this little bit of paradise?' He tried to be light-hearted, not wanting her to know how the thought of her leaving distressed him. 'The weather's great, the surroundings are near perfect, the company is, well, fantastic.' She laughed. 'And, the water's warm.' He pulled her by the hand into the water and put his arm around her waist. She was barely a foot into the water before he saw the panic in her eyes. She raised her free hand straight up in the air, her fingers pointing to the sky.

'David, please let me go.' The hurt her words caused him made him do just that. Only then did she lower her arm.

'I'm sorry, I didn't mean to upset you.'

She looked into his eyes and smiled. 'I know this, but you cannot touch me like that, you will alarm Matt.'

'Matt?'

'He will think you are going to cause me harm.'

David looked around and noticed Matt for the first time. He must have been walking along the pathway a short distance behind them. He was staring in their direction. David felt the anger rise inside him.

'Why does he always have to be here?' He spat the words out before he could stop them. He saw the sadness in her eyes. 'I'm sorry, Rachel, I'd no right to say that. I was just so glad to have you to myself. I know you and Matt are close but I just thought we could have some time alone together. I'm sorry, really.'

'Let us sit down. I need to talk to you.' She walked out of the water and sat down on the dry sand. She looked across the bay. He sat down beside her, not sure he wanted to hear what she had to say.

'David, I am very fond of you. I enjoy the time we spend together. How much do you want to be with me?'

The question took him by surprise but he too kept his eyes on the horizon. It did not occur to him to hide his feelings. 'I can't stop thinking about you. I have a kind of ache when I'm not with you. I know we've only known each other a short time but I can't help how I feel. In answer to your question, I want to spend as much time as possible with you.'

'Even if there are restrictions, rules that cannot be broken?'

'Whatever it takes, Rachel, I just want to be with you.'

'Then I will tell you a little about my life. I feel in my heart you will not betray me.'

For a few minutes all he could hear was the lapping of the waves on the sand and the distant sound of children laughing. She was silent for a long time and then he heard her take a deep breath.

'I have to tell you about Matt. He protects me. There are people who want to kill me.'

Whatever it was David expected to hear, it was not this. He looked round at her but she continued to stare ahead. 'People who want to kill you, why?'

'Because of who I am, what I am.'

For a moment he thought he must be dreaming—surely it must be a dream.

'Matt looks after me. He stands between me and the people who would harm me. He knows the danger and he is willing to do this for me. We grew up together. He chose this path, to protect me, like Joe has done since I was a baby. Despite this I gave him the choice of walking away, but he chose to stay with me. He has given up much for me. He has chosen to always protect me, which means he will not have what young men of his age usually have—a wife, children. He spends nearly all of my waking hours with me. The choice is his. Our paths are linked forever. To help you understand his devotion, when I lifted my arm the way I did when you pulled me into the water, it was a signal to him I was safe, that you were not a danger to me. If you had been trying to hurt me and I lifted my arm with my fist clenched, he would have stopped you.'

'Stopped me?'

'He would have stopped you hurting me. I know this is hard for you to understand but I cannot explain any further. You will have to trust me. If you want to see me again you will have to accept Matt will always be close and that my people will not allow anything to happen to me. I have places I have to go and I cannot tell you where I am going, what I am doing, or when I am coming back. When the time comes to leave this country I may not be able to say goodbye. Knowing this, I will completely understand if you want to stop it now. There is no other way.'

He was full of questions. She was right—he did not understand. The way he felt about her was beyond his understanding. He was empty without her. He thought of her nearly every minute of his day. He loved her. It had only been a short time and yet he knew he loved her. He knew virtually nothing about her, only the little she had just told him, bizarre and unbelievable as it was. She could go without even saying goodbye. He asked himself if it was worth it. If he let her go now he knew he would be hurt, but how much hurt would there be a month down the track, or six months. The questions in his head lasted but a moment.

'Whatever it takes, Rachel, I want to be with you. I'll live by your rules.'

When Rachel turned to him, there were tears running down her cheeks. She took his hand and stroked it gently. David wished he could hold this one moment in time. As they looked into each other's eyes he felt a connection that could not be spoken in words. He accepted that every second of their being together was worth any pain they would have to endure in the future. They sat there for a long time, their hands joined, her head resting on his shoulder. They did not talk, just felt. When Rachel did lift her head and took her hand from his, David felt an emptiness.

'I have to go now, David, I leave early in the morning.'

'Leaving, where are you ... sorry. Will you let me know when you get back?'

'Of course I will.'

He stood up and took her hand to help her from the sand.

'David, thank you.'

'What for?'

'For caring.'

He kissed her gently on the forehead and then watched her as she walked across the sand to where Matt was waiting. He watched them walk up the path to the roadway and disappear from view.

He sat down again. Despite what he told her, his heart was heavy. Was she delusional? Were people really trying to kill her? He did love her but he could not dismiss the doubts and, if he was honest with himself, disbelief about what she had told him. His head began to ache.

45

David called to speak to Rachel and she asked him if he wanted to go for a walk in the garden with her. She had been gone for three days and he had felt an emptiness not knowing where she was. He took her hand as they walked to the trees at the bottom of the garden and sat down on the grass.

'I missed you.' he said.

'I am with you now. The only thing that is real is this moment.'

He wanted her to say she had missed him dreadfully. 'You see the world differently from anyone I've ever known.'

'There are many people who believe as I do, that all things are possible, in this world and the world beyond,' she said.

'The world beyond. You mean after we're dead?'

She smiled and gently touched his cheek. 'Have you not thought what happens when you leave this life?'

'I suppose I have, now and then.'

Although shaded under the tree, the heat was becoming intense. David felt the warm breeze and closed his eyes for a moment. They sat together with their backs against the tree.

'What do you hear, David?'

He felt her gently put her hand on his arm. 'I hear the birds.'

'What else?'

'The trees moving in the breeze.' He listened for a while longer. 'I hear myself breathing.' He kept his eyes closed and continued to relax. He began to feel a tingling in his arms and legs. It was a good feeling. He felt at peace.

Gradually he felt a strangeness in his body. He was aware of Rachel still beside him but he felt he was sitting under a different tree, in a different place.

'Do you see the forest?'

He opened his eyes slowly. He was fascinated. He hadn't moved but he knew he wasn't in Andrew's garden because he was surrounded by tall trees which reached to the sky. The grass around him was thick and the bushes dense. He could smell the air, clear and cool. Rachel was sitting beside him, smiling.

'Come, I want you to meet someone.' He took her hand as they walked among the majestic trees.

'Where are we?'

'In a sacred place. The man I want you to meet is part of this forest. His spirit lives here and will always remain here.'

He could smell smoke from burning wood. In the distance he saw a figure sitting on a log by a fire. As they approached, the man stood up and smiled. He was not a tall man but stood erect. He had a large blanket around his shoulders and his long grey hair hung down his back. His face seemed very old but when they drew closer David could see that his eyes sparkled with life. Rachel took his outstretched hand and put her free arm around his neck. She kissed him on both cheeks and held him for a while.

'Child, it is good to see you. You bring pleasure to the heart of an old man.'

'Noah, this is David.'

'David.' He said the name slowly. 'You are welcome.' For a few moments the old man stared at him and then he smiled.' 'He has a good heart, Rachel. Come. Let us sit by the fire and talk.' Rachel sat on the log next to Noah and David on the one facing them.

David could feel the peace of this place and yet he did not know how or why he was here but it didn't seem important to him to know. The old man was looking at him, as if waiting for him to ask a question.

'Where are we?' he asked.

'This is the home of my ancestors. My father Schweabe was a Suquamish chief and my mother Scholitza was of the Duwamish people. Our peoples have lived on this land for many generations. These trees are our friends as is the river and the sky. There are many white people here now, more than my people. We have tried to live in peace with them but they do not understand our ways. We cannot understand theirs. They do not listen to what this land has to tell them. They do not listen to the Great Spirit. Their souls are young I think. They will have to wait for the voices of old souls to guide them.'

David realized this was a dream. He was sitting in a forest with an Indian talking about white men. Of course! He'd fallen asleep under the tree and was dreaming. Well, he thought to himself, it's a pleasant dream. He felt at peace here so there seemed no hurry to rush back to reality.

'Do you listen to the earth where you live, David?' Noah asked.

''I love to hear the ocean and the sound of the birds. Yeh, I think I do.'

'You hear the birds and the ocean,' Noah said, 'but that is different from listening. You hear with your ears but you listen with your heart.'

'I never thought about it that way. How do I know the difference?'

'Ah, that is easy. When you listen to the earth and its creatures, you feel a sense of belonging. You feel you are part of the same wondrous life. You have a connection, a tie that binds you to all living things. You can converse with the earth and its many creatures, the two legged and the four legged. You will know the difference.'

'You mean you can talk to animals?'

'Of course. Have you not tried it?'

David laughed. This dream was getting interesting. 'No, I can't say I have. Well, I talk to our dog but he doesn't answer.'

'Do you want to try?'

'Sure, what do I do?'

'Close your eyes. Still your mind, open your heart and listen.'

David closed his eyes. It was easy to relax in this place. After all it was a dream. He could do anything he wanted to do. He could talk to animals if he wished.

He felt a warm stillness in his body. He could almost believe he was floating. He listened. He could hear the birds in the trees and the sound of running water in the distance. A gentle breeze touched his face. Time seemed suspended. He did not hear Rachel or Noah. He heard only the sounds of the forest. After some time had passed, there was a rustling in front of him. He slowly opened his eyes and saw an eagle on a log a short way from the fire. He was amazed by the size of the bird. Its powerful talons gripped the log and he was sure it had the strength to lift it from the ground if it chose to do so. Its feathers were dark brown except for the white on its head and the tips of its wings. Just as he wondered how large its wingspan was, the eagle slowly unfolded them and spread them out to the side. Its gaze never left him. It then folded its wings back against its body. David felt compelled to stare into its eyes.

'You are welcome here.'

He blinked. The eagle had not made a sound but David heard its words.

'You have never spoken with an eagle?'

'No,' the answer formed in his head, 'I've never talked to any animal I expected to answer me back.'

'As it is with most people. We have much to say but people do not listen. We can tell you many things about this world but because you do not want to know, you do not have the questions to ask and thus you have no need to speak to us. Do you have a question?'

He thought for a moment. What could he ask an eagle? 'What's it like to fly?'

'To an eagle it is everything. When we soar above the earth and feel the wind beneath us, it is everything. To an eagle and even to the smallest of birds it is everything. People do not understand this. People take birds and put them in cages. Why do they do that do you think?'

David's excitement at talking with the eagle was overtaken by a feeling of discomfort. 'They admire their beauty,' he replied. 'Perhaps they want a companion.'

'Ah,' the eagle sighed, 'they want. Do they not understand what they do when they put a bird in a cage? There are birds who know nothing else but cages. They are different but even they dream of flying free. But to take a bird that has known flight and cage it, this is to take from the bird everything.'

David's feeling of discomfort grew.

'We are all born to fly,' the eagle said, 'and humans so easily give up the dream to rise above the earth. They choose to stay in their cages. They allow others to tell them it is where they belong.'

Suddenly the eagle spread its magnificent wings and flew away. David watched it as it soared above the trees and then disappeared from sight. When his gaze returned to earth, he found Rachel and the old man looking at him.

'You talked with the eagle?' Noah asked.

'Yes.'

'Remember his words. He does not speak to everyone and his wisdom is valued.'

Rachel smiled at the old man. 'David and I were talking about death before we came here. I remembered the day you gave a great speech to your people and the white men. Your words stayed with me.'

'I remember. I am pleased you also remember that day, Rachel.'

'Many people remember that day, my friend. Your words have touched many generations.'

'Is this so?' The old man looked pleased. 'This old Indian's words live on.'

He turned to David. 'You wondered about death, David? I know the answer to be simple and true. There is no death, only a change of worlds.'

David was silent. He repeated the words in his head.

'We will go now, Noah. It has given me great joy to speak with you again.'

'And I you, Rachel.' He held out his hands to her and she took them. She lifted them slowly to her face and kissed them.

The old man then turned to David. 'You are welcome here. I hope one day you will return.'

'Thanks, Noah. It's been interesting.'

David followed Rachel away from the fire and before they reached a clump of trees he turned and looked back. The old man was seated by the fire. The eagle had returned and was sitting on the log. The two seemed deep in conversation.

'Who is he, Rachel?'

'Noah is my friend. He is a chief among his people. Some call him by a different name. They call him Seattle.'

When David opened his eyes he was sitting under the tree with Rachel. She still had her eyes closed. He had been dreaming. It was a strange dream. As he went over it in his mind, he saw something floating above him. He protected his eyes from the sun and followed its path. He could have sworn it was a dark feather with a white tip.

46

'David, go for a walk or something, you're driving me crazy,' Jenny said. 'What's up with you? You can't seem to sit still for two minutes. Are you feeling okay?'

'I'm fine Mum, I just ...'

'Jenny, leave the boy alone. He's got a lot on his mind. Why don't you take Robbie into the garden for a while and you can both let off some steam.' John smiled at him, a knowing kind of smile and David realized his father understood what he was going through.

It was a perfect night. The stars seemed to sparkle so brightly against the night sky. The silence comforted him but did not calm his restlessness. Robbie had wandered back, smelling the scones his mother was baking, but he felt reluctant to leave the solitude of the garden and kept on walking until he was out of sight of the house.

'David.' Rachel's gentle voice drifted in the air. He looked up to find her a short distance away.

'Rachel. I was just thinking about you.' He felt his heart soar.

'I know. This is why I came.'

His eyes greedily took in her face but his heart still ached with the need to touch her. He felt as if time had slowed as they walked towards each other. He savored the feeling of wanting to touch her.

His eyes held hers every step of the way. He felt her before he reached her, and it made his body tingle. He stopped in front of her and slowly lifted his hand to her cheek. He ached to pull her body to his, to wrap his arms around her and hold her. Her smile told him everything he needed to know. Gently he lowered his face to hers, their eyes still locked. Her mouth opened slightly as his lips touched hers. Gently they kissed as their bodies touched. It felt so familiar to him, as if he had kissed her this way before. When eventually they drew apart, Rachel put her head on his shoulder and he stroked her hair. She nestled against him and he held her tight.

'It has been a long time,' she said. 'I have missed you so.'

He held her closer. 'You know I love you, Rachel. I don't think there are words to describe this feeling.'

'We will find the words again.' Rachel's voice was but a whisper. Again he thought how strangely she used words.

'David, I have to go now, the others will feel me gone and I do not want to make them anxious.'

'You're a grown woman, Rachel, surely you can do what you want.' David was instantly ashamed at the annoyance he heard in his own voice. Rachel drew slightly away from him and looked at him intently. 'Please don't go just yet.'

'I have to.'

'When will I see you again?'

'Soon.'

She kissed him briefly on the lips but before he had time to reach for her, she was gone.

He stood there in the darkness, feeling empty. He wanted to hold her close and protect her, and most of all to love her. He still tasted her mouth and the softness of her skin. He thought how his life had changed since he met her. Nothing else seemed to matter to him but being with her. He wondered if this was how being in love felt for everyone. Did his father feel like this about his mother? He smiled because he knew he did. He tried to imagine how it would be, being married to Rachel, having children together, spending the rest of their lives with each other. A flush of pure joy filled him for a second and then sadness suddenly took hold of his heart. He took a deep breath and walked slowly back to the house. He knew the path ahead would not be easy but loving her was all that mattered.

47

She made her way quietly out of the house to the bottom of the garden. She stopped once she was through the gap in the fence. The moon was full and she could see him waiting by the pool. She knew he was watching for her but that he would not see her until she stepped out from the bushes. She savored the moment of just watching him. How she loved him. There had been a moment long ago when she had watched him like this and felt the same depth of feeling. When David had told her John and Jenny would be away for two days at a wedding in Sydney and asked her if she would come to his house so they could spend some time alone together, she had been engulfed in a feeling of destiny, of walking the path she had chosen so long ago. In that moment she knew all the events, the experiences, of her lives were joining together to complete a circle. The prophecy would be fulfilled. She did not question. She did not falter as she feared she would.

She smiled and walked towards him. Robbie wagged his tail when he saw her, and then curled up again in his basket, as if sensing this night was only for them. The only light in the garden came from the moon and the candles. Soft music drifted from the house.

'Would you like some wine?'

'Thank you.' They sat together on the garden sofa. The moonlight sparkled on the water in the pool and made stars of the light. There was a warm breeze and it gently moved the chimes hanging outside the door.

'Let's have a toast,' he said. 'To us, and whatever the future holds.'

'To us,' she said, holding her glass to his.

They sipped their drinks and talked like two ordinary people in love. He took her hand and gently stroked it with his thumb. There was no other world but the space surrounding them.

She rested her head on his shoulder. For this moment in time he completely surrendered his heart and his love to her.

'I miss you every second we're apart,' he said.

'My heart aches to be with you.'

They walked together into the house and she took his hand as he led her into his bedroom. There was no need for words as he slowly undressed her, his eyes never leaving hers. He cupped her face in his hands and gently lowered his face to hers. He felt her lips tremble at his touch and then she wrapped her arms around his neck. He slid his hands to the softness of her back and then downwards, pulling her so close that she would have been in no doubt about the depth of his need for her. He took his time undressing her, kissing her skin as he did so. She moved away a little and slowly unbuttoned his shirt. She smiled as she struggled with his belt. He kissed the tip of her nose and did it for her. When he too stood naked, she moved towards him, wound her arms around his neck and drew his lips to hers. For David that kiss could have lasted a moment or a lifetime, such was the ecstasy of her touch. They moved towards the bed and as they lay on the soft white sheets, their bodies entwined, the outside world stood still. Their kisses deepened and became more urgent. There was only this moment, this point in time when two hearts beat as one and love engulfed them and bound them together forever. When they had both satisfied their need for each other, they still clung together, their eyes locked in recognition of a moment that would stand apart from all others. Any doubts David had of wanting to be with Rachel forever floated through the skylight above them and was captured by the moon. He pulled away a little so he could look into her eyes. There he saw his desire, his love, reflected there. They again made love, not with the initial urgency of the first time, but with deliberate intention to give slow, and sometimes teasing, pleasure to one another.

'I'll remember this night always, Rachel. No matter what happens I will remember this perfect night.' David felt the wetness of her tears on his chest.

Later as they walked hand in hand back through the house to the garden, they saw and heard nothing but each other. When they reached the back of the house Rachel stopped, closed her eyes and stood perfectly still. Then she turned to him and held his gaze.

'David, do you know the meaning of your name?'

'No. I just know I was called after my grandfather.'

'It means beloved. You are my beloved. I have loved you a very long time, David. I will love you always.'

His heart ached at the sadness in her voice and he stopped to look at her. 'You sound like you're saying goodbye.'

'Not goodbye, David.' She turned from him and walked out onto the patio. David saw the man almost the second he stepped into the moonlit garden after Rachel. She put out her arm and stopped him from going further.

'I would appreciate it if you both stood exactly where you are,' the stranger said. 'I won't hurt you.'

'Patrick.' Rachel smiled at the stranger.

'You know me?'

'We have travelled a long time together, Patrick.'

'What's going on?' David asked. 'Who is he, Rachel, and what's he doing here?'

'He will not harm us. He is a friend.'

'A friend!' Patrick said.

'Have you not been with me on my journey? When I was a child and first became aware of your presence, I had no fear of you. Your silent guardianship has been a comfort to me.'

'You don't understand,' the man said. 'I was never there to guard you. I was sent to ...'

'Watch me? And this is what you have done.'

'You really don't understand. He wants me to ...'

'You will not give me up to him, Patrick. You have a good heart.'

'You know why he wants you?'

'Yes. The Cardinal and I go back a long way. His fear of me has lost none of its strength.'

'He told me to bring you to him when the time was right.'

Rachel slowly turned to David. She lifted his hand to her mouth and kissed it gently, her eyes holding his. 'The time is right,' she whispered and turned again to Patrick, 'but you will not give me up.'

Patrick felt the warmth of her smile. He felt the love radiate from her heart. He knew she was right. Somewhere along the way he had changed from spy to guardian. He knew in that moment he had stayed to protect her from the Cardinal. He could pretend no longer.

'Rachel.' It was the first time he had said her name. 'You're in danger. He'll stop at nothing. You must leave immediately.'

'I knew you would betray me.' They all turned to the voice which came from inside the house. The Cardinal stepped through the doorway, flanked by Philippe and two other men holding guns. It was the first time Patrick had ever seen the Cardinal out of his robes. He seemed much smaller, much older.'

'What the hell's happening here?' David shouted. 'Who are you? What are you all doing in my home?'

Philippe stayed by the Cardinal's side and the other two moved towards Patrick who was reaching inside his jacket.

'No, Patrick,' Rachel said, 'it is of no use. Please.'

Patrick slowly lowered his gun to the ground.

The Cardinal walked to stand in front of Rachel. David and Patrick both made to go to her but guns were aimed at their heads.

'I suggest you stay where you are or my men will shoot you dead,' Philippe said.

'Well, here we are,' the Cardinal said. 'I have waited a very long time for this day, witch. You know why I am here?'

'Yes. But you will not have what you want.'

'Oh I think I will, I think I will. Finally the Church will be rid of you.'

'The Church is not you, Cardinal. There are those in the Church who believe in me, in the message I bring. They know I am not what you say I am.'

'They are foolish.'

'You are wrong. The Church has always been full of good, honest men who are not blind to the truth because the words come from a woman.'

'You and your kind would have the Church run by women. You would have the world ruled by women. Little by little you have all ingratiated your way into positions of power with your witchcraft. You believe you have a direct line to God. I know you have been gathering people to your cause for a very long time. There are the weak among us who cling to your words. They are blinded by your evil, by the sweetness in your voice. The devil is strong in you. I have made it my life's mission to destroy you. This illusion needs to end. I will stop you once and for all, and all the bricks of the house of evil you would build will come tumbling down and be lost forever.'

'Why do you hate me so?' Rachel said. 'You must know my words are true. You know in your heart who I am and yet still you fight me. I can help take away your demons and show you the true light of God.'

'You vile instrument of the devil. You want to take away my demons? You want to show me God? I know God. I know God has given me the task of destroying you and returning you to the arms of your evil master to burn in hell forever. When I first came across the scroll in the archives when I was a young priest, I knew when I read it, I knew in my heart what it said about you was a lie.' The Cardinal's eyes were aflame with hatred and those watching him saw his madness.

'Take her,' the Cardinal ordered. The two men kept their guns aimed at Patrick and David while Philippe moved towards Rachel.

'Rachel. Stand still.' Matt's voice came out of the darkness. Matt and Joe, and the four men David had seen in the garden with Rachel, surrounded her.

'Ah, the precious Guardians are here,' the Cardinal said.

'You think we would not know you left Rome, your Eminence?' Anton said. 'As you watch us, we also watch you.'

'Kill them all, except the witch.'

The two men with the guns turned towards the new arrivals. David heard one of the guns fire but at the same time he was aware of a slowing of his senses. At first he thought he had been shot. A white light appeared in front of Rachel and then it was as if time just stood still. The bullet that was making its way towards Matt stopped in mid-air. The Cardinal and his men also seemed unable to move. David saw Matt put his arm around Rachel and pull her away. Joe indicated to Patrick to follow them. As they headed into the darkness, Rachel looked around at David. He saw such sorrow in her eyes. Then she was gone. They disappeared leaving him and the others still motionless. David did not understand why he was unable to move. The white light remained but slowly it moved to his side. Just as if someone had pressed a restart button, he felt his body move again.

'Follow them,' the Cardinal shouted, 'do not let them get away.' It was then that the men realized their weapons had gone. They stared at each other and then at the Cardinal whose eyes were ablaze with fire.

'We will take him with us,' the Cardinal said.

As the men moved towards David, the white light intensified and grew. The men stopped in their tracks. The Cardinal stared at the light.

'I will not give up,' he shouted. The light grew larger. 'Leave him,' he said to the men, 'he must be of no importance to her or she would not have left him behind.'

The Cardinal headed for the door followed by the three men. Just before they disappeared back through the house the Cardinal turned once more to the light.

'I will not give up.'

David found himself alone in the garden. The light had simply disappeared. He knew Rachel was gone and there would be no use trying to find her.

'He must be of no importance to her.' The Cardinal's words would haunt David and would fill the empty space Rachel had left in his heart.

She stood by the shoreline. The sky was dark blue, almost black. The moon was full and made a pathway to her feet. The sea was calm and the waves lapped gently onto the sand.

The peace of it all. Here she could think clearly and empty her mind of thoughts. She merely had to experience the beauty of the night.

He walked slowly from the furthest point of the crescent of the shore. There was no hurry. She knew he was there and the knowledge brought her comfort. She continued to experience the moment. He drew close when she was ready, as she knew he would.

She melted into his outstretched arms. She breathed him in as she clung tightly to him. He kissed her forehead and the tears on her cheeks. She smiled and touched his face.

'Only you can make the sorrow leave my heart,' she whispered.

'Much has been asked of you, child, and you have given more.'

'There is nothing you can ask of me that I would not give.' She stayed in his arms and felt her doubts fade and her fear subside. She lifted her head from his shoulder and looked into his eyes.

'Of all the memories I carry with me of this world, the one that has sustained me in my times of sadness, was when we danced together so long ago at Cana. Do you remember?'

'Yes,' he said. 'I remember.'

'Will you dance with me again now?'

He smiled and took her hands, and together they danced on the sand in the moonlight.

48

David walked in the garden. He felt the warmth of the sun on his body but it brought him no joy. It was so quiet. His father had died a month ago. Robbie was long gone. His mother had taken herself off to Scotland on an extended holiday with her relatives but he knew her visit would do little to ease the sorrow that filled her heart.

His mind went back 15 years to the day he had first set eyes on Rachel. Fifteen years! Had it been so long? A lot had happened in that time, some of which was faded in his memory. He had a failed marriage behind him. Fortunately there had been no children. The choice had been his and had eventually caused the breakdown. His career had been a very rewarding one. He had spent years working in London and New York. Despite his success in business and his acquisition of material possessions, he felt empty. He returned to Australia at least once a year to visit his parents and catch up with Jack who now had a lovely wife and two beautiful children. The rest of his spare time he spent travelling to different parts of the world. In his heart he always hoped that somewhere he would come across Rachel, but he never did. He had never been able to completely erase her from his memory because he dreamt about her often, dreams so real that the wakening from them broke his heart all over again.

He missed his father. He had been overseas when his mother phoned to say he was in hospital after a massive heart attack. It took David two days to get home. When he entered the hospital room he expected to find his father barely alive.

'Oh David.' His mother rushed to hug him. She looked so weary and there were lines of worry etched on her face. 'I'm so glad you're here.' Tears welled up in his eyes.

'How is he?' David went to his father's side. He expected to see monitors and tubes but instead he lay peacefully asleep on the bed. He sat down and took his hand.

'What did the doctors say?'

'He doesn't have much time.'

'Why aren't they doing something?'

'He refused everything. He doesn't want the pain killers or any medication.'

'Why not? Surely they can do something for him.'

'It's my time, David.' John's eyes opened and he smiled.

'Dad. It's good to see you. You're going to be okay.'

'Of course I am. I'm going home.'

'Oh, Dad.' David shook his head. He had spent the last 15 years avoiding any conversation with his parents about their belief in life after death. They had been devastated when they heard how Rachel had left. David refused to speak about it, or her, again.

'Let the doctors give you something. Let them try to help you.'

'I'm not afraid. I don't want this experience clouded by drugs.'

'Try to rest.'

'We have to talk, David.'

'We will. I promise. Right now I want to talk to the doctor.'

Later David sat in the room alone with his father who was now slipping in and out of consciousness. His mother had gone out to get some fresh air. David was staring into space, sorrow engulfing him.

'Don't look so worried.' John smiled and reached out his hand to David.

'Dad, I'm so sorry.'

'Don't be sad for me.'

'Dad, I wish...'

'No regrets, David. I love you very much and I know you love me.'

'I don't want to lose you.'

'You can never lose me. I'll always be around.'

David laughed as he wiped the tears from his eyes. 'You really believe that, don't you, Dad.' His father's eyes were sparkling and held no fear. 'You really believe we live forever?'

'I don't just believe it, I know it.'

'How can you know? I want to believe you but how can you know?'

'Rachel told me.'

'Rachel?' Her name still cut his heart like a knife.

'Yes. We've had many talks all those years ago. She told me then and I believed her. She told me again last night.'

'Last night? Rachel was here?' He felt his heart race.

'Not in the sense you mean it. She came to me while I was sleeping. She said she just wanted to check I hadn't forgotten. She said she would help me make the transition.'

'You dreamt about her,' he said, disappointed.

'Not a dream, David, not a dream.'

David stared at him. His father was losing his mind. He did not want to argue with him, not in his last hours.

'You don't believe me,' he said.

'As long as you believe it, that's what counts.'

'She loves you very much, son. She said it just wasn't your time.'

'I don't know what that means. I just don't know what it means.'

'I'm sure some day you will.'

'What else did she tell you in your dream?'

'She hopes you will not abandon her but the choice will always be yours.'

He stared at his father. Why did he use that exact word—abandon. He remembered the dream he had not long after he met Rachel. His head ached.

'She was the one who abandoned me, Dad.'

'I don't think it's that kind of abandonment she was talking about. You don't know who she is. She wanted to tell you but you weren't ready to understand.'

'I know you believe in all this spiritual stuff of hers, living forever and talking to ghosts, but....'

'I know it's true, David. I can't convince you of it but I know it. When I had the heart attack I was taken to a place I can only describe as paradise. I felt no pain, no regrets, nothing but joy. I was filled with love. I felt a love for every living thing and I felt I was loved. I wanted to stay there but then I saw Rachel. She told me I had to go back. I said I didn't want to, that I wanted to stay there. She said I had one more thing I had to do and once I'd done it I could return.'

'What did she want you to do?'

'She said we should have the chance to talk and I was to tell you where the journal was.'

'What journal?'

'Rachel gave me one of her journals for safekeeping until it was needed. It belongs with you. It's in the safe in my office at home. Do you remember the code?'

'Yes. It's our birthdays. Dad, will Rachel come back for it?'

'One day. But read it. You'll realize why she left it with me. Now I've told you, I'm ready to go.'

'No, Dad, no. Please hang on. Please don't go.' Panic overwhelmed him.

'I want to go, David. There's nothing I've left unsaid to your mother.' He smiled.

Just then the door opened and his mother rushed in. 'I had this feeling I had to get back. Sweetheart, are you okay.' She rushed over and took her husband's hand.'

'Yes. It's just that it's time for me to go. I want you both to know I love you very much and I'll be around to keep an eye on you.'

Jenny sobbed uncontrollably.

'I'm not afraid, truly I'm not.' The smile of his lips reached all the way to his eyes. David reached out to press the buzzer for the doctor.

'Please, David, don't do that. Please let me go the way I want to. I don't want them to try and stop me. I'm going home. I know what that means now. I'm going home.'

David looked at his mother. She had stopped sobbing but the tears still ran down her face.

'Let him have his way. It's what he wants.'

'Thank you, my love.' *He smiled and reached out to touch his wife's cheek. She took his hand and kissed it. Slowly he closed his eyes.*

49

Reliving that day brought a lump to David's throat. He walked down to the bottom of the garden. The new neighbors had fixed the fence not long after they moved in. Andrew Graham died somewhere in Pakistan where he had gone to help flood victims. He left his affairs in order which included an express wish there be no funeral for him. He was to be buried where he died. It seemed strange to David at the time as he assumed Andrew would want to be buried with Helen.

David thought how everything changed when he met Rachel. He wondered where she was. Then he remembered the book, or journal as his father called it. Wearily he made his way back to the house. He opened the safe and found the book in a small box, wrapped in a white linen cloth. It was very old and worn, as if it had been read many times. He sat down in his father's favorite armchair, took a deep breath and gently opened the first page. In beautiful handwriting someone had written "1664, France".

David was unaware of how long it took him to read the book. He slowly closed it. He felt as if he had just woken from a dream. Emotions, good and bad, excitement, sadness, he felt them all. He was confused. If Rachel did indeed write this story, why would she want him to read it? She said she did not write fiction but this told of a woman's deep love for two men, of poverty and plague, of children dying in the arms of their mothers. Who were these people Rachel wrote about? He did not know why this book was so important to her but he would honor his father's wishes and take care of it. He re-wrapped it carefully and put it back in the safe.

A restlessness took him to the beach. He parked the car and walked down to the water's edge. The air still held the late summer's warmth and the waves lapped gently on the shore. The few people remaining there appeared to be packing up to go home. He felt lost. In his mind he saw his father's face as he died. How did he get to be so peaceful? He looked out across the bay, but he was not really seeing it. He felt he was standing in a whirlwind. He missed his father. It hurt. The words of the book raced around his head. He had acted the same as Edward had with the woman he loved. He wanted her love, her complete love, and yet knew he could never have it. David recognized Edward's feelings of frustration, of not understanding his need. He again wondered why Rachel had left the book with his father.

'David.' Now he was hearing her voice in his head.

'David.'

He turned to find her standing a few feet away from him. He held his breath, not sure if she was real. She had changed little. Still slim with her dark hair framing her beautiful face. And her eyes. He was being pulled into them.

She smiled. 'I am happy to see you again, David.'

'I can't believe you're here. I was just thinking about you.'

'I know,' she said gently.

'What are you doing here, Rachel? I thought I'd never see you again.' The ache in his heart seemed somehow greater than it had ever been.

'I came to see if it is now our time.'

'Time for what?'

'Time to understand each other. Time to bring our destinies together.'

'You say it so easily. I wanted it to be our time 15 years ago.' He still held the anger of her leaving.

'There is so much unsaid between us. Come, sit with me. I will answer all your questions. We will talk and perhaps we can bring the past to the present and it can be one.'

She still talked in riddles. He sat down beside her on the sand and they both stared out across the bay. He closed his eyes for a second and felt her beside him as he had done all those years ago.

'You are thinking of the last time we sat here together.'

'Yes. The only thing missing is Matt. Or is he watching us?' He felt the jealousy resurface.

'Yes,' she said. He did not turn around to look.

'My father's dead.'

'I know. You must miss him.'

'Have you come for the book you gave him?'

'Yes.'

'Tell me about it. Why is it so precious?'

'It was about a time in my life.'

'Your life? I don't understand.'

'I will tell you my story. I will tell you who I am. Open your heart and let the words find a place there.' She closed her eyes for a moment and took a deep breath. 'A long time ago, in another lifetime, I was born to a woman named Mary and a man named Joseph. I had an older brother, Yeshua. The world knows him as Jesus.'

David sighed. His head really ached and he was filled with sadness. How he loved her still. He looked back at the ocean. For a moment he had dared to think she had come back to him and perhaps they would have another chance, but with her words his dream of loving and being with this woman for the rest of his life slipped away. He felt himself disappearing into a dark pit. 'How can you be?'

'I do not have the same body but I am the same spirit,' she said. 'The same spirit who has lived these centuries and learned and grown to become the woman who lives in this body. I know now what I knew then and what I have learned since. I have lived many times. My body is different but my spirit, my soul, who I am, is the same.'

He moved so he could look at her face. She did not appear to be crazy. 'Rachel, how can this be true?' he pleaded.

'It is a long story.'

'I have the time.' He was not ready to let her go.

'Yeshua is described as the Son of God. The truth is we are all children of God. Our body is the vessel which holds the soul. Our body, our mind, our thoughts, they can belong to whoever we wish to give them to, but our soul belongs to God, forever. We each have a great destiny and the power to do wondrous things. My brother was like everyone else, a child of God. What made him special was that

God chose him to remind the world of the very essence of what life is about. Jeshua saw God and his destiny was to show the world how we could reach out with our hearts and not only feel God's power but to understand we are part of the creation of all that is. Yeshua was aware of his destiny and had the courage to follow the path that led him to its fulfillment.

'A Messiah was expected by the Jewish people, although they believed he would be a real king who would release them from slavery and subservience–give them a land they could call their own. They wanted him to be someone who would save their earthly bodies and give them peace and prosperity. Yeshua offered them a way to live a life of spirituality, growth and love but they wanted material things, they wanted what they thought God had promised.

'I remember every detail of growing up with him. I remember the laughter and the tears. All of it. I followed him everywhere he would allow and I wrote about him in my journals. Times have changed so much since then. Great good and much evil have been done in his name. His message was so simple, "Love one another as I love you". He showed us how to love. He loved all living creatures and saw the beauty in everything.

'Did you ever wonder why one man could attract so many people to him? They would follow him everywhere. The day he gave the sermon on the hill, the people just kept coming. They were not the ones looking for a messiah or someone to set them free. They just wanted to be near him and to feel his love for them. It was that simple. We felt his love, his total unconditional love for us. Our souls know there is more to our lives than just our bodies and our existence in this part of time. In his presence we connected to our souls. Once you have that feeling you never want to let it go. You would do anything to keep it. There were many who died because they followed him. They lived in the moment of feeling that love. They looked not to the future or the pain they might endure.

'I was with him when he healed the sick and brought peace to the souls of the suffering. I walked each step with him as he carried his cross to the hill and I watched as his spirit left his body. They say he rose from the dead. He did not die. We do not die. Yes, our bodies do but not us, not who we truly are. We are not this body. We are Spirit. We are a part of the Creator and of a universe beyond imagination. Many religions teach that we will one day be reunited with God. How can that be? We are never separated from Him. Yeshua understood this and wanted us all to know the truth. He saw my pain at his leaving and his Spirit returned to me as I wept at his tomb. In my pain I had forgotten the truth.

'We tried our best to keep his teachings alive in the hearts of those who had known him and to enlighten the hearts of those who had not been given the chance. We did not want his simple message distorted. It was not easy. Some of those who walked with him were afraid. They did not know which way to turn. They were lost without him. They did not believe I could still converse with him. I could see his Spirit and used to talk to him in front of the others. They thought I was mad but then they realized I could heal like him. I tried to explain to them he was standing next to me when I laid my hands on the sick. They argued over what should be done with me. My mother was so afraid I would have the same fate as Yeshua. Eventually we gathered a small group around us who only wanted to spread his words of love and peace.

'Peter thought the words of Jesus were only for Jews. Then later there was Paul. After Yeshua spoke to him on the road to Damascus he left his hatred of us behind and wanted to convert the world. Paul was arrogant and fiery. His intention was good but his enthusiasm clouded his judgment and sometimes blocked out the spirits who tried to guide him. He took the words of Yeshua to the Romans and the Greeks, to anyone who would listen. His courage and faith could not be doubted.'

Rachel smiled. 'I remember the first time I met Paul. He wept. I had not expected that. I think a sea of regrets washed over him at that moment for it was not my hands he ached to hold.'

'You remember everything?' Although he could not believe her, he was fascinated by her story.

'Oh yes. It is not as if it happened to someone else. They are my real memories; part of my life.'

'Why have I never heard of you?'

'I was a woman and at that time women could not teach men. It was unacceptable. There are still those today who feel the same way. After my brother's death there was a fear I would draw his followers to me. There was mention of me in writings but it was removed. I disappeared as the story was rewritten and retold. It did not seem important that the Christ had a sister. It mattered not, for my God had other plans for me.

'Tell me. I want to know.'

'I was very fortunate. I had help from those in this world and in Spirit. God allowed me to heal and bring comfort. I was greatly blessed by the gifts given to me. When it came time for me to depart this world I knew I would return. Those who guarded me knew it also. I cannot tell you the sorrow I feel when I encounter those who are afraid of death. Remember what Noah said to you in the forest?'

'Noah! I thought that was a dream.' David remembered also what the eagle had said, that to take a bird that had known flight and cage it, was to take from the bird everything. He realized he had tried to do that to Rachel. He had tried to cage her in his world when hers was as endless as the sky, at least in her mind.

'He said there is no death, only a change of worlds. His words are true. We go to a place where there is no pain, no fear, no time. The light of God shines on you and through you and you realize our life on this earth is but a moment in our eternal existence. To have that is to have everything. When I feel the light of God, I struggle to let it go and return.'

'You've seen heaven, Rachel? There's actually such a place?' His whole body filled with tingling excitement, but also a fear this was all a dream.

'Perhaps not as people imagine it to be, but yes, there is a heaven. And God is not someone you can see with your eyes. I have been asked what God looks like so many times and yet all I can say is that God is in every living creature on this earth and is an energy that touches all you have been, all you are and all you will become.

'But I am no different from you, David, or anyone else. We all have a destiny. Some souls are young and they have yet to understand that there are no limitations to what they can experience, what they can achieve. Other souls have lived many lifetimes and bring an awareness of what is possible to the life they are experiencing now. Every living soul holds greatness and the power to change the world but so many doubt the power they possess. So many are yet to recognize the light which shines within them.'

'My father knew this before he died?'

'Yes, he knew.'

'I thought he was crazy.'

She laughed. 'Like me?'

He looked at her for a long time and then suddenly all the doubts disappeared. He saw now what his father had seen in her from the beginning. He reached out and took her hand in his. 'Tell me.'

'I have lived many lifetimes on this earth, David. I remember only one lifetime before I lived as the sister of Yeshua. One day I will tell you about that lifetime, about a man named Alexander.' Rachel paused for a moment, a smile on her face.

'I am reborn when there is a need for me to learn, to be of assistance to other souls. Archangel Michael carries my soul home, like he did for my mother, Mary. When is it time for me to return, he is the one who carries my soul back to this earthly existence, but his gift is that I am aware of my other lifetimes and my destiny. My guardians in this reality keep the memory of me alive and pass it on. Whenever I am reborn I am expected and eventually they find me and again guard the way for me.

'I have seen such terrible things through the ages, David, all a consequence of man's greed and need for power. I have stood in battlefields where blood has covered the ground like a blanket, blocking out the power of the Earth to heal herself. I have felt the fear and the despair of souls crying for release. I help where I can. I let the healing light of God flow through me and ease their pain or I walk with them towards the light when their souls cannot remember the way home.'

'The journals the Cardinal wanted, they were about your different lifetimes?'

'Yes, but the ones he wants the most, the ones he would kill for, are the ones my brother wrote with his own hand.'

He stared at her. 'You have journals written by Jesus?'

'Yes. We would sit together writing. He would take my journal and say "What have you written about me today, Little Sister?" I can still hear his laughter and see his smile. He shared his thoughts with me and I wrote down all I could. I wanted there to be a record of how he lived his life and how he tried to explain he was no different from anyone else, but both this followers and his enemies did not believe him. There was so much left out of what was written about him.

'I wrote also of his death and the years that followed. I cannot understand why people like the Cardinal would want his words, his thoughts, his teachings destroyed. In all my lifetimes there have been those who somehow knew about me and the journals and did not want to accept the truth. God choosing Yeshua was not good enough for them. They needed Yeshua to be the Son of God.

'Those friends who were left after my physical death passed on not only a memory of me but the journals. The Guardians have kept them safe for over 2000 years. Some have died to protect them. I know where they are and I know they are safe.'

'One night I came to see you,' he said. 'You were sitting in the gazebo and then I saw Joe come out of the house with four men. Was that them?'

'Some of them. They brought the journal I gave to your father.'

'Rachel, how do the people who guard you and the journals find you each time you come back?'

'Like me they are open to communication with Spirit and they just know. Sometimes they do not find me until I am grown but they always find me. They know me by this.'

Rachel pulled up her shirt to show three thin red marks on her right hip. 'After we took Yeshua from the cross, I held him. Later all the blood washed off except these small patches. I have carried these marks since then.'

He gently touched them. 'I remember feeling these that night ... that last night.' He held her gaze, knowing she too was remembering.

'I have also shared my life with people I loved on a physical level and that has often caused me to question my destiny. In all my lifetimes knew I could not bear a child. There were those who loved me enough to accept this, and those who walked away. Some said it would not matter but it did.'

'I would still love you.'

'You told me this before.'

'I don't understand.'

'You read the journal I gave to your father?'

'Yes.'

She smiled at him. 'You do not remember?'

'Remember what?'

'We have known each other before. This is how I knew your heart was good that first day. We loved each other before.'

He stared at her. 'Edward! You're saying I was Edward?'

'You are Edward. Your heart knew mine then as it does now.'

David closed his eyes. A warmth began to spread through his body. He realized now why he felt he had always loved her. That wonderful feeling of loving her. They merged with the feelings he had for her 15 years ago and the feelings he had now. They merged into one. He knew she was telling the truth.

'I had a dream just after we met. I was searching for you in a storm. I could hear you calling me, asking me not to abandon you.'

'Your spirit was remembering the last time we met.'

'Yes, and probably remembering the guilt I would have felt at not accepting you as you are. I abandoned you then and in a way I did it again 15 years ago because I loved you but I didn't believe in you.' He opened his eyes and looked at her. 'How can you forgive me?'

'There is nothing to forgive. All that matters is now.'

'Why didn't you go back to Edward? In your journal you said you loved him very much.'

'I loved him, you, with all my heart. I knew instantly the love I had for you would be forever. I know I hurt you then by leaving but I had much work to do. The plague that struck the people of London in the summer of 1665 spread quickly. I knew I had to help. God used me to save many lives during those terrible times and to guide others to the light. I could not go back to you. There was always more work for me to do and you would not have understood. I knew we would meet again. God would not have allowed me to find you and then lose you forever.

'What you do not realize is you had a destiny to fulfill in that lifetime as you do in this. If we had not met at that particular time all those centuries ago, you would have gone to London earlier. Perhaps the plague would have taken your life and that would have affected your family and those you had yet to meet. We cannot always understand the reason for all that happens to us but never doubt there is one.

'You have always been part of my destiny and I learned so much from our time together. It was then I realized what stood in my way. It was my ego. I thought I could be perfect and should be before it would happen. I thought my importance so great that I would let nothing interfere with what I had to do. There were those who tried to tell me this but I did not believe them.

'I remembered a time in the Temple when Yeshua became so angry at the traders and the moneylenders defiling the house of God, he smashed things and shouted at them. I realized how foolish I had been. He was not perfect so why did I think I needed to be. It would have come to this anyway.

David smiled and touched her cheek. 'I never really thought about having a destiny but I'm happy though that we are part of each other's. Where did you go when you disappeared?

'To Scotland. The journals my brother wrote are kept in an old church there. I felt the need to touch them. To read them again. They restored my spirit.'

'Are all the others still with you?'

'All except Patrick. He passed five years ago. We miss him. It was a great joy to have him "watch my back" as he used to say. Your father and Andrew were also of great assistance to us after we left.'

'You saw my father after you left?'

'Not physically.'

'He told me you visited him in his dreams. I thought he was losing his mind.'

'We had long conversations,' Rachel said, 'and still do.'

David smiled. 'I'm sure you do. Will you just keeping doing this, Rachel, over and over again?'

'No. Not forever. There is another reason people like the Cardinal want to destroy me and the journals. I told you I have never borne a child. My destiny has always been that one day, when the time is right, I will bear a child who will change the world. The seeds of hope and love I have tried to spread through my lifetimes will bear fruit. We will gather people to us, the healers and the Guardians, and those open to Spirit who recognize the existence of their souls and that their souls are part of God and that we are all part of each other, part of the whole. There are so many people who know this, more than you can ever imagine. More and more people are awakening to the truth. With my child to lead us we will take our love and healing to the world. We will teach all that matters is love. Love of God, ourselves and each other. We will give them proof, not just ask them to have faith.'

'Why have you come back now, after all this time? It is just for the journal?' Pain passed through him at the thought she might leave again.

'I brought your daughter to meet you.'

'Daughter! I have a daughter? I don't understand. You said you couldn't have children. You said ....' He looked into her eyes and knew the truth of what she was saying to him.

'Why didn't you tell me?' His mind was spinning.

'My life and hers were in danger. The Cardinal did not stop looking for me. He knew I was carrying a child when I left. If I had stayed with you, you and your family would also have been in great danger. The Cardinal knew I would guard my child with my life and I would not take the risk of contacting you again.'

'What's she like, Rachel?'

'So beautiful. I called her Mary. She has always known who she is; why she is here. She loves like my brother did. People are moved just by being in her presence.

'When she was old enough we went to where we were needed, where wars raged and people suffered. We helped where we could. David, she just has to look into their eyes and all their fears disappear. We have met with people from every religion all over the world who are ready to help us. These people have been working quietly to spread the truth. There are even those in the Roman Church who are ready to stand by us when we reveal my brother's journals and his message, and to tell them of Mary. There is much work to do.'

'Can I meet her?' David asked.

'She is here.'

'Where?' He looked around. He recognized Matt, Joe and Anna standing on the pathway by the trees. Next to them was a girl wearing blue jeans and a red jacket. Her long dark hair was tied back in a ponytail.

She slowly walked towards them. David felt her energy even before she was close enough for him to see her eyes. They were the same deep blue color as Rachel's. She smiled and her beauty took his breath away.

'Father,' she said softly. 'My mother told me of her great love for you and of what you shared.'

'Mary.' David could find no other words.

She held out her hands to him. 'Will you walk with us on our journey, Father?'

As David walked hand in hand with Rachel and his daughter along the beach, Anna, Joe and Matt by their side, only he was unaware of the many who walked with them.

THE END

Notes

King Louis XIV - Louis XIV lived from 1638 to 1715 and was the most famous of France's kings. He was known as the Sun King and believed in absolute monarchy. He operated his court and government from the Palace of Versailles.

Noah - Noah was the Catholic baptismal name of Chief Seattle for whom the city of Seattle was named. He was born around 1786 and died in Port Madison reservation in 1866. He is known for his intelligence and courage, and excerpts from a speech he made in December 1854 are still quoted today.

Alexander - Alexander the Great was born in 356BC and died in Babylon in 323BC. He conquered and ruled a large proportion of the known world by the age of 21. When Alexander's father, King Philip, was murdered, there was speculation Alexander was involved in the death of his father's new son by his last wife, making Alexander sole heir and King of Macedonia. The two great loves of Alexander's life were Bucephalus, his horse, and Hephaestion, his long-time friend and lover.

Michael - Archangel Michael is said to have carried the soul of the Mary, the mother of Jesus, to heaven. He is the angel of strength and protection.

Prince Henry Sinclair - Prince Henry Sinclair was a Scottish nobleman born around 1345. He was Baron of Roslin, Earl of Orkney and Shetland. In 1398 Prince Henry is believed to have led a fleet of ships from the island of Orkney, for a new land across the ocean. Among those who accompanied him were a contingent of Knights Templars and Sir James Gunn. They landed in Nova Scotia, wintered there and later explored the eastern seaboard. An effigy of what is thought to be Sir James Gunn, who died on the expedition, was found carved on a rock face at Westford, Massachusetts. In 1401 Prince Henry and the Templar fleet returned from North America but the Prince was assassinated before he could lead a second expedition. Ninety-two years later Christopher Columbus voyaged to America. Prince Henry's voyage is immortalized in stone at Rosslyn Chapel near Edinburgh which was built in the late 1400s by his grandson, Sir William Sinclair.

The Spear of Destiny - The legend of the Spear of Destiny, which is said to have pierced the side of Jesus on the Cross, says that whosoever possesses this holy object and understands its power, holds in his hand the destiny of the world for good or evil. Many people throughout history believed in this legend, including Hitler. When he marched his army into Austria in April 1938, Hitler removed the Spear from the museum in Vienna and sent it to Nuremberg. Seven years later, Hitler committed suicide shortly after hearing the Americans had taken Nuremberg and the Spear was in their hands. The Spear again resides in the Hapsburg Treasure House Museum in Vienna.

Also by Cathy M. Donnelly

There is a Place

The year is 1513. Michael Craig's brother is among the 10,000 who were slaughtered with King James IV of Scotland at the Battle of Flodden Field. The tragedy ignites in 16-year-old Michael the ability to see the dead. A mysterious monk shows him how to use his gift to help the lost spirits who wander the blood-soaked battlefield. Michael discovers he can also heal the living but is unable to banish the demons that stalk his own life.

He journeys to Rome and France and makes a pilgrimage on the Camino de Santiago, but always his demons follow him. He returns to Scotland an Augustinian Priest and is appointed chaplain to John, Lord Erskine. He earns the respect of the Knights Templar and becomes entwined in the lives of King James V, Marie de Guise, and their child, Mary Queen of Scots.

When Michael meets Alice he recognizes a kindred spirit. He becomes her mentor and guide and they share a friendship that will bind them forever.

In a time of danger, Alice is thrown through time into a world that is not her own. Will Michael be able to bring her home?

CATHY M. DONNELLY

For more information on the author

please visit

Website:

http://www.cathymdonnelly.com

Amazon Author page:

http://www.amazon.com/Cathy-M.-Donnelly/e/B01A0BXFA0

Printed in Great Britain
by Amazon